THE

CROW

CHILD

TRILOGY SAGA...

Sherrie Todd-Beshore

www.patchworkpublishing.com

Cover concept by s.t.b.

Other books for Preteen/Young-Teen readers by this author:

Mystery *Series*: MOSQUITO CREEK DETECTIVE CLUB

- Book 1 - *Mosquito Creek Inn*
- Book 2 - *Black Eagle Pass*
- Book 3 - *High Stakes Gamble*
- Book 4 - *Dakota Mist*
- Book 5 - *Toy Master*
- Book 6 - *Grandma's Red Convertible*
- Book 7 - *WingMan*

The compiled stories in the following pages are entirely a work of fiction.

All characters and all events are a creation of the author's imagination…

CONTENTS

At times

we feel small, helpless,

at a loss for our direction and purpose

then *something* unexpected happens.

Perhaps that *something* even appears insignificant

like only a word, an idea, a single thought,

maybe a fleeting event.

But if we're paying attention–

what *seems* insignificant

might

create a change to our entire destiny…

PART ONE - *The Crow Child*

WHITE

CROW

CHAPTER...1

"Have you decided what you want for your birthday, Elijah?"

Grandpa Clearwater stirred his grandson's herb tea slowly with a fresh cinnamon stick. The cloves and ginger broth was still too hot to drink.

"It's 2016 and in thirteen days you'll turn thirteen on April thirteenth that makes your age *on* your birth date, an exceptionally special birthday."

Tree sap sizzled and spit as a fire crackled in the cast iron wood stove.

The warm kitchen wrapped Elijah in aromas of burning pine, his grandfather's strong coffee and steaming spices. He looked up from his bowl of fresh raspberries mixed with applesauce. "I want a new bow, a bigger bow!"

Rock Clearwater ambled over to the table with his coffee mug and Elijah's spiced tea. The man's brown eyes almost disappeared when he smiled behind wrinkled brown skin, tanned by years in the sun and his Sarsi Tsuu T'ina heritage. "I see. Well then eat up."

"And finish this too." He pushed Elijah's mug across the wide cedar wood table. "If you want a bigger bow, you're going to need more muscle, not those spindly birch branches you have now."

Elijah giggled and caught juice that dribbled from the corner of his lips as he swallowed. "Why do you always make me laugh when my mouth is full?"

His grandfather pretended to be serious. "It is all part of your archery training–to develop concentration."

"G-r-a-n-d-p-a?" But Elijah's laugh started painful coughing spasms.

Grandpa Clearwater reacted quickly. Pushing Elijah's head down he thumped his grandson's back with his cupped palm to help clear his grandson's lungs, then held the nebulizer mask up to Elijah's nose and mouth.

After two full minutes Rock Clearwater eased his grandson to sit upright again on his kitchen chair then pulled a second chair closer so he could sit next to Elijah. "Well I guess now we don't need to use your chest-clapper before you go to bed tonight."

With his head resting on his grandfather's chest it was several more minutes before Elijah's pulse returned to normal and he could take deeper breaths again.

Elijah closed his eyes focusing his mind on the rising and falling of his grandfather's breathing. He could hear the muffled beat of his grandfather's heart and it calmed him.

Later propped up by two pillows in his loft room bed, Elijah's face was slightly flushed. He was tired, but smiled for his grandfather. "I have another birthday *want* that's really more of a *don't*-want. I really, really, really don't want cystic fibrosis anymore, Grandpa."

His grandfather frowned. "I know son, I know me either. Have a good sleep."

And Elijah did, drifting to a faraway place and time…

****

…A few members of the clan had hidden beneath a rock ledge in the river canyon for two sunsets and three sunrises.

Prince Dade stirred the fire embers looking up the length of the steep, rocky slope across from his watch point. Reef and Tann still hadn't returned from their early morning scouting. It was late afternoon and there was less than three hours of daylight left. Dade worried.

As he checked over his shoulder toward the sandstone wall his mate Ona cradled their infant daughter as she slept. She had been diligent about keeping their child quiet so the sound of the tiny piercing voice would not give away the location of this camp.

Their oxen remained staked deep into the forest so the trees and underbrush could muffle their sounds if they made any. But mostly they had grazed quietly which was fortunate.

If his cousin Torr was able to discover more than two of their previous resting places then he could guess their direction. Following the river was a risk because Torr would check along its banks for his men and his lieutenants Baza and Kauji, as they would need water too.

A faint light flickered from a hand-held rock of mica a mile down the river on the opposite side of the bank. Dade stood and moved closer to the ledge, but he could tell from the signal it was Tann. Tann was returning with Reef.

Relieved Dade added more broken branches to the dwindling fire, ensuring that any thin smoke plume was under the rock overhang.

When Prince Dade's trusted guards reached the wide sheltered ledge Reef reported first. "Torr stopped to make a night camp. Then I found him again as he crossed through the forest to reach water."

"I'm sure Torr does not suspect our exact destination yet. When I saw him at first light, he was with these fighters," Reef held up both hands with all fingers spread, "but not Kauji. Much later at the river he was with only Baza and these fighters." The guard held up just one hand with all of his fingers spread.

"Torr and those with him are one sunset and one sunrise from us in that direction." Reef pointed southwest.

"The others led by Kauji have remained in the open plains attempting to track us in that direction." Tann extended his arm straight east. "They have separated to cover more area. When I ceased watching them they were moving a greater

distance from Torr and by first new light will be another sunrise away and of no threat. We are now of the same number as Torr's smaller tracking party."

"We stopped so Ona could deliver." The prince reminded his guards. "She is good, but still recovering. She is unable to power a sword and because of her milk should not use her bow for several more sunrises."

Scooping damp soil he had gathered to smother the small fire Prince Dade shared his plan. One side of his dark blonde hair, blown by the wind fell across his chiseled cheekbones with strands stuck in his beard.

"Quickly eat the fish Ona's mother cooked then we clear this camp of any sign we were here. If we use Torr's camp time to continue, we can also use the dark as cover until the moon is high to get closer toward the land of Erdini."

****

Grandpa Clearwater reached the top metal step on the wide spiral staircase, to the loft where Elijah slept. He had to stoop slightly until he reached the peak of the pitched roof where he could stand up straight.

Elijah's king-sized bed was set on a thick hooped rug on the floor. Open box style shelves stacked from the floor to a height of four feet were set just below the start of the sloped roof. They held Elijah's clothes and toys. Toys, especially his bins of Lego were often mixed with a pair of socks or t-shirts, or a sweater.

Watching his grandson sleep, he remembered the first few nights when Elijah first came to live with him and his late wife. They had slept with three year-old Elijah between them after their son Glen and daughter-in-law Margaret were killed in a winter car accident.

Even two years later when he was five Elijah's grandmother still worried that he might choke if he coughed at night. So she had insisted they keep the larger bed for their grandson which allowed them to take turns sleeping beside him.

The head of the growing youth with the unruly mop-top of dark curly hair turned on the pillow. With a deep sigh, Elijah opened his hazel eyes. He saw his grandfather, but said nothing at first only looking beyond Grandpa Clearwater with a vacant stare for several seconds.

"I was just about to wake you. Do you want me to thump your back now or would you rather strap on the chest-clapper?"

Elijah sat up and stretched. "The clapper, but after we eat. I'm starving, and I hav'ta pee. Is it snowing?"

"Not yet, but it will be in another two hours by the time your school bus arrives." Rock Clearwater returned to the top of the staircase and started back down. "When you go to the outhouse wear your rubber boots and not my house slippers," his head was just above the floor, "or I'll make you go barefoot." He winked. "Hurry, our oatmeal is ready."

Elijah settled into a chair waiting for his morning oatmeal. "I had the weirdest dream last night or maybe it was this morning. I mean it was weird but not. It made sense kinda like I was watching a movie."

Grandpa Clearwater filled two bowls with oatmeal. "I see. That happens sometimes."

The fire burned quieter in their kitchen stove that morning. Elijah noticed there was less bark on the split logs in the fire box.

"Was there a bow in your dream?" He handed Elijah a small pitcher of maple syrup.

"Mmm," Elijah swallowed a bite of his pear. "Not really, there was this guy who seemed to be a leader of some kind and he talked about a bow. Oh, and a sword! And the guy's wife, least I think she was his wife knew how to fight with a sword and use a bow too!

Grandpa stirred maple syrup into his hot oatmeal. "Your dad taught your mom how to shoot a bow. She had never touched a bow before she moved to Alberta from Ireland and she got pretty good too and so was your grandmother."

Elijah stopped blowing on his oatmeal filled soup spoon. "Why didn't I know that?"

"Well, you were three when your parents died and you were four when your grandmother had her first heart attack. Your Uncle River didn't start archery lessons with you and your cousins for two years after that. You and Jayson were six,

James was eight and Joseph was seven. Sarah was only four and Jorge and Spring were still in diapers then."

The wall clock chimed half-past the hour.

"You better finish and we can do ten minutes with the clapper before you get dressed, unless you plan to wear your frog pajamas to school."

Half a mile from the end of Elijah Clearwater's driveway, the bright yellow Canmore County school bus rounded a wide bend when he spotted the first snow flakes. He was still trying to catch the wide, late spring snowflakes on his tongue when the bus stopped and the driver Mrs. Deerling opened the front side door.

He threw his backpack on the bus floor ahead of him then climbed the two deep steps. He quickly scanned down the first few rows of occupied and unoccupied seats before deciding to sit beside Sasha Deerling who always sat right behind her mother, this route's bus driver.

Sasha was in grade four with his cousin Spring Blackelk. Sasha had blonde curly hair, a sweet smile and dark brown eyes with the thickest glasses he'd ever seen anyone wear except his late grandmother.

That morning Elijah wasn't in the mood to lug his backpack any distance down the center aisle of the bus *and* hoped to avoid his least favorite kid the big-*wart* Larry Swallowtail.

"Hey stick-boy!" Larry hollered from six rows behind him.

Usually the older kid was distracted playing a video game, but obviously not this morning. "Catch a lot of snow with that big mouth of yours?"

Elijah knew from their turbulent history together that if he didn't acknowledge the annoying lump, the tormenting just got worse for several days. He turned in the direction of Larry's voice and waved, with a thin lip smile.

Larry sat by the window sharing a bus seat with Elijah's older cousin James Blackelk. His other cousins Joseph and Jayson sat in the seat behind them. He didn't see Sarah, Jorge or Spring.

When Larry was around Elijah thought his two oldest cousins acted like brainless zombies. Larry had been held-back two school grades. He'd been partially raised by two foster families, his sometimes absent mother and his sometimes sober father.

In January Larry's grandmother had taken him and his parents into her house on her turkey farm north and west of the Sarsi Reservation. Soon after that Elijah began to wish Larry was still in the Calgary school system or better still at the other end of the country somewhere on the east coast of New Brunswick.

CHAPTER...2

The entire seventh grade class got detention, less than ten minutes after the last Monday morning bell rang.

This week wasn't beginning well. First Elijah's day started with Larry Swallowtail. Next, his perpetually dieting teacher whose nerves were generally on the verge of igniting, suffered a complete collapse of what was left of her sense of humor.

Mrs. Birch had been at the chalk board with her back to her class when she sneezed. It wasn't just any sneeze. Elijah looked up when he heard it and recognized it as the kind that reshuffles a person's ribs.

Besides that, the force of Mrs. Birch's sneeze was too much for the fragile seams her tight cotton blouse. Both side seams tore simultaneously and it reminded Elijah of the Hulk.

The sudden shredding of cloth echoed loudly and the entire classroom erupted in spontaneous laughter.

When she spun around Elijah expected Mrs. Birch might turn green like the Hulk, but she didn't it was worse. Her eyes bulged against a bright red face that screamed in a piercing bark. "You're all on detention – for a week!"

She vanished with the slam of the classroom door behind her.

Nothing moved.

No one took a breath.

Then barely a swallow in time, later the principal, Father Philbrook, flew into the room followed by Mrs. Birch who wore a large black cardigan. Without looking up she pulled her purse from the bottom drawer of her desk and was gone again.

The priest's glare shot nails at every student while he lectured them the importance of character and the consideration of others. "You have upset your *devoted* teacher so severely she must go home to recover from your cruel brutality!"

He rummaged in the supply closet then opened a package of plain white copy paper. He pulled out several sheets. "Here, hand these out, one to each of your fellow *clowns*." He dropped the paper on the desk of Elijah's cousin Jayson.

"So the first order of the next hour will be that each of you creates a get-well card for Mrs. Birch with a sincere apology note printed neatly inside."

No one was allowed to talk, or even fold the paper with any noise. Everyone had to sit still with their feet together, soles flat on the floor under their desk tops. Father Philbrook paced up and down the rows of students frozen in their desks - like he was the warden of a prison.

At first Elijah was miserable at the thought of being confined to the classroom with extra homework for every recess and lunch break for the next five days. But when he gave it more thought, detention seemed better than trying to dodge his two cousins and Larry every day – that was until Father Philbrook announced he would fill in for Mrs. Birch for the entire week.

By the end of the morning Elijah was almost looking forward to Larry's shoving and James' verbal insults. It was a misery-tossup between an irritable priest on the warpath or a bad-tempered school bully.

Grade seven kept working through their recess and when lunch period arrived they ate in total silence. When each student in turn finished eating Father Philbrook insisted they hold up their hand and wait for permission to be dismissed to go to the washroom.

The hall outside the boy's washroom was empty so Elijah hurried in. He was relieved there was no one inside either. But when he came out Larry with James and Joseph were coming down the hall toward him.

"Well if it isn't the sick-stick-boy."

Elijah had no time to hide or escape. Larry, James and Joseph were between him and his prison classroom. But facing them in the hall was preferable to retreating back into the isolation of the boys' washroom. In March he'd barely escaped having his head dunked in one of the latrines.

"You got anything to hold while ya pee, you snot-body defect?" Larry elbowed James and they both laughed. Joseph smiled awkwardly.

His cousin James was in grade nine, he'd be fifteen in the summer and was eleven inches taller than Elijah's four feet, six inches. Larry was already sixteen and another five inches taller than James. Joseph was in grade eight and six inches taller than Elijah. The trio towered over him.

Maybe it had been Larry's sarcastic remark on the bus that morning. Or maybe it had been Mrs. Birch dumping her class with detention. Or maybe it had been the confining morning with warden Philbrook... But Elijah suddenly realized he'd likely be stuck with Larry Swallowtail until high school graduation. And in that moment on this decaying Monday, Elijah decided that he was going to stop praying on his rosary for God to send Larry to another school, preferably in another country.

Ignoring Larry he looked directly at both of his cousins. "My dad was your mom's brother ya know. We have the same grandfather! Why are the two of you hanging around this insect? If we get Jayson that's four of us against one! Larry needs you more than you need him!"

"Think about it! He's going to get you into trouble someday. Don't be such stumps!" Elijah's last few words were a raspy effort.

With his heart punching his ribs he pushed by Larry and between his two cousins then walked chin up, shaking all the way back to his classroom where he thought for sure he'd throw up his lunch.

There was no sign of Larry or James after class while the reservation and farm students gathered to wait for their buses.

Curious, Elijah had asked his cousin Joseph, who was still playing the big-shot. "None'a your business."

"I'm telling Mom." Jorge appeared with Spring.

"Yeah? What are you telling Mom?"

Jorge looked unsure. "That you said 'none of your business' to Elijah."

"So?"

"So you weren't talking nicely."

"Shut-up. You're just as stupid as he is." Joseph pointed to Elijah and walked away.

Elijah's cousin Sarah joined the family group and retied Spring's hair ribbon. "Who's stupid?"

Spring got her older sister caught up. "Joseph said Jorge and Elijah were stupid. Here comes our bus!"

Jayson whispered behind Sarah as the kids jostled to get in line. "Larry and James had to stay after school."

The line to get on the bus moved slowly.

"Why?" Sarah looked from her brother to her cousin Elijah and Jayson looked around for his older brother, but couldn't see him. "Joseph wasn't sure completely, but Larry passed James a note in chemistry that James passed back to Larry and Mr. Fiche caught them. Something about Mr. Fiche being a *fag!*"

Elijah had kept his eyes closed for the entire bus ride home. When he jumped from the bottom step of the bus to the gravel on the road he stood for a moment relieved this day was over.

Only the high pitched whinny of his horse Arrow brought his head up.

The south section of the corral fencing extended five feet beyond the trees along Grandpa's driveway. Half dragging, half carrying his backpack he ran toward the big gentle, fury birthday gift he got when he turned seven.

"Arrow!" He dropped his backpack at the side of the driveway and climbed up using the lower fence rails to sit on the top.

His horse whinnied again and shook his head excited. When Elijah leaned over to lay his cheek against the horses' nose Arrow stood still.

"Man! This day was poop, Arrow."

The horse listened to the boy's voice then nudged him with a throaty response.

Elijah jumped to the ground inside the corral and they walked to the barn together. "First Larry started in again. You don't ever want to meet him! He's a mistake of nature!"

Climbing the ladder to the hay loft Elijah pushed open one of the hayloft doors that swung out over the corral. When the door opened Arrow looked up and backed out of the way.

After snipping the binder twine Elijah threw chunks of hay from the bale to the ground below. But Arrow waited.

Back on the barn's lower floor, lifting the lid of a wooden bin, Elijah scooped three cups of oats for Arrow. "Then, my whole class got a detention when Mrs. Birch ripped her own blouse, cause *she* can't stay on a diet."

He poured the oats into a wide, shallow plastic salad bowl. "The blouse was too small anyway."

Arrow savored his oats.

"I don't even know how she got it buttoned up."

When Arrow finished his oats, Elijah picked up the bowl and spread the clumps of hay from the dropped bale around on the ground for Arrow to eat. Then he got out the stepstool and brushes to groom away some of the heavy winter coat Arrow was starting to shed.

"So Mrs. Birch has this hissy fit and goes home." He leaned on Arrow's back for a moment. "And then we get stuck with Father Philbrook who's like some kinda genius, but a majorly grumpy genius and it's been like a hundred years since he was twelve anyway."

Elijah jumped down to brush Arrow's main. The horse turned his head bumping Elijah with his nose.

"And then Larry shows up again and those knuckleheads James and Joseph are with him. I know there's nothing in Larry's head except deer droppings – seriously. But James and Joseph listen to him!"

He stood back. "You look much better."

Arrow raised his grey colored head with a double white star on the bridge of his nose. The nine year-old gelding was part Quarter Horse part Appaloosa with the distinctive markings of the Appaloosa across the top of his rump.

"Let's go check on Dart. Maybe she can come out for an hour."

Arrow followed Elijah all the way into the barn to a closed stall. Inside, a small black mare covered by a horse blanket whinnied a greeting. Holding her halter, Elijah took Dart's temperature in her ear with a gage left by their veterinarian.

"Hey you don't have a temperature today at all. We can let you stretch your legs for a little while." He opened the stall gate wide.

The two horses greeted each other then trotted outside.

Elijah split open a second bale and pushed it out then closed the upper hayloft door. He gave both horses a hug then headed back to climb the fence. When he picked up his backpack Arrow was eating the hay and Dart had her head lifted to the wind.

Elijah mimicked the mare. The air felt damp and heavy with the scent of wet dirt and if the temperature dropped it would snow again instead of rain.

Inside the back door Elijah could smell Grandpa's meatloaf. It was the best. Not even Aunt Dawn could make meatloaf like her father.

"Grandpa?"

"Right h-e-r-e." Rock Clearwater's head came up. He'd been bending over an open cardboard box. Between the sofa and the split rock fireplace on the far side of the A-frame cabin's living room main floor, were three more open cardboard boxes.

"I fed and brushed Arrow already Grandpa." Elijah kicked off his boots and hung his jacket. He pulled his backpack behind him only as far as the kitchen table then left it to see what his grandfather was doing.

"I checked Dart and she didn't have a fever anymore, so I let her out of her stall, is that okay?"

Rock Clearwater stopped sorting through photos in an envelope and looked at his grandson and then his watch. "That's perfectly okay. But let's make sure we get her back inside in about an hour. How was your day?"

"Like I told Arrow, it was poop." He dropped down on one end cushion of the sofa. Then, as with Arrow, Elijah candidly shared his Monday mess with his grandfather.

"You called Larry an insect?"

"He is! He's a slithering millipede."

"How, is calling Larry Swallowtail an insect going to improve your situation?"

Elijah shrugged. "I tried ignoring him. I tried not talking to him. I tried praying for him to *go* away - back to Calgary – somewhere, anywhere 'cept here!

Grandpa Clearwater turned his head slightly to one side. "I know Larry's grandmother Eliza very well. Eliza and her late husband Lorence Snow were good friends of your grandmother and mine when we were kids in school together."

"But Lorence died when Larry's mother Lilly was your age. Larry's mother was the youngest by ten years to her next sibling and was sent to stay with an older sister while her mother Eliza coped with her grief. Lilly ran away from her sister's house with Larry's father when she was only fifteen."

"Are you saying I should feel sorry for Larry Swallowtail? Cause both my parents died, and so did my grandmother, and I was born with CF!"

Rock placed a gentle hand on his grandson's knee. "Compassion is what we must feel for anyone who is hurting."

"Larry's too *mean* to hurt."

"Everyone has a story Elijah, everyone. Larry's unhappy. We know this because happy people don't seek to torment others. Mrs. Birch is unhappy too. And unhappy people *can* be a worry."

"I'm *not* trying to *excuse* Larry or even Mrs. Birch – just explain them. Do you think you can understand the difference?"

Elijah nodded. Then he frowned, "But what about Father Philbrook?"

"Father Philbrook is not an unhappy person, just a perfectionist who gets frustrated when his neat and tidy plans are interrupted."

"Ugh!" Elijah put both hands on top of his head grabbing his hair. "How do you tell the difference?"

Rock Clearwater smiled. "By observing people carefully, and giving them the benefit of your doubt."

Elijah shook his head. "Yeah? Well today I *observed* one people who wanted to punch me in the head, a second people who gave me detention. I've never had detention! And a third people, who tortured me in my desk – *all* – day. We had to sit like we were statues, barely breathing."

They ate Grandpa's meatloaf, mashed sweet potatoes and green beans in silence for several minutes.

Rock watched his grandson eat. "Any cramps today?"

"No. My gut was good. That was the only good thing about today. I really liked the new dressing on my lunch salad, what was that?"

"A raspberry vinaigrette."

"What are you doing with those boxes?" Elijah pointed behind him with his fork.

"I was looking for the photo album your mother brought with her from Ireland. We can trace your First Nations heritage in Canada back four hundred years, but we have nothing about your mom's family, the O'Day clan from Ireland."

After putting Dart back into her stall for the night Elijah tried to read one of his mystery books from the school library, but fell asleep. When the clock struck at midnight he woke up, turned off his bed lamp then fell asleep again...

****

...Prince Dade walked alongside the oxen that carried his mate and newborn daughter. The second oxen carried Ona's mother Lee and her sister Tao. Tann walked several paces ahead, while Reef walked several paces behind.

They had kept a slow, steady pace along the tree line in short grasses where deer grazed so they wouldn't be so easy to track if Torr's men came this way. When the moon was high they had stopped to sleep.

Before first light an owl called out and awoke the restless prince. He sat up careful not to disturb the covering over Ona and their baby.

The cool morning air was thick with the scent of blooming clover. Its' sweet flowers were a favorite of their bulky oxen and the impatient wild bee.

As he looked around their rest spot, the edge of the small meadow was a perfect find. In the moonlight Reef had discovered tall thick grass already flattened by a small herd of deer. They staked the Oxen to graze along a naturally worn dirt path used by raccoon, and fox.

Dade watched as the owl that woke him glided down from a tree and captured a small rat with its clawed feet.

Cousin Torr's treacherous betrayal had flashed shock throughout the entire O'Deaghaidh Clan dividing members along ethical lines. Torr had gathered artificial loyalty among many farmers, merchants and military who had been convinced to follow him with the promise of land and rising to a higher rank.

His father's pet parrot Ut had squawked the alarm from an open window in the Great-House the moment of Torr's treasonous strike. But the bird's warning had been too late to save Dade's father Chieftain Dea and older brother Prince Rol.

Murderously assassins had assembled in twos for each victim. Just as everyone attending the council meeting was seated they were rushed and all nine died in a flood of blood by frenzied men driven by greed.

Dade too had been expected to attend the meeting, but had been delayed when Ona went into labor, or Torr would have been free to claim the crown of O'Deaghaidh Clan Chieftain for himself right there and right then.

With Reef and Tann's help Prince Dade and what was left of his family had managed to flee Gangani and hide between the lakes of the Setius River. If they could make it north as far as the Pavius River in Erdini they could count on the protection and support of the Fennanagh Clan as Chieftain Darrin was the mate of Dade's older sister Eba.

The baby stirred and instantly Ona too was awake.

Prince Dade reached over and picked up his tiny bundled daughter. The infant blinked several times then starred at the face before her. "I think this little lady should carry the name T'ull". He looked at Ona.

Ona smiled. "That is a perfect name." She leaned toward Dade and found his lips with hers. Then she rewrapped her baby in clean linens and began to nurse her.

"Good morning Sire." Tann reached the resting place coming through the trees. "Reef and I took turns sleeping and watching. There is no sign of Torr, Baza, Kauji or their armed followers."

Ona's mother Lee appeared from the other side of the meadow carrying a basket. "I have raspberries and black berries to go with the last of the cold fish."

Lee set down the basket. "Teo waits by the oxen and they are fine."

Reef joined them and they gathered around the basket of wild fruit and the cloth wrapped fish to eat quickly then leave before the sun rose any higher.

CHAPTER...3

"You don't look so good this morning." Grandpa Clearwater flipped a slice of French toast frowning. "Do you have cramps?"

Elijah rested his forehead on the edge of the heavy pine table. "No, I have murdered people in my head." He talked to the space between himself and the table.

"I dreamt about those same people, you know the guy with the bow and the sword. He's some kind of prince or something important, but he had to escape cause this other guy, his cousin, killed his dad the chief and his older brother."

Grandpa Clearwater watched his grandson listening carefully. He set down a platter of French toast. "Here dig in while it's hot."

"I actually saw blood Grandpa! The prince's cousin slit everyone's throat, it was a mess!" Elijah shook his head. "I'll just have maple syrup this morning, no raspberry sauce."

Rock Clearwater smiled. "Too red for you this morning?"

"It was like I was there! The prince had this real cute new baby too. She was only a few days old."

"The prince is on the *run* from a nasty *cousin* huh?" Grandpa took a bite and chewed.

Elijah grinned. "Oh yeah, that makes sense. I have a nasty cousin I try to avoid so I dream about a prince who runs away from his cousin."

Grandpa shrugged. "One never, knows." But Grandpa had his suspicions and considered a meeting with the Reservation Council.

Neither Larry nor Elijah's cousin James were on the bus Tuesday morning so Elijah was far more relaxed until he got to the door of his classroom.

Father Philbrook had devised a new form of suffering. Instead of a math lecture followed by practice in their notebooks every one of the twenty-six students were lined up practically shoulder to shoulder, facing the chalkboard - on decimals and fractions.

When his lecture began, he droned on and on and on while he patrolled around the classroom looking over everyone's shoulder "Typically coinage is expressed in two decimal places. Show me how you would write twenty-five cents, two dollars and thirty cents then one hundred and sixteen dollars and no cents."

"This is baby stuff. No *cents,* is about right for this morning." Elijah whispered to himself frowning.

Twins Tracy and Tina Stone heard him and giggled.

Like a phantom Father Philbrook appeared right behind them. "Is there something amusing about decimals that the three of you would like to share with the rest of the class?"

Their chalk stopped moving.

"Turn around all three of you and someone better answer my question."

Fearless Tracy spoke up. "Elijah just made a little joke about decimals making *no c-e-n-t-s* instead of no s-e-n-s-e." She spelled the two words.

Elijah was saved by Tracy's quick thinking.

The annoyed priest looked over the tops of his bifocal glasses. "Sense and cents, Mr. Clearwater I didn't realize you were that clever." He waved his right arm in a wide sweeping motion. "Back to the boards!"

"Three friends had a lemonade stand and sold all of their lemonade in one day. In that one day they made twenty-eight dollars. How is twenty-eight divided by three expressed in decimal places?"

He made a final patrol of the room. "Quickly, quickly ladies and gentlemen."

Scanning along the back of each student's head. "Mr. Clearwater, you're the *smart* one. What did you discover?"

Elijah stepped away from the board slightly and pointed to his answer. "With three friends the total is divided by one-third.

Each friend gets nine dollars and thirty-three cents, but the decimal place goes on and on kinda forever."

"I think the correct word you're looking for Mr. Clearwater is *infinity*. But what happens to the remaining point zero one cent Mr. Clearwater?"

Elijah shrugged. "Rock, paper, scissors?"

The kids laughed.

Father Philbrook ignored it. "Since the change is thirty-three cents if you were required to round to the nearest ten cents, would you round up or down?"

"Since it's below five I'd round down to thirty cents."

The bell for recess rang however, no one in Mrs. Birch's class moved.

"Erase your work and return to your desks. Take out your World History book then read chapter eight on Ireland, formerly known as *Hibernia*."

For a room of twenty-six twelve and thirteen year-olds on detention - reading about people who had been dead for six-hundred years from a faraway country they didn't think they'd likely see – was more boredom.

Only two facts that Elijah discovered about the Irish were even remotely interesting. Their tribes were called clans, and the leader of each clan was called a chief, like the Native Americans and Canadian First Nations. Otherwise he didn't see the point.

By the end of the second day of detention he was considering a visit to the veterinarian who had put a sick goat to sleep on a neighboring farm.

"Ugh! Arrow! I wish you could go to school instead of me." Elijah spread hay for both Arrow and Dart.

This time Dart nibbled some of the hay and then drank a little water from the trough.

He brushed them both. "The only good thing about today was I never had to look at or listen to Larry Swallowtail, or my mouthy cousin James."

"Cause both those guys are on a two week suspension!" He put away the brushes then hugged them.

He checked the hen house, retrieved a single egg then headed for the back door. In the oven Grandpa had pork chops baking in mushroom soup and Elijah was immediately ravenous.

Grandpa came through the back door a few minutes after Elijah dropped his backpack by the kitchen table. "I was a little late feeding the pigs this afternoon. I checked the chickens before I left this morning, and our older hen Greta is slowing down. How was your day *today*?" He took off his cowboy hat and Hudson's Bay jacket.

Elijah poured himself a glass of apple juice and shook his head. "This was from Greta's nest." He held up a single egg. "Maybe she's not slowing down maybe she's just getting later."

He then shared the decimal point lesson with his grandfather. "When doc Miller put Mr. Ingersoll's goat to sleep - could he like put people to sleep too - but only for, say, one week?"

Grandpa laughed out loud and made fresh coffee for himself. "It could be worse. I had lunch with your Aunt Dawn. Larry and James are in a heap of trouble."

Rock Clearwater pulled out the vegetable bin from the fridge. "Here, you clean carrots, I'll pull the leaves from the corn."

"I know they're suspended. Jayson is in my class and Joseph was quieter and not such a snot to me on the bus home today. But did Larry and James really accuse Mr. Fiche of being a gay guy?"

"It appears so."

After dinner Elijah labored an hour over his class questions for the history chapter on Ireland. And because his cough had returned he spent thirty minutes strapped to his chest clapper.

He brushed his teeth then took the melatonin that helped him fall asleep when he was keyed up then Grandpa read a chapter of the mystery they were both following.

Rock ran his fingers through his grandson's hair. "You need a trim at least. You're starting to look like Mr. Ingersoll's dog."

"Well I know how to herd his sheep and goats." Elijah laughed.

His grandfather chuckled. "And that's a fine skill to have with an interesting career ahead of you."

Elijah laughed harder and then his coughing spasms returned.

"Aw, we didn't get enough of the gunk from your lungs did we?" He held a small bowl while Elijah spit.

After a few minutes his breathing returned to normal. "I'm good now grandpa. I'm too sick to do some things, but not sick enough to get out of homework."

Grandpa hugged him then let him lay back on his pillows. "I never liked homework either. Now I wished I'd paid more attention then and can't seem to get enough time now to read everything I want to, decades later." Rock Clearwater stood and headed for the top of the spiral staircase that connected the loft down to the main floor. He winked, "Have good dreams son."

"I think I will Grandpa, I think I will…"

****

…As they trekked closer to Erdini the hills became steeper and more plentiful while the flat grasslands disappeared behind them.

With a feeling of unease he could not explain Dade had sent Reef to scout behind them, but in the direction of the rising sun. And then Tann he had sent back to check along Setius River to gage the distance Torr and his group might have reached.

Prince Dade, with Ona, Lee and Teo on the oxen had made it all the way to the southern tip of the west lake fed by the Pavius River. He was pleased with their progress. Only the upper half of that day's sun was visible.

The spot was perfect for a resting camp. There was water to wash and drink and cook, with fallen leaves piled deep beneath the trees from previous seasons, on which to sleep and cover their presence when they left.

Ona saw a weak tiny flash from the top of a faraway hill. She tapped Dade's shoulder. "That is either Reef or Tann?"

Dade nodded and tried to signal back, but only the upper round rim of the sun shone a soft orange glow to the west. "Not enough light to respond well, but Reef or Tann must have seen where we stopped. All we can do is wait until one of them reaches us here."

Several paces from the water on the lake's shore Dade started a small cooking fire behind a grouping of large rocks, while Lee set several rabbit traps and Teo set traps in the trees for low nesting pheasants.

Ona wrapped baby T'ull in clean dry linens then washed the soiled cloths at the lake's edge. Ona was nursing her infant when Tann reappeared panting.

Tann dropped to his knees bent over with cramps from running.

The prince quickly handed his guard his water pouch, then refilled Tann's from clean water scooped several feet out into the lake.

"Thank you Sire." Tann struggled to slow his breathing so he could speak.

Lee returned and uncovered her basket with what was left of the raspberries and blackberries. Then Teo returned with several small apples carried in the hem of her robe. She spilled them on the small rug by the basket.

"Sire," Tann splashed water from the pouch onto his face then reached for two apples. "Torr follows the river now with his entire party. Both Baza and Kauji are with him and they have come a great distance."

Dade bit into an apple. "We will easily reach the Pavius River fork that feeds into the east and west lake before another sunset. From there we are in the province of Erdini then one of the farmers can get word to the Chieftain Darrin and my sister Eba."

Tann shook his head. "They have reached the southeast edge of the lake that joins the Setius River on the north. Because of your sister Torr may have guessed at your purpose. They travel much faster than we do and will catch up with us by the time the sun is high midday tomorrow. If they do not stop to camp tonight they will reach us even before that."

"To eat then continue after dark is what they shall do..." Reef's voice came from the dark shadows of the trees just before he collapsed from fatigue and his wound.

Prince Dade, Tann and Teo rushed to where they heard Reef fall. When they carried him to the soft sand by the fire they saw the sword wound in his left side.

Lee quickly caught the end of a small branch that extended from the low flames then pressed the glowing end against the bleeding tissue to clean and seal the wound. Reef jerked in pain and opened his eyes. With a small rug rolled under his head Lee held the opening of the water pouch to his lips.

Teo returned from the edge of the forest with fresh moss. Carefully she laid a palm sized piece of clean moss against Reef's wound then held it in place wrapping a band of cloth torn from her sleeve, around his waist. Reef closed his eyes again.

They heard a sudden snap then a sharp squawk deep in the trees then the call of an owl. Teo and Lee ran toward the sound to check the rabbit and pheasant traps. They soon returned with two birds and one rabbit for roasting.

Reef slept. Everyone else in the party was quiet and they rested too as their food cooked over the low flames of the open fire.

This time two owls called to each other from across the narrow lake. Reef stirred then grimaced and opened his eyes.

Teo held more water to his lips. After he drank, she offered some raspberries. "If you like I can wash your robe?"

He shook his head and took her hand. "That is not necessary. After crawling through grass a few more stains will not matter. Besides I'm not expected at a council meeting." Reef smiled at her.

His fellow guard Tann moved closer to Reef. "I saw Torr, with Baza, Kauji and the rest of Torr's treacherous hounds following the Setius River. Did you come upon them after me?"

Reef turned his head to look at his fellow guard and to Dade his clan's new and rightful Chieftain. "No I stayed to the open grasses on the sunrise side of the trees that grow between the grasses and the river. It was there I came upon two of Torr's jackals."

"They were returning to the rest of the disloyal gang after checking to see if we were perhaps heading for Ebla, and the clan of your grandmother Sire. I killed Fra the carpenter easily, but Ver the blacksmith had a longer sword and pierced my side."

Then Reef smiled remembering. "However with his sword in me his heart was that much closer to the point of my sword."

Tann shook his head smiling.

Prince Dade nodded. "Very good." He looked from Tann to Reef. "I thank you, loyal friends."

With the word 'friend' Reef knew that if they all survived then his rank and Tann's would rise from guard to knight. As a knight he would own land and could then ask for Teo to be his life mate.

Dade stood and walked away from the fire and the others along the side of the shore. He knew they could not defend themselves against the numbers who followed Torr.

When he returned to the gathering, the roasting food was ready to eat and the prince had an idea.

CHAPTER...4

Grandpa Clearwater had always been careful with Elijah's diet however, Elijah wasn't always so careful.

From time to time, no matter how diligent Grandpa was with the food Elijah ate, his grandson didn't always take enough pancreatic enzymes when he ate fatty foods nor drink nearly enough water to keep his viscid packed body hydrated.

Wednesday morning Elijah woke up in pain from gut cramps.

When Grandpa walked up the tight winding stairs to wake his grandson Elijah was laying on his side with his knees pulled up to his chest. "Oh no, when did this start?"

Rock turned to get the medication Elijah's doctor had given him when Elijah had been hospitalized the previous Christmas. "You been in pain long?"

Elijah opened his eyes. "No it woke me up, but it's getting much better now. There was a sword fight!"

Grandpa hurried to retrieve the Gastro-grafin from a small locked cabinet on the east wall by the small loft window. Elijah's comment about a sword fight concerned him and he rested the back of his hand on his grandson's forehead to check for a fever.

"Can you sit up and take this?"

Elijah rose up on one elbow to sip some water with the gel-capsule. "I think I shoulda taken two more digestive enzymes with dinner last night." He lay back down. "We had those pork chops."

His grandfather nodded and sat on the side of the bed. "I wasn't thinking either and should have reminded you, but we've talked about this before. I'm not always going to be here. And you're getting old enough now to understand that your condition is something you're going to need to monitor."

"Who's that friend at school, the girl in your class with diabetes?"

"Julie Bates."

"Yes, now I remember, Julie Bates. You said that she had to learn to give herself insulin injections a few months ago. And you mister, don't drink enough water or water or water…"

"But Grandpa! So much water makes me *pee* all the time! Mrs. Birch said I could just get up and go whenever I needed to, but *warden* Philbrook makes us put up our hand and then he makes such a big deal about interrupting the class."

Smoothing the hair from his grandson's forehead he let out a deep breath. "I'll remind Father Philbrook about your situation when I call the school to report you absent for today. Remain still and let the medication do its' job." He checked for any sign of a fever again. "I'll be back with some apple juice for you."

Elijah drifted back to sleep...

****

...Dade pulled away the roasted bird's thigh with the upper part of the leg. He was hungry and this tasted good. He chewed and swallowed. "If we can't outpace Torr then maybe we can confuse him."

He finished his portion then reached for an apple. He looked at Ona. "Our daughter is now three sunrises and three sunsets – if you feel up to it, we can likely travel faster without the oxen."

Ona smiled and brushed the side of his cheek with the back of her fingers. "It would be good for me to walk," she nodded.

"Good then this is what we shall do. Reef should not be walking for two maybe three sunrises. So we rest until the moon reaches there he pointed upward. Tann and I will keep watch until then."

"After we have rested, we will all leave this camp at one time. Reef will ride one oxen in the direction of the rising sun toward Ebla and gather support from my grandmother's brother Chieftain Ni."

"Tann will lead the second oxen behind Reef only as far as the valley before the Rujinda River. Follow the river as far south as Rheba then return to the direction of the setting sun and our land of Gangani."

Tann smiled. "With Torr not there in Gangani I can gather a greater number of our loyalists to condemn him."

"My plan is that even if Torr can pick up each of our trails after he leaves the shores of the Setius River, he will have a problem. One trail will clearly lead in the direction of the land of my grandmother's birth. A second trail will lead in the direction of the province of my sister's mate. A third trail will lead away from the first trail – which he will correctly reason leads directly back to our home and the place of his betrayal."

"Torr won't know which trail that 'I' have taken and may assume I have chosen the third trail to claim my birthright. Either way he must divide up his band of traitors into three smaller groups and decide which one he shall lead."

"Whatever choice Torr makes he will have reduced his large number of bribed loyalists by one-third leaving his forces more vulnerable if he can't overtake us before we reach each of our three destinations."

Prince Dade leaned forward searching each face intently. "We must reach each of our destinations."

****

"Elijah, Elijah wake up son."

When Elijah opened his eyes his grandfather sat beside him on his bed. His grandfather rubbed his back with one hand and held a tall glass of apple juice in the other.

"Oh oh, Grandpa the medicine is working!" Elijah sprang from his bed and ran for the stairs. At the back door he put his feet into his rain boots then just grabbed a sweater and rushed outside to the outhouse.

It was overcast again with a light drizzle falling.

Later Elijah sat on the long narrow window seat beside the high, wide living room window holding a mug of hot chocolate. As he watched the school bus pass by the end of their driveway he felt relieved, almost weightless like a helium balloon.

He turned around as his grandfather started a fire in the fireplace. "This is your best batch ever Grandpa."

Rock squeezed the bellows to fan the smaller flames. "You're just saying that because you get to have a day away from school." He chuckled then picked up his coffee mug to join Elijah on the bench.

"How are you feeling now?"

"My muscles are a little sore, don't really feel like eating anything yet, but I had a great poop," he grinned. "So I know I don't haveta go to the hospital again."

Elijah took another swallow. "How come you kept checking my forehead?"

"I thought when you first woke up you might be running a fever. Some of the first words out of your mouth were about a sword fight. That's a strange comment first thing in the morning even for you."

"I had another dream about that prince again he's still trying to run away from his nasty cousin."

"That's interesting." Grandpa checked the fire then took another sip of his coffee. "Was it the same dream or a different dream?"

"Kinda the same, but different. It's like a TV episode. The prince's dad who was the chief and his older brother were killed by the older cousin who wants to be chief. The cousin needs to kill the prince now cause the prince is the real new chief. The prince is trying to get to where his sister lives with her husband so they'll be safe."

"I see. Sounds like a pretty unusual dream." Rock Clearwater watched his grandson closely.

"Yeah it is. It's weird. It's not scary, just sort'a tense. I hope the good prince who's supposed to be the chief doesn't get killed by his mean cousin who wants to be chief."

"Gosh, now I'm tense too."

Grandson and grandfather sat silently together for another eight minutes watching cattle grazing in the field across the road through the rain spattered glass. The fire behind them warmed their back.

A log fell from the iron grate and startled them both.

Grandpa's coffee had grown cold. "Well let's get some chores done o'l man. Do you feel like collecting the eggs, while I feed the pigs?"

"Can I stay in my pajamas?"

"Y-e-s, you can stay in your PJs." Grandpa walked toward the back door. "Put on thick socks inside your rubber boots and wear your lined windbreaker." He turned to face Elijah who had followed him, "with the zipper pulled all the way up."

Elijah wrinkled his nose then grinned. "Okay *warden* Grandpa! What about Arrow and Dart?"

They stepped out onto the wide back deck, then down to the winding gravel path to the out buildings behind the house.

"I'll get their hay if you get their oats then you need to lay down again for a rest at least until lunch."

The damp spring air bit into Elijah's cheeks by a gusting wind that hit him as he came around the corner of the hen house. "Wow." He had to grab the door from slamming into the outside wall.

"Sorry ladies." He stepped inside and several chickens scurried at his feet. They ran outside then ran back in again after they encountered the sharp wet wind.

Only half of their fifteen chickens had laid a single egg, so gathering them didn't take long. He filled their water tank, scattered seed inside and out and then set the egg basket on the deck floor by the back door on his way to see Arrow and Dart.

Both horses were outside and damp, but it was a warm damp. They came up to him, lowered their heads and nuzzled him. It was easier for Elijah to hug Dart around her neck because she was so much shorter than Arrow, but he loved them both.

"I think you guys should be inside." He led them to separate stalls directly across the walkway so they could still see each other.

"Good thinking." Grandpa stood behind Elijah. "Dart shouldn't be out all day in this for sure. I'll get her blanket while you wipe down Arrow."

The tall windows of the A-frame cabin rose from the floor to the peak of the open beam ceiling. If Elijah stood at the half wall railing across the front of his loft bedroom he could see through the upper glass far across the west pasture. From the smaller square window behind his headboard he could see out to the east pasture, the pig barn and the henhouse.

Back in his bed after the animals were fed, Elijah realized he was exhausted and fell asleep beside his second mug of hot chocolate after just two short breaths…

****

...Torr with eighty-six men left the banks of the Setius River and jogged through the narrow band of trees between the river and the grassy plains. The plains soon changed to steep rises where they had to take more and more rest stops.

Two of his scouts still had not returned, he was curious about their fate, but only mildly so. He had a mission and that mission would not be stopped. He had been the only son of the chieftain's younger brother, who died defending the clan, and Torr felt cheated by a birth order he intended to change.

Up and over the grassy hills Torr led his fighters toward the west lake that was fed by the river Pauius. Just beyond the river was the land of Erdini.

He was wild with excitement and expected to come across his cousin and small defenseless party at any moment.

The sun was not yet high in the cobalt sky when one of Torr's scouts discovered Prince Dade's last resting place next to a lake. He had followed the faint scent of cooked pheasant and rabbit that still hung in the air.

The campfire had been left almost undetectable covered by sand and scattered beach rocks. The scout was sure he would be rewarded handsomely for this and he was also sure he could tell what direction the prince had gone beyond this camp.

The scout rushed back through the trees and signaled with a flag tied to the end of his spear.

The next scout spotted the flag then he waved back to the next hill. Torr and the rest of his army was only one mile away when the series of signal flags reached him.

Torr was elated. He could almost taste his cousin's blood. If Ona had given birth the child of course would need to die too then Ona would be his mate.

At the site they regrouped and followed the first scout through the trees and into an open meadow where it was obvious that three distinct trails led off in three separate directions.

Anger ignited like wheat dust and he ran the first scout threw with his sword then turned to a second scout. "I was told," he bellowed, "that Dade left with only his mate, her mother and sister and two guards!"

"Captain?" One brave guard stepped forward. "We confirmed that and the two oxen to carry his mate with child and her family. The oxen would certainly have slowed them down as well as a woman expecting."

"Then how is it possible there are three distinct trampled trails, fresh and early this day?"

The second scout stepped forward. "Let me follow the trails for a short distance Captain and report back."

"No! We will follow all of them now! We waste time!" Torr spit his orders loudly to the men, resentful that he had been forced to divide up his army.

With his army carved into three smaller groups of twenty-eight each, Torr had two new difficult decisions – which *group would he lead and in which direction? He was certain that his cousin would not take the route east to the province of Ebla – his grandmother's birth place.*

That left either north or south. Would his cousin send Ona to the safety of his older sister's home in the land of Erdini while he doubled back to Gangani?

Torr selected his fittest runners to follow the trail south. "Baza I am certain that my cousin heads south to claim his birthright. Catch up to him and kill him and bring his head back to me!"

"Kauji, follow this trail east quickly and stop that party from reaching Ebla the land of Dade's mother's mother. When you reach them, bring their heads back to me."

He chose the second fastest runners for his trek north then he took aside his two trusted lieutenants. "I have no doubt that we will overtake Ona, her mother and sister. If by chance Dade reaches our clan in Gangani before you can kill him and he secures his place as chieftain – send word to him that I have Ona and shall kill both his child and his mate unless he surrenders the crown to me then leaves our clan."

The main body of the army disbanded into three smaller units running in three different directions.

****

When Elijah opened his eyes he had expected see a thick grove of wild apple trees.

He blinked several times then sat up. Glowing red numbers beside him showed twelve thirty-six. In the loft space the aroma of corn chowder drifted up from somewhere below him then he heard footsteps.

"Oh good, you're already awake." Rock winked at his grandson standing partway up the spiral steps. "You slept for two hours, how do you feel?"

At first his grandson scanned his surroundings as if he wasn't entirely sure where he was.

"I'm actually hungry." But Elijah didn't move.

"O-k-a-y." Grandpa came up the last four steps and crossed the loft space to the foot of Elijah's bed. "What is it?"

"I was *there*, really there." He recognized his grandfather.

"I could smell the apples on the trees, lots and lots of apple trees and no one even planted them. It was an apple tree forest."

"But the mean cousin Torr is getting closer! He has a lot of men with him and Prince Dade won't reach Chieftain Darrin and the safety of Erdini in time!"

Elijah's expression was almost frantic. "Reef is wounded and riding an ox to Ebla, but another group of Torr's men will overtake him, I'm sure of it! And Tann has taken the other Ox south back to their home of Gangani, but even though he's not wounded he's still all alone against more than twenty other guys!"

Rock Clearwater was paying attention, shaken by the fact that he suddenly realized his grandson wasn't just dreaming he was actually living the legend and straddling *time.*

The Sarsi Tsuu T'ina had descended from the Blackfoot Nation and there was a legend his grandfather shared with him. Rock Clearwater had been younger than Elijah, only eleven, but he remembered the words and what they meant vividly and his heart raced that the truth of the legend and the signs from Elijah's birth that might be coming true.

"Did you talk to any of these people, or did you just listen from a short distance?"

"I'm everywhere and I'm talking and I'm listening."

"Do you understand what these people are saying?"

"Yes. They speak an old sort of English. They sound like the people on the BBC, but different."

"Your mother was from Ireland, she was often mistaken for English to anyone who didn't know the difference in accents. Did they sound like your mother?"

Elijah looked at the framed photo of his parents set between his digital clock and lamp.

"Do you want to listen to the answering machine tape again?"

"No grandpa I remember." Then he nodded, "Yeah they sounded Irish."

He smiled for the first time and seemed to be completely in the present and back in Alberta.

"We're reading about Ireland in history, but Father Philbrook called it..." Elijah thought for a second, "Hibernia. Father Philbrook said Ireland was known as Hibernia in ancient times."

CHAPTER...5

...Prince Dade felt a sudden panic.

He looked over at his courageous wife who had matched him step for step. She carried tiny T'ull in a sling from her shoulder. Her mother Lee and sister Teo were only a few paces behind.

The sun was now high. They were just beyond where the river Pavius forked, but he knew they would be found before they could reach the safety of the clan of his sister's mate in Erdini.

Reaching the base of a wide trunk of an old apple tree, Dade held up his hand. "We need to rest here." But the prince did not sit.

Lee leaned her back against the tree trunk and closed her eyes. Teo fell back onto the tall grass.

Ona sat beside her mother and watched has her mate climbed up through the gnarled branches of the tree.

From the vantage point at the top branches the prince spotted movement far to the south crossing the river at its fork before the line where the apple forest began. He knew the movement was not a band of local hunters, it was Torr. The band moved quickly and was no further away than six-thousand paces.

Dade's heart began to race. Torr and his men would reach them much sooner than Reef had thought.

He cleared his mind as he descended. When he reached the ground, he had a plan. "Teo."

She sat upright.

"Come with me."

They rushed to the eastern edge of the small forest.

"There, over that ridge and one more beyond, starts Erdini." Dade made a small cut in his palm just below his thumb. He squeezed his blood on a strip of cloth that he wrapped just behind an arrow point.

Raising his long bow he shot the arrow high and it disappeared beyond the first ridge. "Follow where the arrow went, as quickly as you can, running as much as you can."

"When you reach my arrow, use your bow to shoot my arrow in the same direction beyond the second ridge, so you stay on course. Perhaps my arrow will attract the attention of one of Darrin's patrols and when they see the blood, that is a sign for distress."

"Why are you staying here? Why are we not going on together?"

"Torr is no more than six-thousand paces south of the tree I climbed. By you running north I hope Torr will think we have all moved on, but your mother and Ona can't keep the same pace that you and I can. I must hide them and then run to join you."

Teo nodded then sprinted across the tall wild grass in the direction of Dade's arrow.

As he turned to hurry back to the large old apple tree he trotted through a small open area surrounded by younger, thicker apple trees. 'Little T'ull,' he thought, 'my baby apple.'

When he reached Ona and Lee he had to put the second half of his plan in place. "Torr is running in this general direction from the place where the lakes fork into the river. I sent Teo to the border of Erdini where one of Darrin's patrols should spot her."

"But Torr will surely find us before that occurs. We must be prepared." He looked at Ona. "Will using your bow be possible for you?"

"Only my small bow."

"That is still fine."

"Let's follow the tracks Teo and I made to the edge of the trees."

Ona and Lee stood and followed Dade. At the forest boundary they turned and he led them to the small open area.

"Here the trees are younger and thicker. Lee I want you to climb that one. I'll climb that one to the south. Ona can you *climb that one carrying T'ull or should I hand her up to you?"*

Ona touched his cheek and smiled. "Your daughter weigh's barely anything. I can climb much easier now than I could before she arrived. What is the reason we do this?"

"Hiding. But hiding so that if we are discovered we are higher than Torr and his men and we can shoot at them from three vantage points, behind cover. Do not shoot from your tree unless you see me shoot first."

Lee hugged her daughter and kissed her sleeping granddaughter then climbed up through the branches of the tree Dade selected.

Dade kissed his daughter's forehead then Ona's lips. "You realize we may not survive this..."

Ona interrupted Dade. "I understand. I understand very well what may happen, so does my mother, so does my sister, so did Reef and Tann. But we had to try and we had to try for you, our rightful leader, our true chieftain."

They kissed again and parted.

From Dade's tree he could not see Ona or Lee. If he had not selected the trees for them he would not know they were there.

He closed his eyes and thought of his father and older brother. He had not been able to see to their funeral and fumed all over again at the thought they died at the hands of not just a traitor, but that they had been betrayed by a member of their own family.

Birds stopped singing, even the trees became still. Far to his left he heard low voices, then feet breaking twigs coming through the trees. Torr's men were walking in a line, shoulder to shoulder.

Abruptly the feet stopped about the location of the old apple tree. Then Torr did what Dade hoped he would do, he signaled for his men to stop searching in a line for a trail - because Torr thought he'd found it.

Prince Dade could hear a dozen feet moving away then the sound of more feet following the trail to the point that Teo ran to the ridge toward Erdini.

But unexpectedly a human line of Torr's followers appeared to his left at the edge of the small clearing. Eight men walked east in the direction of the edge of the apple tree forest.

Dade's bow was ready.

He had a clear shot, and he knew that he and Lee and Ona could kill these eight, but didn't want to give away their location unless he had to.

Then amazingly Torr and all of his men appeared in the small clearing between the very trees he had led Ona and Lee.

Torr immediately gestured with his arms, pointing. Torr assigned four men to stand point at four places with their backs to the main group. Looking out they watched into the trees for a possible ambush. Three of the men stood only a few paces away from each of the trees in which Ona, Lee and Dade were hiding.

Where Torr stopped toward the center of the clearing, Dade could hear what was being said.

"We still do not know how many guards came with Dade, but it appears that no more than two people have gone on to Erdini. Following that trail is a risk. We're very close to Chieftain Darrin's border, so hurry but remain watchful."

Eight more of Torr's followers left the clearing in the direction Dade had shot his arrow for Teo.

Out of the original band of eighty-six fighters – Dade had managed to reduce the threat from his rival to the twenty-one men standing below him. If it was Reef and Tann hiding in the other two trees, Dade with each of them could have easily killed or wounded all of those who remained.

Dade's bow was ready. As soon as he could get a clear shot of Torr – he was certain the rest of the traitors would flee. The loyalty of these men was for personal reward and with Torr dead – there would be nothing for any of them to gain.

But, Torr kept moving and remained between two guards who were protective, as if they knew that with one arrow Torr's importance had the substance of air.

Torr lowered his voice. "One trail went north toward Erdini then a second partial trail led back into these trees, which tells me that someone in Dade's party is unable to travel."

"Ona may be about to give birth which means her mother and her sister will be with her too." Torr stopped speaking and listened. His men were barely breathing.

"Dade who could travel much faster alone may have gone on alone or with one guard – leaving another guard here." He turned away and then began to scan around the perimeter of the entire clearing. *"From that entrance point those left behind must have split up so they wouldn't leave a new trail."*

Torr's voice faded as he thought out loud looking around once more. "And they didn't leave any bent grass or broken twig. There's no sign at all that anyone crossed from there," he pointed, *"to somewhere else."*

He motioned to five more of his men then pointed. "Follow that entrance trail back around returning to the large old apple tree. They may have doubled backed from here. See if there is any sign of another path from the old tree besides the one we found. Search these woods carefully from the old tree to the river."

The glen of wild apple trees was a short narrow strip of land in the shape of a shallow dish. To the west was the Pavius River, to the east was the open plains of tall grasses.

The Pavius River was wide and shallow not narrow and steep as the Setius had been with a canyon of rocks for shelter. So the only place to hide was in the forest – and Dade knew, that Torr knew that.

Prince Dade couldn't feel his legs and his upper arms and shoulders had begun to ache. He worried that Ona and her mother Lee would be feeling the same and unable to move or shoot if they had to. With five more men sent to search from the old apple tree to the river there were now only sixteen men with Torr.

"We must begin to search carefully from this clearing to the old apple tree. People can't fly across this forest." Torr's attention was distracted by a pair of Robins.

When they flew between the branches of the tree beside the one where Ona hid they disappeared. Neither they nor their nest was visible.

Suddenly Torr looked up searching the branches of the trees around the clearing.

Dade's first arrow killed Torr's guard to his left.

The prince's second shot killed Torr's guard to his right.

Another arrow came from Ona killing the lookout below her tree.

Dade's third arrow hit Torr's right shoulder as he shielded himself with the body of his first fallen guard.

The lookout below Lee's tree fell mortally wounded.

Two more arrows shot from the branches of Lee's tree killing two more guards as the confused and terrified men scattered for the underbrush.

Dade killed another guard who tried to help Torr run for the woods.

Another one of Lee's arrows hit Torr in the back of his leg.

When Torr stumbled, Dade shot again, but hit the fourth lookout who had been running for the cover of a fallen tree.

One of Torr's men blew their distress horn, as the remaining men began to blindly shoot arrows into the trees around the clearing.

Then everyone heard the cries of a newborn infant from up in the branches of the tree that grew on the north perimeter of the clearing.

Every movement stopped.

There was no other sound except that of the child of Ona and Prince Dade.

Dade's arrow was ready in his bow and pointed at the place where Torr had crawled to hide, but he saw no movement.

Eternity passed.

Silence.

Abruptly no sound came from the upper branches of Ona's hiding place.

No sound came from the men hiding in the forest.

No sound came from any birds or animals.

With his heart kicking at his ribs Dade watched all around, then his tree, and Lee's tree, and Ona's tree, but still he saw nothing.

And then in one swift flaming mass, nine arrows wrapped in tar soaked linen shot into the grass below Ona's tree.

Dade watched in horror as his sly – cunning cousin prepared to burn his mate and tiny child.

The first nine flaming arrows were followed by another nine.

A rush of energy he had felt only twice before filled his entire being and he rose up on the tree branch.

His bow and arrows fell to the ground.

A flash of white light surrounded Prince Dade transforming his physical form to that of a giant white crow with a wing span that touched the tops of the trees.

In a single sweeping flurry the prince stepped into the air and filled the clearing with his light then sent a giant wave of wind with his right wing that snuffed out the flames below Ona's tree.

Desperate Torr limped into the clearing with a flaming spear in his left hand followed by all of his men armed with flaming spears. As one body ten spears sailed toward the hovering white essence of Prince Dade, the White Crow.

The flames shot upwards then became dust before they could hit him.

White Crow became brighter growing even greater in size.

The white light altered to violet – sending a second massive wave of wind that sucked the air from the lungs of every traitor in the apple orchard, and on the path to Ebla and on the path to Gangani.

One by one as the traitors awoke they discovered they were mute. Their voices had been taken from them.

When the wounded Torr stood to get his bearings, he saw Prince Dade helping his mate Ona down from her tree. Torr tried to yell orders for his men to attack, but no sound came from his throat.

GREY

CROW

CHAPTER...6

Thursday morning, Elijah was wide awake and alert just before sunrise.

Sensing his grandson was up and might need him, Rock went directly to the kitchen, made his coffee and boiled water for Elijah's spiced herbal tea.

When Grandpa Clearwater reached the top of the spiral stairs Elijah was sitting up. "Good morning Grandpa. My tea smells good. Thank you." He reached for the mug as his grandfather sat on the side of his bed.

Rock Clearwater took a large swallow of his coffee. "Well my friend you look like a new person, but you're up before our rooster." He grinned relieved that his grandson was feeling even better, than better.

"No," he smiled. "I'm up before the *crows*! Grandpa, Prince Dade sure showed his nasty cousin who was in charge. I could hardly believe it! There was only the prince, his wife Ona and her mother all outnumbered by ten or fifteen of Torr's creepy men..."

Then Elijah went into great animated detail recalling the battle and the magical transformation of the hero prince in Elijah's continuing dream. A dream so real, it had seemed to bewilder him.

"That was quite the dream. I don't think... No I know I've never known anyone before who had dreams even close to those."

"Now I really gotta pee." Elijah handed his empty mug to his grandfather then rushed to the stairs.

Rock took a last swallow of coffee and glanced at one of Elijah's pillows as he stood. There on one of pillow's from the bed that had belonged to his late parents lay two large white feathers.

Grandpa Clearwater blinked hard twice sure he was seeing things, but when he looked again both feathers were still there.

When he reached for them they felt warm to his touch. They were perfectly formed, as large as his forearm in width and from his wrist to elbow in length. Now he had confirmation and knew he needed to meet with the Tribe Elders of the Sarsi Tsuu T'ina Council again.

As he waited for the familiar yellow school bus, Elijah was tempted to dip into his lunch bag for an early snack. He still didn't feel full from his breakfast of three scrambled eggs, four strips of bacon and a bowl of sliced strawberries.

By the time the bus reached the school, he had finished all of his apple slices and started on a small bag of carrot sticks.

He felt good. He had no gut cramps, no cough, no Larry Swallowtail or cousin James on the bus and only two more days of Father-warden-Philbrook.

He felt like this was going to be a great day – then the bell rang for class. On his desk were three bottles of water.

"Mr. Clearwater, you're not contagious?"

"No sir."

"Excellent. I received a call from your grandfather. Homework was to finish reading chapters eight, nine and ten on Ireland, so we could discuss them."

"I read them sir."

"Good." Father Philbrook began to wonder up and down the rows of desks again, but today it didn't bother Elijah.

"Who can tell me what similarities they found between the ancient people of Ireland, then called Hibernia with Canada's First Nations and our southern Native Americans?"

Elijah's hand shot up. "The ancient Irish had tribes too, called clans and at the head of each clan was a leader called a chieftain."

"Well, you were paying attention."

"I'm only half Sarsi Tsuu T'ina – the other half is Irish. My late mother was born in a village called Ruan, in Munster, but in ancient times the province was called Gangani."

Then it hit Elijah. Had he been dreaming about some ancient Irish relatives? Was Prince Dade a great, great, great, great,

great something of his? Suddenly the odd series of dreams had more meaning for him, and he had trouble concentrating on the rest of the history discussion.

"That's very interesting Elijah. Anyone else in the class have Irish roots of which they are aware?"

When the bell rang for the recess break Father Philbrook called him aside. "Mrs. Decker will sit in for me for the next two hours, while I have a very important meeting in my office. When you are done in the boys' washroom, come immediately to my office."

Out in the hall, Elijah caught sight of his cousin Jayson watching him. When he nodded Jayson turned to walk back to their prison classroom.

Waiting by the secretary's desk, Elijah heard raised voices coming from behind the closed door of the principal's office. Then it was deathly quiet.

When the office door opened the chemistry teacher Mr. Fiche left the front reception area at a brisk march. He had a pinched expression on his face as if he'd bitten into a lemon.

Through the partially open door Elijah was startled to see his Aunt Dawn and Uncle River, with his cousin James.

As they passed him, his uncle winked and his aunt bent down to kiss his cheek, but his cousin sneered.

Then thanking Principal Philbrook was Larry Swallowtail's grandmother Eliza Snow. As she backed out of the priest's office Larry looked at him and Elijah's heart constricted.

Mrs. Snow stopped. "How is your dear grandfather, Elijah?"

But Elijah had trouble paying attention. Larry's hand gesture was impossible to miss.

"Elijah dear?"

He stood. "Oh I'm sorry Mrs. Snow. He's well thank you ma'am."

"Please say hello to him for me. I will give him a call sometime in the next few weeks." She smiled and they left.

Behind her followed her guerrilla grandson glaring at Elijah and mouthing, '*You are dead.*' as they left.

Two minutes later Father Philbrook appeared and waved Elijah into his office that looked more like a mini library. It was amazing to Elijah that the priest could actually meet with people. There was barely room for anything else in the crowded room.

Two walls of book shelves, as far back as Elijah could remember from when he was in grade one had been packed tight. Since then the floor space had slowly been occupied with stacks of more books, then windowsills and the room's round table and chair seats.

Oddly the top of the principal's desk was always nearly bare, with only a desk phone, day-timer, penholder and note pad. But today stacks of books normally resting on chair seats had been moved to the desk top.

"Because James is one of your cousins, you have no doubt heard that he was temporarily suspended from classes for the past week, pending any other ruling by the school superintendant?"

Elijah nodded, wishing he could morph into a crow like Prince Dade and fly off.

"Larry Swallowtail has also been suspended, but his circumstances are more serious and his suspension is permanent."

He didn't hide his surprise and really, really, really wanted to ask what Larry had done.

"Thanks to the courage of your cousin Jayson – more of Larry's activities in partnership with James and to some extent Joseph as well – have come to light. Apparently you have been on the receiving end of many of Larry's creative bullying activities."

"For the record would you care to share some of those experiences?"

Elijah's entire body felt numb. He looked down at his hands and his feet to make sure they were still attached. Earlier relief that Larry would no longer be on the school bus was replaced by a turbulent panic wondering exactly *where* Larry would be *located*.

"Is Larry…?" Elijah barely had a voice. He cleared his throat. "Is Larry moving away?"

"I made some recommendations for other schools, but that's up to his grandmother at least until he turns eighteen. The fact that Larry was almost seventeen and still in grade nine was certainly not ideal, and that became a challenge for both him and our school."

"Do you need my experiences with Larry Swallowtail for a file of some kind?"

Father Philbrook could sense that Elijah – like most bully targets – was reluctant to say anything. "Not really, but it would be one more person's story to complete a pattern that we have already compiled on Larry. He pretty much picked on anyone at least once, however the students he harassed on a regular basis are important to know."

"There were a few incidents, but my cousin James never let Larry go too far. In February, he started picking on me after I called him a prehistoric Mastodon when he made Sasha Deerling cry. You know the school bus driver's daughter?"

The principal nodded.

"She wears really thick glasses, and when he took them off her face she couldn't see. She's only in grade four. Well he was holding them up out of her reach and she needed to go into the school to the bathroom, but she couldn't see."

"When I called him a Mastodon, he said, '*What did you call me?*' And then I said if he didn't know what a Mastodon was he must be as dumb as he was big! He hit me in the chest, I fell backwards and then he threw Sasha's glasses all the way from the side doors to the swings. My cousin Spring ran and got them for Sasha."

"Now I feel awful, I could have been more tactful – I didn't know then how old he was. What I said must have made him feel real bad when I called him dumb." Elijah looked down at his hands.

Father Philbrook folded his hands together on top of the table. "This is a lesson for all of us Elijah. It's not always easy to understand, but bullies are more often the ones hurting too for some reason, that's *why* they pick on others. It doesn't excuse their behavior, but can sometimes explain it."

"So we should be *nice* to bullies?"

"No, be patient and try to look for what motivates them? Do they feel insecure? Are they not getting enough attention at home? Are they being bullied at home by a sibling or parent or care-giver? Has there been a divorce or new step-parent? What motivates someone to bully could be a number of upsetting life events."

Father Philbrook stood. "We're done here, Mr. Clearwater. If you'd like you can get your lunch and your water," he smiled, "then eat in the library. You might remain there for the rest of the afternoon so your curious fellow classmates don't hassle you with questions."

The librarian made Elijah finish his lunch before she'd let him check out the book, *Irish History 1300 to 1500*. He knew his mother had been born in a more modern Ireland though in 1980 there were no cell phones yet, but he wanted to know more about the time in Ireland when Prince Dade had lived.

When Grandpa Clearwater heard the back door slam he called to Elijah. "I'm working on your Irish family tree!"

Elijah shuffled half sliding half walking to the front room still wearing his thick boot socks. "I have this history book when Ireland was really old – eight years before Columbus."

Grandpa Clearwater worked on his laptop that rested on a TV tray in front of the fireplace. Family photographs were placed in four separate piles. "Well I'm pretty sure I can't trace your mother's family back that far. I can only trace our Tsuu T'ina side three or four hundred years."

Elijah sat on the raised hearth. "I wanted to know more about the time of Prince Dade. Just curious that's all."

His grandfather nodded. "Well how was today? You've only got tomorrow with *warden* Philbrook," he ginned, "then you're back with your homeroom teacher Mrs. Birch."

Elijah told his grandfather about waiting outside the principal's office, Larry Swallowtail, Mrs. Snow, his Aunt Dawn and James – and his talk with Father Philbrook.

Rock Clearwater turned off his laptop. "This has been some week. I think we need to feed Arrow and Dart then drive into town and have a thick juicy hamburger at the Mountain Creek Café."

"Yes! And Elijah was at the back door with his boots back on his feet before his grandfather took one step.

That night after a twenty minute session with his chest clapper – Elijah took his melatonin and then had the best sleep he had had for months. There were no dreams, and know one running away from a cousin with murderous motives.

CHAPTER...7

At breakfast Elijah ate his bran muffin with peaches looking more rested than his grandfather had remembered seeing him since Christmas.

"So, a bigger bow, with longer arrows huh?" Grandpa peeled the paper from his muffin. "I'll see what I can do?"

Elijah swallowed. "And while you're at it just ask Great Aunt Lucille if she'd like to contribute to a new bow and arrows. Please no more of her homemade pajamas, I'm gonna be thirteen."

Grandpa laughed out loud almost choking on a swallow of his coffee. "Not a chance. My sister is famous for her knitted sweaters and flannelette sleepwear – and you're not getting off so easy. I happen to know she already finished your birthday gift, but this year the pattern is more grownup..."

He started laughing again, "they're..." he tried to collect himself. "They're bears with fishing poles by a lake!" Grandpa Clearwater had to put down his mug so he wouldn't spill the coffee.

Elijah shook his head.

The only remotely positive part was knowing that his grandfather's sister sewed nightgowns for all of the girls and pajamas for all of the boys, no matter what their ages, for everyone in the family. She bought fabric by the bolt, so each year everyone got the same pattern, which made the embarrassment complete for the entire family.

There was still no James on the school bus. Jayson sat beside him and Joseph sat behind them and they just talked about their weekend camping plans. Life was pretty easy without Larry Swallowtail.

When the bell rang, Jayson and Elijah hurried to their classroom, expecting Father Philbrook, but Mrs. Birch was back.

After all of her students were seated, Mrs. Birch closed the classroom door and was about to say something when Charlotte McKenzie stood up. "Mrs. Birch, I know I speak for everyone in your homeroom class when I say we are so happy to have you back."

Then *little-miss-suck-up* sat down.

Mrs. Birch looked slowly up and down the rows of desks then smiled. "Well Charlotte *and everyone*, that's very gratifying to know." Mrs. Birch was wearing a loose fitting sweater and looked like she'd actually lost about ten pounds.

The rest of Friday just went. Elijah wasn't sure what he'd learned in any of his classes, all he knew as he stood waiting for the bus was that the day was over and so was this long constipated week.

Both Arrow and Dart whinnied as he came up the driveway.

Elijah dropped his backpack at the side of the road and ran to the fence. "Hi you guys." Leaning over the top rail of the fence he lowered his head between theirs and felt every worry vanish. "You're the best."

He rubbed both of their soft noses then jumped to the ground. "Let's have dinner." After he spread their feed around on the ground by the barn, Elijah cleaned out their stalls. He then rested on an over turned bucket. Both Arrow and Dart chewed slowly with bits of hay sticking out from the side of their mouths.

"Wow, what a crappy week. Though not entirely crappy, cause Larry is not at my school anymore."

Arrow nodded his regal head with a throaty response then picked up another mouthful of hay.

"I'm gonna be thirteen in eight more days that makes me a teen now, not sure if I'll feel any different though. I'm a little taller, but don't feel a whole lot different than I did when I turned from eleven to twelve last year. I wonder why that is?"

Both horses looked at him still chewing.

Elijah shrugged. "I'm not even sure I'm any smarter than last year and I'm almost done with grade seven!" He stood, and patted their necks then retrieved his backpack.

Inside the back door he could smell sausages frying. "Grandpa? You're soon gonna be sixty-one right?"

Rock Clearwater moved the heavy cast iron skillet off the heat. "Yes, too soon." He ladled batter into the heated waffle maker. "Why?"

"Do you feel different now than you did when you were thirteen?"

"Yes. If I tried to jump a fence now, I'd break into several dozen pieces and I'd be a pile of bones in the grass." He winked checking the first waffle.

"Oh."

Grandpa removed the first waffle then ladled more batter. "Actually no." He quit teasing.

"To answer the question I know you were asking my real answer is *no*, not up here." Rock tapped the side of his head.

"Getting older is actually an odd experience. Our bodies change, our faces change, we know more *usually*, but no one I know actually *feels* that much different. I'm always surprised to see myself when I look in the mirror." He smiled then gave his grandson a hug.

"Are you ready for breakfast-dinner?"

"Yes."

"Well get us both some plates and cutlery, and we can eat a little early tonight."

"How come we don't feel different when we get older?" Elijah handed two plates to his grandfather.

"How many sausages do you want with your waffle?"

Elijah thought for a moment, holding the forks and knives. "Three."

They sat at the kitchen table.

"That's an interesting question." Grandpa poured maple syrup over his waffle. "Most people just seem to reach a certain age - somewhere between thirteen and thirty then stay 'feeling' exactly that way until they die."

"That's really, really odd Grandpa."

"Or maybe – it's only *odd* people I know."

They made popcorn and then watched an old John Candy movie, *Uncle Buck* then both grandfather and grandson fell asleep half way through a second old movie, *Grumpy Old Men*.

...Thunder and lightning persisted as a cloudy late afternoon became a starless night. Rain pelted straight down and there was no shelter in the thin growth of poplar trees that grew along the lake.

The band of twenty Blackfoot braves could do nothing except wait out the storm by their staked and jittery horses.

Chief Talkingstone rolled his buffalo sleeping rug tighter, skin side out to keep the buffalo fur from getting wet.

Saturated clouds hung low and rain blocked much of his view, but he kept watch for any sign of movement. He didn't want to risk leaving the cover of the few trees there were until the storm subsided enough for them to follow the lake shore around to the south ridge.

He dozed sitting under the belly of his horse for warmth and shelter.

Eventually a predawn breeze replaced the assaulting night rain and he was shivered awake. They could have no fire, as they were upwind from their prey. Even though most of their enemy were French soldiers with five experienced trappers – the Blackfoot knew three Iroquois trackers also rode in front with the leader of the men in uniform.

Talkingstone had heard during good trades with the Assiniboine that even though some Iroquois travelled with the French - who always smelled of many sunsets without bathing – the Iroquois could sniff the wind as well as any bear.

When he stirred all of his braves stood, anticipating his orders.

He stood patted the shoulder of his horse Ghost then covered his back with a dry deer hide mat. He wrapped himself with his buffalo cape and swung up onto Ghost's back urging him from inside the stand of trees.

In single file the Blackfoot chief led his braves the long way around the lake to avoid the steep rocky shore to the north – then through a narrow pass east that opened out onto the plains.

Drops of rainwater clung to tall wild wheat and foxtail grass soaking the legs of their horses as they went.

Chief Talkingstone's scout Whitegoat rode close behind him. Two hours later clouds had cleared and they were within half a mile from the overlook where Whitegoat had spotted the French military raiding party.

The Blackfoot band stopped and everyone dismounted, but only Talkingstone and Whitegoat continued on foot. When they were forty feet from the edge of the overlook they both dropped to their knees then crawled through the thick prairie grasses.

Eight inches from the edge with undisturbed grass for cover the chief and his scout were in time to watch. The French were making the last of their preparations before they moved further south into Blackfoot territory - just as the wounded Sarsi brave had warned them.

Keeping low and crawling backwards they rejoined the others. Staying up wind, but following the French soldiers in small groups of three and five the Blackfoot shadowed their enemy until just before sunset.

The Blackfoot braves were outnumbered ten to one and the weapons of the soldiers' were superior, but as the day faded Talkingstone had developed a plan...

CHAPTER...8

When Elijah awoke, the fresh smell of rain washed grass still lingered in his memory and he took in a deep breath through his nose.

Then he heard the back door slam, the scent of wild grass was substituted for baking ham and bran muffins. As he lay perfectly still, looking straight up, open sky had been replaced by his loft ceiling of knotty pine.

Often too warm he had thrown off his covers in his sleep, but a slight shiver prompted his blander. Elijah grabbed a sweater then he hurried downstairs.

"Well good morning..." Rock Clearwater's grandson flashed by him, wearing only slippers, pajama bottoms and a sweater on his way to the outhouse.

When Elijah returned he stood scowling just inside the back door. "Grandpa! Isn't it time that you added a bathroom to this house? Everyone else on this road has indoor plumbing."

Grandpa smiled slicing ham. "Would you rather have plumbing for your birthday or a bow?" He placed ham and a muffin on a plate for Elijah.

Elijah sat at the table pointing a fork with speared ham at his grandfather. "I would 'rather' have a bow for my birthday and plumbing for Christmas."

"Have you been conspiring with your Aunt Lucille? She threatened last week to back my truck into our outhouse."

"No, but if she needs my help," Elijah started to giggle, "she only has to ask."

"You made your point. Guess I should add a proper bathroom on to the back before we both develop arthritis in our old-age."

"Grandpa, you mean it! Really?"

Rock nodded. "You obviously had a good night's sleep you're peppy, pushy and talkative."

Elijah got up to get another bran muffin and slice of ham. "I had another dream last night." He sat down and reached for the butter.

Grandpa stopped eating. "Did your friend the prince run into another disloyal relative?" He asked casually watching his grandson.

"No, this dream wasn't about Prince Dade in Ireland this one was about a Blackfoot Chief named Talkingstone. He and some of the men from his village were tracking a lot of French soldiers for some reason."

"The land was really pretty flat so it might have been Saskatchewan a long, long time ago or maybe North Dakota." Elijah shrugged and swallowed the last of his ham.

Grandpa kept his comment casual. "I don't know anyone who has more interesting dreams than you do. At least not lately." He checked the clock above the stove. "Let's strap on your chest clapper then you can get dressed."

The rest of the weekend flew by. The weather prevented them from spending extended time outdoors, so movies, Scrabble and Elijah's Irish family tree occupied their time.

Monday morning his cousin James was on the bus, but he sat on the last seat in the back row. Not even Joseph sat close to him. And the expressionless stare on his cousin's face made Elijah a little uneasy.

Mrs. Birch wore a black, loose fitting dress, and Elijah was relieved that his grade seven homeroom was safe from a fashion fiasco this week. Even though he had seen another side of Father Philbrook the previous Thursday he really, really, really never, wanted to be a student in the priests' class again.

Though Mrs. Birch wore a smile and seemed in a happy disposition of forgiveness their English assignment looked suspiciously like a form of revenge. She wrote the titles to five book 'classics' as she called them, on the chalkboard. From the short list each student could choose one book title to read then write a ten page typed report that included a one page biography of the author.

'Ugh!' Elijah thought as he tried desperately to pick something: "*My Cousin Rachel*" by Daphne duMaurier – "*Of Mice And Men*" by John Steinbeck – "*Brothers Karamazov*" by Fyodor Dostoyevsky – "*Gone With The Wind*" by Margaret Mitchell" – "*The Robe*" by Lloyd C. Douglas…

As Elijah looked around at his fellow sufferers the perplexed expressions on their faces seemed to match his own confusion.

And their bewilderment didn't improve any when Mrs. Birch cheerfully explained the basic plot of each book in fact, it only made it worse. None of the books were less than four-hundred pages and he was pretty sure that Mr. Ingersoll's oldest daughter, Monica had had some sort of reading assignment for a dude named John Steinbeck. And Monica, was a journalism major, at Mount Royal University!

'Clever, very clever Mrs. Beck.' Elijah thought. Suddenly he wanted to take back the apology he wrote and the card he made that Principal Philbrook insisted everyone in the class send the week before.

Reluctantly, Elijah chose "*My Cousin Rachel*" by Daphne duMaurier. Even though it was about a girl, it had the least amount of pages. The report wasn't due until the third week of May, but Elijah hurried to the library. This assignment felt like a trip to the dentist – just better to get it done and over with as soon as possible.

****

Rock Clearwater met again with his chief and eleven fellow Tsuu T'ina Council Members. "My grandson Elijah had his second dream last night. He remembered the first part of it, but so far not in much detail."

Geraldine Runninghawk was the lone woman Council Member. "His age in this time will reach thirteen at thirteen minutes past midnight, six days from now on the thirteenth day, correct?"

Council Member Rock Clearwater nodded.

Chief Paul Tenbears had not been present to attend the first meeting and neither had Geraldine. "Then the rest of his dream will come to him in the next few days as did the first. Inform us when that has occurred."

****

Grandpa Clearwater finished unloading crates of discarded cabbage from the market for his pigs. Coming from the hog shed he spotted Elijah walking up the driveway kicking his backpack ahead of him as he went which gave Rock a pretty good idea that his grandson's Monday had curdled like sour milk.

"Hey there buddy."

The ill-fated backpack had almost reached the west front corner of Arrow and Dart's corral.

Rock hurried to meet Elijah. "Let's feed and visit with our favorite critters together." He reached around his grandson's shoulder and gave him a hug. "I'll spread the hay if you get their oats."

When Elijah looked up at his grandfather, Elijah's color was pale and he looked tired again.

Grandfather and grandson walked across the corral. "How was this Monday compared to last Monday?"

Elijah set the hose in place to add fresh water to the trough. "On the 'poop-scale' last Monday was a nine." Then he filled the oat bucket. "This Monday was a seven, only because Larry wasn't part of it, but James acted creepy. He stared at me this morning on the bus like he was made of wax, then lining up for the bus after school he did it again."

"And I know exactly how Mrs. Birch spent her weekend." Elijah sat on an overturned aluminum water bucket.

"You sound annoyed by how she spent her weekend." Grandpa finished spreading the horses' hay.

"I am! She spent it plotting the revenge of her homeroom class!"

Grandpa leaned against Dart with his arm draped across her back. "I'm afraid to ask."

"You should be." Elijah lowered his voice as if Mrs. Birch might overhear. "That teacher is a devious woman! Her five-week-assignment is in my backpack, I'll show you."

Rock was worried that his grandson had not had enough water that day. The natural moisture surrounding all organs of healthy people was lightly moist, but it was thick and sticky with cystic fibrosis interfering with or blocking much of the normal organ function. Dehydration – a serious condition with anyone – was an even more acute situation for those with CF.

"Let's get you inside and we'll drown your sorrows with your favorite; Caesar Salad and leftover ham, root beer and fresh raspberries from the market. But first water! Lots and lots of water!"

"Aw Grandpa."

After dinner, Elijah dozed off twice trying to read the book "*My Cousin Rachel*." Then still concerned the water he drank after getting home might still not be enough to avoid severe stomach cramps, grandpa sent him to bed early to rest after ten minutes longer with his chest clapper.

Grandpa set down the small camping toilet in the far corner of Elijah's room. "You've had so much water since dinner I didn't want you running outside in the dark," he grinned.

"But besides this," he pointed to the pot. "I had another idea. Why don't you read the book that was your homework assignment out loud to me? Then I'll know what the book's about too and maybe it won't seem like such a chore."

Elijah closed his eyes smiling. "That's brilliant Grandpa, so bril..." But he fell into a deep sleep.

Grandpa turned out the light and went downstairs, deciding to turn in early himself.

...With dusk, Chief Talkingstone and his braves had followed just far enough behind to the east and from the north to know when the French soldiers stopped to set up their camp for the next night. Talkingstone expected the enemy would arrange their night camp exactly as they had done before – and they did.

Only eighteen members of the raiding party rode on horseback three Iroquois, five fur trappers and ten officers in uniform. The other eighty men walked or jogged behind the saddled horses followed by the food supply wagon pulled by four horses.

After the French soldiers stopped, the Blackfoot braves shadowing the raiding party, watched laying flat in the tall grass. Two soldiers drove four stakes into the ground then tied rope from one stake to the other forming a corral area. Then each horse was loosely tied to a section of the rope with a shallow water bag and allowed to graze in place.

The rest of the camp was laid out in a compact rectangle shape. The rope corral, for the horses, was located on the east corner with the supply and cook wagon close beside the corral.

Two rows of eight ten-men tents were pitched in two groups of four lined up across from each other running east to west. Two officer's tents and the trapper's tent were at the far western edge of the camp. Three campfires were enclosed by stacked stones and centered thirty feet apart on the grass between the tent groups. Their damp kindling sent a spinning plume of smoke skyward from each fire pit.

Chief Talkingstone and his nineteen braves looked on patiently waiting for their opportunity. These soldiers needed to be stopped, or they would devastate all of the Blackfoot villages as they had the two Sarsi villages they found in their thieving, destructive path.

They kept watching silent as the smoke, while the soldiers ate then drank the gut-fire that the Sarsi brave had warned the Blackfoot made these men turn feral like a squirrel with rabies.

CHAPTER...9

Grandpa Clearwater had difficulty waking Elijah the next morning, which was never a good sign. He felt Elijah's forehead, he was warm perhaps running a low-grade fever.

When Elijah opened his eyes they were rimmed with dark circles, his cheeks were flushed, but the rest of his skin was pale.

Grandpa propped up two pillows then handed his grandson a large glass of warm water. "Start drinking this slowly and don't stop until it's empty. Do you have any cramps?"

Elijah shook his head as he sipped. He knew he hadn't had enough water during school the day before. He didn't object to his grandfather's order now because he didn't want to go to the hospital again.

"I'm going to call the answering service at the school. You can stay home today and read that book."

"No Grandpa," Elijah swallowed. "I'll be okay, really I will and I promise to drink my water all day long. I don't want to miss anymore days."

Reluctantly, Grandpa Clearwater nodded then returned to the main floor.

With just half of the water still in Elijah's glass, he felt the first wave of cramps. They weren't the sharp stabbing cramps that told him the sticky substance that surrounded and filled his intestine had thickened somewhere creating a block - this was just the squeezing kind of cramps, but the squeezing kind could turn into the stabbing kind.

Elijah sat straight and breathed shallow sipping more water, hoping the water worked its way to moisten where the sticky-gunk was blocked. He focused on the smiling photograph of his mom and dad – trying to relax away the rippling cramp that seemed a little stronger this time. Then he stood. Standing felt somewhat better. He put on his robe and slippers and hurried to the outhouse.

Grandpa watched Elijah closely when he came through the backdoor. "How are you doing?"

"I'm good," he nodded. "I'll have some more of that water and one of your amazing bran muffins."

He hadn't seen his staring cousin James on the bus that morning, but was startled just before first bell to be pushed into his locker by his cousin Joseph.

"You're big mouth got my brother into trouble and Larry tossed outta school." His words came out like the hiss of a cat.

Elijah's heart raced as he looked up to face Joseph. "You know that isn't true." He hardly recognized his menacing cousin, whose eyes had narrowed to slits.

"Whatever it was that Larry got James to do in Mr. Fiche's class - got both of them in trouble."

The second bell rang and the hall began to clear.

He tried to keep his voice down, but Elijah struggled against a rising panic that Larry Swallowtail had managed to turn his two oldest cousins against him. "And Larry picked on me and so many other kids he was bound to be seen. The principal called a lot of people into his office, not just me!"

The third bell rang.

Joseph turned away and Elijah hurried to his class, forgetting his water.

The U.S. Space Race was the farthest topic from Elijah's mind as first period history started. 'Why did they want to put a man on the moon anyway,' he wondered? 'Would people be nicer to each other if they lived on the moon or even another planet?'

An hour later, just inside the door of the chemistry lab Elijah dropped to his knees with a sharp shooting pain. He felt like several jagged blades were sawing back and forth and stabbing him at the same time.

The chemistry teacher Mrs. Lund rushed over. "Everyone please go sit at your lab stations. Jayson you may stay with your cousin." She dialed 911 then Elijah's grandfather.

He couldn't stand. All he could do was lay his head on the floor and pull his knees up to his chest. He closed his eyes to shut out the fear on the face of his cousin Jayson and the stares of the other kids...

****

...With the singing of the men who drank from the brown bottles, and the noise from the activity of the camp still echoing into the night sky, Talkingstone sent two of his braves to wait by the horse corral so the horses would be at ease with them. He tasked two other braves to bundle several thick stocks of wheat bound with foxtail grass.

As the hours past Talkingstone followed the stars that formed the shape of the Little-Dipper as they moved in the night sky. Most of the soldiers stumbled then fell sleeping outside of their tents on the ground.

Then it was time.

Talkingstone and Whitegoat knew where every member of the French raiding party was and who might still be awake, though both guards were asleep at their post.

The Blackfoot braves split up, with eight following Whitegoat to the north side of the camp and Talkingstone leading eight to the south of the camp. Five archers in each group spread out behind the rows of tents with their bows ready.

The two braves at the rope corral silently untied and led away all of the French raiding party horses - while Talkingstone and Whitegoat each with three men cautiously moved between the tents toward the smoldering fires.

Suddenly the tallest Iroquois, the wounded Sarsi brave said was named Fish, appeared from the opening of the farthest northeast tent. The alarm he attempted to scream became only the hiss of an arrow that came from the bow of one archer on Talkingstone's side of the camp.

Tips of the bundled-wheat torches ignited then Whitegoat and Chief Talkingstone backed away to the perimeter of the camp.

With all torch carriers in place Talkingstone raised his flaming torch and waved it in an arc as the signal.

Simultaneously the back of each tent became a blaze.

Then the torch carriers knelt in place with the other archers ready with their bows.

Soldiers running from flaming, stained and oil-seasoned-canvas were struck down by arrows woven through the air from all sides.

In thirty minutes the French raiding party that had attacked two peaceful Sarsi villages, was cut down by either fire or arrows or both.

As Talkingstone gave the signal to retreat greedy flames still sliced the air lighting the predawn sky.

He worried that a few of the raiding party might have survived – though alone he doubted they could live long out in the open prairie. But would more soldiers come to Blackfoot and Sarsi territory if these men were not heard from?...

****

Grandpa dozed as he sat in the hospital recliner. He began to slip sideways and awoke with a jerk of his head. With several blinks to clear his vision, he saw that Elijah was awake. "Hi there, you."

Elijah smiled. "Normally I hate this place, but I feel real good."

"That's probably because the paramedics gave you a mild sedative. You were one giant knot when they arrived at the school my friend." Grandpa rubbed the back of his neck then stretched his arms high above his head. "When did you wake up?"

"Just about two minutes ago. Is that clock right? Is it really eleven at night?"

"Yup. Your Aunt Dawn and Aunt Lucille left just before ten."

Elijah turned over from his side to his back carefully so he didn't shift his medicated IV line. "I dreamt some more Grandpa."

"Your head's a busy place these days. The Irish prince or the Blackfoot chief?"

"The Blackfoot, Chief Talkingstone."

"Some nasty soldiers in a French army joined with some other Indians from another tribe and raided a couple of Sarsi villages. The soldiers took all their buffalo and deer hides, took their food, burned their teepees and chased away everyone they didn't shoot."

"Entire families were left without shelter or food, with many wounded. One of the Sarsi survivors made it to the first Blackfoot village by coming down the river. Even though he was badly hurt he warned the chief these soldiers were heading in their direction and they should get ready.

But Talkingstone didn't sit and wait for the soldiers he found them first and burned their butts – like for real!"

"Sounds quite disturbing."

"No, I didn't see any dead bodies or anything. Talkingstone and his men were sooo outnumbered, but he came up with a really smart plan to punish the soldiers."

As Elijah related more details of the battle from his dream, Rock Clearwater relaxed. He was relieved the medication in Elijah's drip had taken less time to start clearing the mucus block in his small intestine. Other times it had taken longer than twelve hours, much longer. His grandson's energy was back and so was his color.

"I don't remember being scared." He frowned. "Odd though I do remember being worried, like I was responsible or something, but Chief Talkingstone is pretty cool."

CHAPTER...10

The next morning, Elijah was so hungry when he looked at some magazines at the end of his bed he began to wonder what paper might taste like.

The medication had cleared every sticky block in Elijah's small intestine and he stated to the nurse that he was ready to eat one of Grandpa's pigs whole – ears and all. Fortunately, for the pigs' ears, he happily settled for two poached eggs, four slices of bacon, two apples and a large oatmeal cookie.

"If you're done eating then I guess it would be safe enough to give you a hug?" Elijah's Great Aunt Lucille stood in the doorway with a fruit bouquet and a Scrabble game.

Aunt Lucille was a slightly shorter version of her brother. Her parchment textured skin tanned by heritage and decades of gardening crinkled when she smiled, which she did often and easily. Her waist length grey hair was always coiled and wound in an elaborate knot at the back of her head.

Grandpa came out of the bathroom just as is older sister stopped by Elijah's bed. "Food! Good call. Now we can't keep him full. About an hour ago it was worth your arm if you got too close."

He pushed a chair from the corner of the room and set it next to the hospital recliner. He looked on as Elijah tore open the basket's plastic covering and selected a large chocolate covered strawberry.

In spite of Elijah's happy disposition Rock felt the uneasy energy of invisible storm clouds beginning to gather close by. His grandson would be thirteen in four days and he had to trust that Elijah's dreams would prepare him for the challenge of assuming his destiny.

Lucille settled into the recliner. "Oh this is a nice one. Maybe I should have a recliner at home?" She smiled.

The nurse named Catherine came into Elijah's room. She took his temperature, his pulse and his blood pressure. "The doctor has scheduled an MRI after lunch and if the test results show no more dark shadows then Elijah can be discharged tomorrow morning." She patted Elijah's hand, pulled up his blanket then typed his vitals into his computerized chart and left.

Elijah closed his eyes.

Grandfather and Great Aunt watched him for a minute then Lucille leaned toward her brother and lowered her voice. "I stopped at Dawn's place you know. She and River are having quite a time with James these days and a little of that has rubbed off onto Joseph too."

She looked over at Elijah who was now sound asleep. "Apparently the grandson of that old school flame of yours, threatened to hurt Sarah if James and Joseph didn't join him and do what he ordered."

"Dawn's real upset because apparently Elijah was also one of Larry Swallowtail's targets and neither James nor Joseph defended him."

Grandpa Clearwater let out a deep sigh. "Yeah I know, but I didn't realize just how extensive Larry's bullying went. At Elijah's birthday dinner there will be an opportunity to heal the family."

He shifted in the smaller chair. "And stop calling Eliza Greyowl-Snow my old flame!"

Lucille covered her mouth, chuckling. "I brought the Scrabble board for you and Elijah. Since he's asleep again do you want to play a round?"

Rock nodded, wondering if he should tell his sister of Elijah's dreams and his second meeting with the council. He was surprised she hadn't asked him about Elijah sooner, as she was one of the midwives at his birth and recognized the *sign.*

"Here's the bag. Count out your seven tiles." She set each of her tiles side by side on the wood tile rack. "Oh for heaven's sake how am I supposed to make a decent word with a Z, three As, one P, and two Ss?"

Her brother looked up puzzled. "Seriously? *PASS,* or *ZAPS.*"

"Well I'm certainly not going to use Pass, and Zaps is only 15 points."

"We just started this game. That's pretty good for only four letters. You can't expect a triple word score from the center."

And when Elijah awoke the aging brother and sister were down to eight tiles in the bag and bickering as they had when they were children. Elijah smiled to himself observing them. They were usually more entertaining than just about any television show.

Nurse Catherine returned with a wheelchair for Elijah and his grandfather looked up. "You want some company?"

"Na, I'm fine Grandpa."

His grandfather feigned fear. "Please, let me go with you. I need to be rescued…"

"That's only because he's losing – huge, huge, huge." Lucille interrupted.

Elijah looked up at the nurse. "He's okay – those two are always like that."

Catherine smiled and nodded. "We won't be too long."

With three tiles each, Rock was searching the board for a place to put even one of his tiles when Lucille reached across and tapped his arm. "I bumped into Geraldine at the market. She began talking to me about Elijah's dreams…"

Rock suddenly looked alarmed.

"…only because I helped to deliver him and you're my brother. She's not the type to talk-out-of-turn, especially with Council matters. So how's he doing?"

Grandpa Clearwater shared what details he knew of Elijah's first dream then the progress still evolving with the second dream.

"What do you think will happen Saturday - anything?

He shook his head and shrugged. "Hard to tell Sis, hard to tell."

CHAPTER...11

When Grandpa Clearwater walked into Elijah's hospital room at 7AM Thursday morning Elijah was sitting up and dressed in the clothes he brought with him two days before.

Rock grinned holding up a small canvas tote. "I brought fresh socks and underwear with a clean shirt and jeans." He shook his head.

"When did you wake up?"

"Before the roosters." Nurse Catherine stood behind Rock in the doorway."

Grandpa turned around startled.

"They just started serving breakfast." Catherine checked her watch. "But I got him one bran muffin, two slices of raisin toast and apple juice an hour ago. Then he ate all the pineapple slices from your sister's fruit basket."

"I'm ready to go!" Elijah moved from sitting on his hospital bed to stand by the recliner to prove his point.

"Hold onto your boots cowboy the doctor still needs to sign you out first." The nurse began to take Elijah's temperature and blood pressure. "You know how thrilled I get with the paperwork around here."

Elijah smiled and relaxed.

Catherine had cared for Elijah on and off since he was five. She had never met his parents, but had grown close to his extended family and grandparents. She was sad too when Elijah's grandmother had a second heart attack then died only a few months after he turned five. Some of Catherine's patients had become particularly special to her *and* Elijah was one of them.

"When do you expect the doctor?"

"Any time now, she started her rounds at six this morning."

Catherine finished noting Elijah's temperature and blood pressure into his computer file just as Dr. Sinha walked in.

"Ohhh, you're not anxious to leave at all are you?" She smiled at Elijah.

"Mr. Clearwater, good morning." She nodded to Rock.

The doctor walked over to Elijah then sat in the small chair indicating the recliner for Elijah. "As you can tell by how you feel, we managed to clear your system very quickly this time, which is good. But do not forget for even a moment that you can be casual about your fluid intake, especially water. Lots and lots of water as well as high water content foods." Keta Sinha smiled, "in addition to lots of chocolate."

Impulsively he gave his doctor a hug. "Thank you, again and again." He looked from Dr. Sinha to Catherine. Their faces were as familiar to him as his teachers at school, though the hospital staff had been part of his life much longer.

"Catherine," Dr. Sinha stood, "since the Calgary Children's Hospital can no longer afford to continue feeding this ravenous young man, we better send him home."

She stopped just before the door to the hall and looked back. "Have a wonderful day on the anniversary of your birth."

Out in the parking lot Elijah ran to his grandfather's truck. A soft, warm breeze carried the scent of a slowly budding spring.

"Every time I leave the hospital I feel like I've been released from prison." He opened the passenger door, "though technically I'm only paroled because I always need to go back every four or eight months."

Grandpa Clearwater turned the key in the ignition, but didn't back out right away. "I realize that as you've gotten older these trips to the hospital, are draining on your mind and I'm sorry about that. But you must admit that as *prisons* go this is a pretty great place."

He put the truck in reverse and as Rock drove away Elijah looked through the rear window at the giant Lego styled building, brightly painted in primary colors, still visible from several miles south down Shaganappi Trail.

Grandpa next turned right onto 16th Avenue and then the TransCanada Highway 1 west to Canmore. In minutes they had left Calgary's busy streets behind for the rural spaces between Calgary, Canmore and Banff.

Daydreaming, Elijah watched the acreages and farms flash by, soon Grandpa was turning onto county road #40 then driving south again toward their farm.

"I'm feeling really good Grandpa." Elijah made a face. "Before I have'ta start my homework, do you think I could saddle Arrow for a ride?"

"I think so, but drink some of that water first and take the rest of the bottle with you." Then he turned left onto their driveway. "Dart could do with a little exercise too, how about some company?"

Grandpa stopped his truck part way up the driveway. Elijah jumped out and ran for the fence calling to Arrow and Dart. They both whinnied a greeting as they trotted toward him from around the north side of the barn.

"Hi you guys. Let's blow this place." He ran by them toward the barn.

Sensing that something was different about this spring morning Arrow followed Elijah to the barn, while Dart waited for Rock to open the gate. "We're going too, girl." He patted her shoulder. "Let's get your saddle."

There were still too many large patches of deep snow, so a full gallop wasn't possible, but both horses and both riders embraced the sunny day with zeal, ready for the new season.

"Grandpa what did Calgary and Alberta and all of this, look like when you were my age?"

They were five miles directly east of the farm and had stopped at the crest of a hill that over looked a section of valley to the north of the Bow River.

"I'm not that old you know. It was only 1968 when I was thirteen. This river valley looked about the same."

"There was television, and computers – though they weren't portable and certainly couldn't fit on your lap. Computers were the size of train cars and they filled rooms as big as your gymnasium. Program code was holes key-punched into cards about the same size as a plane ticket."

"Calgary's population was only about 500,000. Canmore was half the size then that it is now, but since the 1988 Winter Olympics it got a great deal more international attention."

Elijah looked over at his grandfather with an expression of pure mischief. "Did people have indoor plumbing and running water in 1968?"

"I've already talked to your Uncle River about helping me add-on to the back of the kitchen in a few months, wise-guy."

Elijah laughed

Rock tapped Dart's reins to the right. "I think it's time we headed back to the house and you did your homework."

Elijah stopped laughing. "Oh rats!"

Grandpa finished drawing the bathroom addition on paper and calculating the cost of roofing materials: two-by-fours, plywood, wiring, pipes, flooring and paint. Next to him Elijah read several more chapters of Daphne du Maurier's book *My Cousin Rachel* for his report – out loud.

After two hours, Elijah's voice became raspy and he stopped abruptly in the middle of a long paragraph. "This wasn't such a great idea."

"It's an interesting story so far." Grandpa looked up from his calculator and note pad. "How far have you gotten?"

"I'm on page 208 with just under half yet to go." Elijah's head dropped forward with his face between the pages of the book. "Ugh!"

"Finish your glass of water and help me with dinner. How do you feel about some of my vegetable soup and cornbread?"

Elijah closed the hardcover book with a sharp snap. "Right now I'd feel better even if you asked me to clean out the hog barn."

"That doesn't say much about my soup."

"It's not your soup – it's this nasty homework assignment."

After dinner Grandpa sent Elijah to bed early to rest. At first he wasn't tired and tried to read more pages, but once again he fell asleep with his beside lamp still on…

****

...The turbulent wet spring gave way to a hot try summer then an early fall. Cooler mountain breezes swooped down on the plains in late August.

Chief Talkingstone and the other tribe elders studied the weather signs and the animals closely. Buffalo began to move south along with migrating geese, ducks and other birds as the leaves began to turn. Antelope were beginning to take on a thicker coat much earlier.

At an early morning tribal meeting Talkingstone presented his observations and concerns of the sifting season. The council agreed with their chief and they voted to begin getting ready to clear their camp earlier too.

Following the buffalo to the higher, but sheltered grasses along the front-range would protect their teepees from the winds and ensure both large and small winter game.

The word went out throughout the camp in less time than it took to take five breaths then anyone who could walk in the entire camp mobilized to pitch in.

Teenage boys and girls began to catch, clean and boil fish.

Young children were sent to make hundreds of bundles of dried twigs and grass for travel fires and fall camp fires.

The younger men broke off limbs of young trees to make travois the horses could pull to carry supplies, small children and squaws late with child.

Elder women and men began to stitch thicker moccasins for walking and for colder weather.

The younger women rolled wild turnip, dried berries, asparagus, dried venison and antelope in deer hides.

On the third day of winter-camp preparations the scent of burning grass propelled by the wind, preceded thick grey smoke. The smoke first appeared from behind low hills to the west then spread just beyond a ridge across to the north.

Their hobbled horses, whinnied an alarm just as Talkingstone spotted two of the camp patrols galloping toward the busy village.

Greyfeather reached Talkingstone first. He jumped from the back of his mount to the ground before his horse stopped. "Chief, a river of flame stretches from the place of the setting sun to the direction from where the hawk glides."

Wetdog reached his chief and Greyfeather. He too jumped from his horse, but held onto his pony's mane. "The wind pushes the burning grass this way."

Patrol riders from the east and the south galloped into camp. They remained on their horses waiting for their chief's orders.

"How much time...?" But as Talkingstone spoke those words the first sighting of flame tips appeared at the crest of the hills to the west.

Chief looked up at the two mounted patrol riders. "Tell everyone to gather all of their ready food and supplies then head for the river."

The patrols parted on horseback and rode yelling orders to the camp.

"We," he looked at Greyfeather and Wetdog, "and the other braves will pull down our teepees. If we don't have time for the poles then we drag our hide walls to the river. If they stay wet we can save them."

Dogs barked at the encroaching wall of fire and smoke.

Panicked horses whinnied.

The elderly fastened travois to a dozen horses to carry toddlers and heavy supplies to the river.

Older children gathered small bundles of hides, and clothing and helped the teen girls carry dried fish and meat.

Teen boys rallied to carry river rock to make a fire barrier as wide as they could as fast as they could, but already the swiftly approaching heat was blistering.

Sparks carried by the wind were sent over their heads and started new spot fires on the other side of the narrow band of small boulders.

Talkingstone was chief to a large Blackfoot settlement, with a meeting lodge and eighty teepees that all the younger braves and women rushed to save.

With winter threatening early they would perish without food and shelter.

While rolling the giant stitched hide of his grandmother's teepee, Whitegoat rushed over and caught his chief's

115

attention. Pointing in the direction of the rising sun Talkingstone looked up.

From a slight rise a quarter of a mile to the east was a long line of uniformed riders. They watched not moving.

Instinctively Talkingstone knew that these soldiers had been sent to find the Blackfoot band who had avenged the two destroyed Sarsi villages.

Squinting through the thickening smoke he spotted two mounted riders who watched at a slight distance from the main body of soldiers.

From their distinctive head dress, Talkingstone recognized those riders were the other two Iroquois, named Runner and Weasel. He knew then how the second band of French soldiers had been led back to Blackfoot and Sarsi territory.

A rush of energy he had needed only once before filled his entire being and he rose up.

His grandmother's teepee hide fell to the ground.

A flash of white light surrounded Chief Talkingstone transforming his physical form to that of a giant charcoal grey crow with a wing span that touched sky beyond the tops of the teepees.

With one sweeping flurry the chief stepped into the air, rising and filling the clearing with his light. He then sent a giant wave of wind with his left wing snuffing out the wall of flames that had blackened a mile of dry grass.

As a single body one hundred arrows sailed toward the hovering grey essence of Grey Crow, but they dissolved to dust before reaching their target.

Thick dark smoke shot upwards.

Grey Crow became brighter more vivid growing even greater in size.

The white light around him altered to violet – sending a second massive wave of wind that sucked the air from the lungs of every soldier and Iroquois scout across the river.

Their horses reared in terror throwing the riders to the ground then as a herd they bolted south.

One by one as the soldiers awoke they discovered they were mute. Their voices had been taken from them.

When they stood to get their bearings, They saw Chief Talkingstone leading his band south away from the smoldering grass. The French captain tried to yell orders for his men to attack, but no sound came from his throat.

BLACK

CROW

Legend

With our cries heard above the roar of fire

Comes *one* who hears those cries.

With

Outstretched wings the *one* who walks as man

Sends wind to protect those who cry and silence

To punish those who take.

This *one* returns as fire cycles the Universe

Then stays to finish the cycle.

As the drum beats

So do our hearts above the noise of the world.

And each time our hearts beat

We feel the tempo of the *one* who comes to us...

CHAPTER...12

Friday morning when Elijah woke up there was an indentation on the side of his face from the edge of the still open book and his bedside lamp light was on.

He sat up and thought about the dream he had with the Blackfoot, Chief Talkingstone. He had smelled the smoke from the grass fire, and he heard horses neighing, dogs barking, children crying and shouts from villagers panicking.

He had been so close to Talkingstone, just like he had Prince Dade, high in the air with them and he had not felt panic or fear, only calm resolve.

When Grandpa Clearwater came up the winding stairs he found Elijah sitting up straight and staring off with his eyes unblinking. Suspecting his grandson had remembered another dream he waited several seconds then quietly said, "Good morning, you still feel like going to school?"

Elijah looked at his grandfather smiling. "Yes. I feel great this morning – but I hav'ta pee!" He rushed by Rock.

Grandpa Clearwater walked to Elijah's bedside lamp then turned it off. As he bent to pick up the book, Rock noticed two grey crow feathers as long and as wide as his forearm. He picked them up and then placed them inside a cedar wood box on one of the shelves beside the two white crow feathers.

Two hours later - that had included two glasses of water, a bowl of bran flakes with sliced pears, another trip to the outhouse and a session with his chest clapper - Elijah was waiting for the school bus.

He was at peace with Mrs. Birch's *revenge* assignment, okay with life in general and excited about turning thirteen. He was finally going to be a teen and he was sure he'd feel more mature, more grown up, more something…

James didn't get off the bus with the rest of the kids, but Joseph had been first off and waved Elijah and Jayson aside. The rest of the kids filed by them chatting.

"We're supposed to meet," Joseph looked around, "at Aunt Lucille's tomorrow," he looked behind them toward the school, "for your big *one-three* birthday."

Elijah and Jayson began to look around too. Elijah had a bad feeling and was suddenly nervous.

The first bell rang.

James stepped off the bus.

Mrs. Deerling closed the doors and then drove away.

121

James no longer had the hostile look on his face, and for a second Elijah dared to believe his older cousin had shaken Larry Swallowtail's hold over him, but then he spoke.

"I have a message from Larry for you." James looked straight ahead, not at Elijah or either of his two younger brothers. "You're to pretend you're not feeling well after school and then not get on the bus. Tell the bus driver Mrs. Deerling you're grandfather is picking you up from school for a doctor's appointment."

The second bell rang.

James walked toward the school without saying anything more or looking back. Joseph rushed to follow him.

Jayson took Elijah by the shoulders. "Are you going to tell the principal or Mrs. Birch?"

Elijah shook his head and then he started walking toward the school's side door.

Jayson walked with him. "What are you going to do? I'll help you fight Larry, I will."

At the lockers outside their homeroom Elijah was still trying to clear his head. His heart tumbled so fast it felt like it was in his throat.

The final bell rang.

He walked to his desk in a daze. 'How could another morning start out so great then turn to pig-slop so quickly?' He wondered.

The morning raced by as a blur. Elijah didn't remember anything from either his math class or his chemistry class. In the lunch room Jayson stayed close, but he was only two inches taller than Elijah so he wasn't sure how helpful his younger cousin would be against Larry.

The only encouraging event was Joseph who came up to his brother and cousin after lunch, first bell. "I'll stay with you after school if you like. We just need to make sure that Sarah, Jorge and Spring get on the bus."

Jayson shrugged. "I don't know maybe we should all stay with Elijah. Spring bit me one time when she was real small. She has pretty sharp teeth."

The last lunch bell sounded and still Elijah couldn't respond. The thoughts inside his head kept spinning. He'd never had any broken bones before, and wondered how long it took for a broken arm or a leg to heal. But more than that, he didn't want any of his cousins hurt either.

During history class he was only half listening to the lecture on events surrounding some important dual between a count and a prince, but he caught enough that it gave him an idea.

Just before the bell of the last class of the day Elijah quietly got all of his books into his back pack. When he checked out the window he could see the yellow school busses lining up. He knew Mrs. Deerling would be in her spot, she was never late.

When the bell sounded – he was first out the door, and first at his locker, and first out the side door sprinting to the waiting busses. He was the first one inside the bus and sitting behind

Mrs. Deerling panting, two minutes before any other students appeared.

"Do you have a plane to catch, Mr. Clearwater?" Mrs. Deerling turned in her seat and winked at him. "Happy Birthday by the way. Hope you have a special day tomorrow."

"Thank you." His breathing returned to normal then a movement across the road caught his attention.

To the side of a spruce tree stood Larry Swallowtail. In his right hand he held a large slingshot taping it against the palm of his left hand.

Elijah turned away from the window, watching the line of riders waiting for their turn to get on his bus. He wanted to make sure all of his cousins got on safely.

When Jayson appeared he sat beside Elijah. "I don't think I've ever seen you move that fast before."

Elijah resisted the temptation to look out the side window toward the park. "I've never had anyone threaten my life before."

Jorge and Spring walked by.

Jayson turned to check where they sat. "Well running away real fast seems as good a plan as any."

Elijah was one of the last students to get off from the bus's normal route. He stood for a second extremely relieved to have arrived at his own driveway with none of his bones broken and no parts of his body bruised or bleeding.

Pleased with himself he ran up the driveway and dropped his backpack on the side of the drive next to Arrow and Dart's corral.

Climbing over the top rail he heard a sharp crack as something hard hit the fencepost beside him. Turning to look in the direction of the sound, a large stone hit him in the chest. He fell backwards then another stone hit Arrow in the shoulder. The startled horse reared up and snorted.

Elijah wasn't hurt when he fell into the loose corral dirt he just had the wind knocked out of him. All three baseball sized stones lay on the ground around him. A piece of paper was tied around the one that had hit Arrow.

When he sat up and reached for the stone wrapped in paper he noticed a welt had formed on Arrow's shoulder. Elijah knew immediately that the rocks and the note were from Larry Swallowtail.

As he stood he decided to ignore the note, just as he had ignored Larry's order to stay after school. Without taking the paper off the stone he tossed it and the other two rocks into the trees that grew beside the horse corral.

CHAPTER...13

Elijah awoke to a loud knock on their front door early Saturday morning and hurried from his bed to watch below leaning over the loft half wall.

When his grandfather opened the door Sergeant Karl Wojuc of the Canmore RCMP Detachment stood on their front deck. A long time curling buddy of his grandfather's, that morning, the police officer was on duty wearing his uniform and not smiling.

"Rock, I know it's early the sun's just coming up," he handed Grandpa Clearwater a piece of paper, "but this little girl is missing. Her name is Sasha Deerling, maybe you've seen her. She's the daughter of Elijah's school bus driver."

Grandpa nodded his head. "I've visited a little with Edith Deerling over the years, but it's been a few months."

"Is Elijah home, Rock?"

"Yes, come in."

They heard the thump of feet coming down the stairs. "Hi Mr. Wojuc. I'll be back I gotta pee."

Shaking his head, Rock Clearwater tightened the sash around his robe heading toward the kitchen. "Coffee?"

"No thanks, I have some water in the van."

When Elijah returned his grandfather handed him the paper with Sasha Deerling's photo and information.

Elijah looked from his grandfather to Sergeant Wojuc shaken. "She's really missing? How can she be missing?"

"According to her mother she didn't get on your bus last night because she was going with another girl on her bus. Sasha had been invited to a birthday party at one of the houses on an acreage north of the school."

"But when we spoke with the little girl who had invited Sasha, she said she hadn't noticed that Sasha didn't get on her bus with the other eight girls. When they reached her house for the party she thought Sasha had changed her mind about coming."

"It wasn't until 8PM last night when Mrs. Deerling went to pick up Sasha that the birthday girl's mother even realized one of her daughter's guests hadn't arrived with everyone else."

"I didn't know there was a birthday party cause my cousin Spring is Sasha's age and Spring got on our bus as usual last night." Then Elijah wondered if he should tell the officer about Larry's slingshot attack yesterday after school. But he decided against it - finding nine year-old Sasha was more important.

"Do you remember seeing her at school yesterday? I realize the elementary students go to classes on the opposite side of the school from middle and high school students."

Elijah shook his head. "Not after she got off the bus in the morning, but ask my cousins Jorge and Spring. Jorge is in grade five and Spring is in grade four with Sasha."

Sergeant Wojuc nodded. "They're on my list. If I need to talk to either one of you later where will you be today?"

Grandpa walked to the front door with the officer. "We're having a family birthday lunch for Elijah at my sister's farm. We'll be there for two or three hours I guess then back here. Do you need volunteers now to search?"

"Not yet Rock, but thanks for asking. I'll call you if that changes. We brought in two of our dogs to the school and amazingly the one we took inside picked up Sasha's scent by a sink in the girl's washroom, however that was it. But neither dog found any residue scent outside, nor the surrounding field."

After Sergeant Wojuc left, Grandpa poured a large glass of water for Elijah then made strong coffee for himself. They sat silent for several minutes with Sasha's picture on the table between them.

"Happy thirteenth birthday, son." Rock got up from his chair and gave his grandson a hug. "Waffles with sliced strawberries and scrambled eggs for breakfast?"

Elijah finished his water. "Not sure, don't feel hungry. It was cold last night Grandpa! What do you think happened to

Sasha? On the news when kids go missing it's not good! And if something happened to Sasha's glasses she couldn't see!"

Calmly Grandpa added more coffee to his half empty mug. "Kids get lost, or kids get abducted and then show up months - maybe years later, or kids get killed. All of that is true, but let's consider a fourth option, kids also hide. Do you remember when Karl said one of the dogs picked up Sasha's scent by a bathroom sink?"

Elijah nodded.

"Well, what if Sasha went to the bathroom after school then had to wait for others to finish or she took too long and when she ran out to get on the bus with her birthday friend that bus and all the other buses were gone. She'd panic right?"

Elijah nodded again.

"And she might feel a little silly too, right?"

Elijah shrugged then nodded.

"Do any of Sasha's friends live close enough to the school that she could walk to their house if she missed the school bus?"

"Not really Grandpa, remember the new school was built at the far eastern edge of Canmore. I think everyone who goes there is bussed cause it's the only Catholic School." Elijah felt slightly nauseous as he thought of near-sighted Sasha who might be stumbling around unable to see…

Suddenly he had an idea. "Wait a minute I know who does live close by, real close, Father Philbrook! The manse is right next to the church and it's just down the road from the school."

Grandpa Clearwater was out of his chair and pressing the numbers to connect to Sergeant Wojuc's mobile phone just as the digital numbers on his coffee pot clock, flipped to 7:33AM.

"Karl, hate to bother you, but Elijah and I have a theory. We think it's possible that Sasha may be hiding. She may have accidently missed her bus and felt embarrassed then looked for a place close by to hide. Elijah thinks you should check the church manse."

Rock listened. "You never know." Then he offered, "When we were kids we made some zany decisions too."

Grandpa pressed the 'End' button. "He's heading to Father Philbrook's as we speak to check. Do you think you're hungry now?"

"Yes."

"Good, because I'm ready to eat the kitchen table. But – before we eat why don't you take a peek under the sofa." Rock winked at his grandson.

Under the sofa Elijah found a long narrow box. When he slid it out, he was able to read the printing: *Summit 48" Recurve Bow*. "This is Awesome! So awesome Grandpa, thank you!"

"You my man are welcome. The tension is adjustable so you can start with a lighter draw weight and work up. I bought you arrows with two different shaft weights as well."

"Can we set up the targets after we eat?"

Grandpa nodded then mixed the batter, while Elijah counted out six eggs to scramble then he set the table. The eggs were done about the same time as several thick browned waffles.

"Your waffles are almost good enough for me to skip any birthday cake." Elijah caught warm butter sliding from the side of his chin.

"Don't even hint at that with your Aunt Lucille. I happen to know she has labored for days on your cake."

Elijah laughed at his grandfather's expression. "You actually look scared."

"Of my sister? You bet. There's no one scarier than my sister Lucille."

Elijah laughed again and then began coughing.

"Let's give that chest of yours' a good thumping. We didn't do that when you got up."

It wasn't until nine-thirty that Elijah felt strong enough to *test-drive* his new bow.

Grandpa set up two targets at two different distances and they both took turns with Elijah's bow. They had been outside only half an hour when the RCMP van turned in at the end of their driveway then stopped beside the house.

For the second time that same morning Sergeant Wojuc approached two members of the Clearwater family unsmiling. They expected the worst, but then he surprised them.

"Elijah, thank you. We did find Sasha Deerling, thanks to your deductive reasoning, but not in Father Philbrook's house."

"Can we go inside Rock? I'll take that coffee now."

Elijah ran to pull the arrows from the targets then joined his grandfather and the police officer inside. "Where was Sasha? Was she hurt?"

Rock made fresh coffee then poured a large glass of water for Elijah.

Sergeant Wojuc took off his hat and jacket then sat across from Elijah. "Sasha was in the basement of the church in a storage cupboard behind the boiler. And if we hadn't had the dogs with us we might never have found her. She wasn't hurt, traumatized though because she wasn't hiding – she had been abducted."

Grandpa Clearwater came to the table with two steaming mugs and then sat in a chair next to his grandson. "Who took her? Can she describe them, him, her or whoever?"

"When the police tracking dogs found her, Sasha was bound with tape over her mouth and a pillow case over her head, pulled down to her waist. After we called her mother it was several minutes before Sasha was coherent. She told us she had hurried to the girl's washroom just before the bell to clean glue off her hands from an art project."

"She had her back to the door when she was pulling out paper towel to dry her hands. Someone much bigger and stronger came up behind her, knocked off her glasses, put wide tape

132

across her mouth then pulled a pillowcase over her head and shoulders."

"The abductor said nothing the entire time he was with Sasha, but it definitely was a *he*. Next whoever he was threw her over his shoulder and then escaped unseen using the rear service door between the girl's bathroom and the janitor's supply closet."

Sasha said she felt the colder air outside and some light came through the fabric of the pillowcase, but even if she had had her glasses on she couldn't have seen anything. The person who took Sasha jogged for several minutes away from the school."

"She said she heard the school bell sound only faintly before she realized the person who carried her was going down some steps. She heard a door open, then a second door then she was dumped onto a hard surface. Sasha thought she was in a box. Her hands and feet were tied and then there was no light at all, everything was black."

With a sudden chill Elijah thought of Larry Swallowtail, but then dismissed the idea. Why would Larry take Sasha Deerling? Mrs. Deerling had little money. She was a widow who shared a house with her bachelor brother to split living expenses.

The officer swallowed the last of his coffee then stood. "I need to be off. Rock thanks for the coffee. Elijah, Happy Birthday. I apologize for not remembering earlier – I was a little preoccupied. You're thirteen today, right?"

"Yes sir. It's official I'm now a teenager." He grinned feeling proud.

"And it's also official," Rock stood to open the back door, "that I'm now a senior citizen – *raising* a teenager!"

"Hey, who's raising who?" Elijah made a face.

Sergeant Wojuc laughed. "Good luck with that one old friend. My twin daughters will turn nineteen in June and my wife and I just might survive until next year – or not."

Grandpa closed the door. "*Who's raising who?*" He mimicked Elijah. "You got some nerve, wise guy. If you're not careful I'll send you to live with your Great Aunt Lucille."

"Nooo!"

His grandfather laughed. "I'll boil some water for a bath in the tub room. Drink the rest of your water mister. We'll leave for my sister's as soon as I'm done."

Elijah wondered into the living room and looked at the hardcover book *My Cousin Rachel* and decided he would wait until Grandpa could listen while he read.

He looked out through the tall wide front expanse of glass smiling as he saw the archery targets. His new bow lay on the cushion of the window seat, the arrows in a pile on the floor beside the front door.

CHAPTER...14

Grandpa had six pots of water steaming on their wood stove.

From his bedroom door that opened into the living room at the foot of the loft stairs, Grandpa carried a clean shirt and jeans toward the kitchen, then turned back to look at Elijah.

"You know, I think it will be pretty fine to have a hot shower in the new bathroom. Then I'll turn the tub-room into a pantry and linen closet."

"Great plan Grandpa. I think I'll practice a little more with my new bow. Don't say it – I'm taking my container of water with me!"

Outside Arrow and Dart whinnied a greeting from their corral and Elijah thought of the piece of paper tied to one of the rocks. He ran to check Arrow's shoulder. The swelling had gone down and there was no open wound. He gave them both a treat of alfalfa pellets then decided to see what rude comment Larry had put on the piece of paper tied to the third stone.

It took Elijah several minutes to find the rock. He'd thrown it further into the underbrush than he thought. Preparing himself for a offensive picture or a lot of rude language – Elijah was stunned by what actually had been written...

IF YOU WANT TO SEE THAT WIERD KID WITH THE THICK BOTTLE GLASES ALIVE THEN TELL NO ONE ABOUT THIS NOTE – I FOUND OUT YUR GRANDFATHER AND GREAT AUNT LUCILE KEEP HUNDRIDS OF DOLLARS HIDEN IN THEIR HOUSES FOR EMERGENTSIES – I'M LEAVING ALBERTA AND I NEED THAT MONEY – YOU GOT TIL 2PM SATERDAY TO GET IT ALL - LEVE IT IN A LUNCH BAG AT THE SOUTH END OF YUR AUNTS RASBERY HEGE – IF YOU DON'T I RING THE WEIRD KID'S NECK FIRST THEN I RING YURS – L.S.

Elijah read and reread the note. His heart pounded so loudly he heard no other sounds.

"You're such a cow-pie!" He said out loud. "If you're going to threaten people at least check your spelling!"

His legs felt like rubber as he walked back through the trees. 'Well you creep, I secretly outsmarted you and Sasha is safe.' Elijah thought as reached the fence then climbed over and into the horse corral. Then taking a post for cover instinctively he looked around quickly and toward the other side of the county road from where Larry had launched the rocks the afternoon before.

He desperately did *not* want anything to do with this kid, but knew Sergeant Wojuc needed to see this note. Then Elijah had an idea...

Running back to the house and to his grandfather's roll-top desk Elijah found an envelope and a stamp then addressed the envelope to the sergeant without a return address. Larry Swallowtail printed the note entirely in uppercase letters to

136

disguise any handwriting style, but his initials would give him away.

Elijah quickly changed his shirt and brushed his hair then tucked the folded envelop into his jacket pocket. He was sitting in his chair at the kitchen table sipping water when his grandfather emerged from the tub-room. Rock had shaved and smelled of Aqua Velva.

"Grandpa no one uses that aftershave anymore."

"Y-e-s they do or stores wouldn't sell it. Just because you're thirteen now doesn't mean you suddenly know everything."

"Maybe not, but I'm not stuck in the 70s!"

"Let's go! And if there was any justice on God's Earth then He would let me be the grandson and make you the grandfather for the next six years!"

The water in Elijah's mouth shot straight out and some dribbled down his chin.

In the truck, Elijah launched the other half of his plan. "Can we swing by the Chevron station on our way to Aunt Lucille's? I want to buy her a *thank-you* card at the Quick-Store."

"Well that's thoughtful, of course you can."

With Larry Swallowtail's threatening note safely in the mailbox – anonymously – to the RCMP Detachment, Elijah relaxed. Heading toward his grandfather's truck he realized he was actually looking forward to getting some new pajamas.

He could feel sorry for Larry. He could feel sorry that even though Larry's mom and dad were both alive they hadn't been the kind of parents Larry could count on. Elijah could appreciate that while his grandmother died two years after his parents he still had his grandfather and his great aunt and his dad's sister, Aunt Dawn, her husband Uncle River and his six cousins.

He thought life seemed strange and he wondered why... 'Larry was healthy with living parents, who didn't seem to care, but Elijah had cystic fibrosis and parents who cared but died. None of that made sense.'

Grandpa brought his truck to a stop just beyond the cattle bridge to Aunt Lucille's farm house. "Oooh look what my sister's done!"

Elijah cringed. "Grandpa, she's tied bright pink balloons everywhere!"

Rock shook his head and got out of his truck. "Be brave. Maybe ten years from now no one will remember that about a hundred pink balloons were tied to nearly every tree and bush in your aunt's front garden."

"Wait a minute! You knew about this!" Elijah stayed behind the open passenger door.

"Hey you only turn thirteen once." He began to walk toward his sister's front porch. "You said it yourself you're officially a teenager - and I can assure you that life get's more complicated after twelve."

Reluctantly Elijah followed. "Did she make my cake pink too?"

Grandpa Clearwater held open the front screen door. "That I do not know, but looking around my guess is that there's *more* pink to come!"

There was indeed *more,* pink.

In the middle of Aunt Lucille's dining table stood a three tiered cake in three shades of pink, with thirteen pink candles. The paper plates were pink, the lemonade was pink, the ice cream was pink, the paper napkins were pink – and – everyone had wrapped their gifts to Elijah in pink tissue paper with pink bows.

Several strands of pink crepe paper were tied from Aunt Lucille's ceiling light to the walls. Everyone wore pink birthday hats and then his Aunt Dawn tied a large pink bib around Elijah's neck that Aunt Lucille had sewn from a scrap of pink flannelette pajama fabric.

Jayson looked stricken and whispered to Elijah. "I hope she doesn't do this for my thirteenth birthday. Last year she only played tricks on James and Joseph."

Elijah remembered the bright yellow lace nightgown Aunt Lucille sewed for James and the large purple sun bonnet she made for Joseph. And those were bizarre enough, but this was well over-the-top even for Lucille.

Father Philbrook stopped by for a quick greeting on his way to see Mrs. Deerling and Sasha. Aunt Dawn and Uncle River had devised a scavenger hunt and when the food was ready,

Aunt Lucille's famous chicken-fried-steak, coleslaw and scalloped cheese potatoes filled everyone almost too full for birthday cake.

At five minutes past 4PM Elijah made a wish and blew out his candles. With the scent of the smoking birthday candles in the air, at first the odor of additional smoke went unnoticed.

Then Spring's high pitched scream caught everyone's immediate attention. When she pointed through the open front door to the porch five foot flames crawled up the front screen door. Uncle River ran to the porch closing the house door behind him to put out the flames, but all the grass and scrubs around the base of the entire house were a blaze.

When Uncle River ran back into the house, Grandpa followed him to the kitchen and the back door. But in the rear of the house hungry flames reached up to the windows there too. They were surrounded by a deliberately set fire and they were trapped.

Grandpa, Dawn and River had left their cell phones in their vehicles, Aunt Lucille only had a land line, but her cable was cut.

Spring, Jorge and Sarah were crying as Dawn huddled against the dining room wall with her three youngest children.

"Lucille!" Grandpa faced his sister as the heat inside her vintage house became increasingly uncomfortable. "Do you have any tools anywhere in the house that River and I can use to make a hole in your kitchen floor? Everyone needs to get to the root cellar below."

Panic showed on Lucille's face. "Just a small hammer for hanging pictures a kitchen screwdriver, scissors and some meat knives." Tears ran down her face. "That's all I have. There, in the pantry."

Uncle River and Grandpa Clearwater rushed to the corner pantry then began cutting into the old linoleum and chipping away at the solid pine plank floor boards with the hammer and the screwdriver as their only tools.

Squinting through the smoke outside the dining room window, Elijah spotted a tall solitary figure watching from the far side of Aunt Lucille's garden at the south end of her raspberry hedge.

Even through the flames Elijah recognized the solitary figure of Larry Swallowtail. Clearly Larry didn't know that Sasha had been found and still had expected Elijah to comply with the demand for money in his threatening note.

A rush of energy he had never felt before filled his entire being and Elijah rose up.

Uncle River and Grandpa saw him through the open kitchen door and their meager tools dropped from their hands. Dawn had spread a table cloth over her head and the younger kids but Lucille, James and Joseph saw Elijah and backed into the kitchen.

A flash of white light surrounded Elijah transforming his physical form to that of a giant black crow with a wing span that touched the top of the farmhouse roof.

Elijah's form filled the room.

With one sweeping flurry Elijah stepped into the air, and breaking the window glass, rose higher out through the flames and filled the clearing with his light. He then sent a giant wave of wind with his left wing that snuffed out the surrounding moat of flames that had blackened the lower half of Lucille's house.

In rapid succession Larry shot large stones with his slingshot at the giant menacing bird that had appeared from nowhere.

The large rocks sailed toward the hovering black essence of *Black Crow* exploding into dust before they were able to reach him.

Thick black smoke shot upwards.

Black Crow became brighter more vivid growing even greater in size.

The white light around him altered to violet – sending a second massive wave of wind that sucked the air from the lungs of Larry Swallowtail.

Shaken, but still defiant when Larry raised his fists and tried to curse the bird, he discovered that he was mute. His voice had been taken from him.

When Larry stood to get his bearings, he saw the form of the *Black Crow* return to the being of Elijah. The boy led his family away from the house with the siding still smoldering. Once again Larry tried to a curse the kid who had seemed to alter into a formidable being, but no sound came from his throat.

CHAPTER...15

By the time the police and county fire trucks had reached the farm, members of the surviving family were on the grass coughing. Elijah showed no signs of his former appearance, but his family was still shaken by not just the fire, but also Elijah's transformation.

Elijah's coughing was worse than any of his cousins and his grandfather rushed to give him his Podhaler, but his breathing became even more labored. An EMT placed an oxygen mask over his face, and then strapped him to a stretcher.

Two ambulances left Lucille's front yard. The first one carried Elijah with his grandfather hovering and worried. The second one carried Spring and Jorge with their mother hovering and worried.

Larry ran away and no one except Elijah had seen him, but the envelope addressed to Sergeant Wojuc was in the mail box.

When Elijah awoke he was back in the Calgary Children's Hospital. His favorite nurse Catherine was lifting a cool gel-pack from his forehead.

"I…" Elijah coughed. His throat felt sore, his voice was raspy. "I have a headache."

"I'm not surprised. You're not supposed to breathe in smoke – certainly not that much smoke with burning paint fumes, wood siding, bushes, grass – you and your family are fortunate."

"Grandpa?"

She smiled. "We gave him a little oxygen too. Your cousins are going to be fine. They're with their mother just two rooms down the hall. Guess you'll be finishing your family party here with the hospital staff, at least overnight."

Elijah closed his eyes.

When Elijah woke up again, his grandfather and his Uncle River stood by his bed. He tried to sit up then to speak, but his throat still felt dry and sore.

"Just rest son," Uncle River took Elijah's hand. "We're all here."

River looked over at his father-in-law. "That was quiet a party." He patted Grandpa Clearwater's shoulder then left Elijah's room to check on his wife and his other kids.

"Aunt Lucille? Her house?"

"She's okay," Grandpa reassured him. "And just the lower half of her exterior siding was damaged, but it can be replaced."

"What happened Grandpa? Did I pass out?"

Grandpa shook his head.

"It was kinda like my dreams, but if I wasn't asleep then..." Elijah thought out loud. "I felt like I was sort of flying, but more like hovering. I looked down on Aunt Lucille's house and waved something large."

His grandfather didn't interrupt him, or prompt him he just waited patiently for Elijah to remember on his own.

Elijah frowned. "Did I put out the fire around the house?"

Rock Clearwater nodded.

"How did I do that?"

"With your wings."

He blinked then shook his head. "My... My what?"

"Your wing span," Grandpa responded calmly and quietly, "from tip to tip when you transformed was forty-eight feet."

"Grandpa what are you saying?" Elijah sat up. "What wings? Did I die and the paramedics brought me back?"

"It's always good to see you back," Nurse Catherine breezed into the room, "though not under these circumstances."

She placed a thermometer in his mouth, put on a blood pressure cuff then took his pulse. "Wonderful. All of your numbers are where they should be." She entered the results into a laptop computer.

"Let's listen to your lungs. Take a slow deep breath, and another, now another. Wow, that sounded pretty good."

Elijah gave Catherine a weak smile.

"Does the doctor still want him to stay overnight?" Rock watched his grandson's color change. He suddenly looked pale.

She nodded, "just as a precaution. We're keeping your cousins too." She leaned over and kissed Elijah's forehead. "Happy Birthday." Then Catherine left the room.

When the nurse was out of sight Elijah clutched his grandfather's sleeve. "Grandpa what!"

Grandpa Clearwater took Elijah's hand in his. "You have fulfilled a pre-historic legend that spans from the primeval clans of Europe to the oldest tribes of North America. You were born to be *The Crow Child.*"

"Every three hundred years an ancient spirit of the intelligent, protective *Crow* returns in human form to bring about change and to shield the defenseless from harm."

Elijah turned away from his grandfather to stare out of the wide window in his hospital room. The street lights had come on. The night sky over Calgary was a deep navy blue as Saturday, April 13th 2016 faded.

In that moment he remembered his entire life as Prince Dade who led his people to a new prosperity through trade with Denmark, Finland and Poland - and he remembered his entire life as Chief Talkingstone who led his people to form alliances with western Canadian settlers that secured peace for the Blackfoot. And in that same moment he felt overwhelmed. He didn't feel like a leader, he didn't feel wise like Prince

Dade or Chief Talkingstone. He didn't even feel thirteen he felt three all over again sitting between his grandparents while two police officers explained the car accident that took the lives of both of his parents.

He lay back against the pillow. "I'm very tired Grandpa."

That night Aunt Lucille slept on the cot in Elijah's room while Aunt Dawn slept on a cot in Spring and Sarah's room. River slept on a cot in Jorge and Jayson's' room. James and Joseph were in the room between their younger siblings.

Worried about Elijah, Rock Clearwater called an emergency Council meeting at his house late that night. "I watched his face after I gave him a simple explanation. He was no longer panicked, but he was very quiet and his color was pale."

"*Quiet* is a good sign." The chief replied. "In that *quiet time* who he was, and who he is would have come to him."

"He was immediately tired because he also realized the weight of his new responsibility." Geraldine reminded Rock.

The council discussed the return of *The Crow Child* for another hour, and how the fire around the house that was extinguished might be explained to the police, and how the reality of Elijah's birthright might be kept quiet from mainstream media for as long as possible…

When Grandpa Clearwater got to the hospital Sunday morning the doctor was making her rounds checking off each one of the family members as cleared to go home.

"Here, Catherine. I think we're done with this bunch." Dr. Sinha signed off on the last chart, and smiled. "Unless there are more?" She turned to Rock Clearwater. "Are there more of you?"

"I hope not."

In Elijah's room, he was sitting up, but Catherine had fitted a Bronchodilator mask over his face to ease his breathing.

"Don't be alarmed Mr. Clearwater." The nurse came in right behind Grandpa. "The doctor wants Elijah on this for another ten minutes to finish out a full thirty minute round before he goes home."

Lucille came into the room looking tired. "He woke up coughing twice in the night." She held two takeout cups of coffee and sipped on one.

"We got his lungs cleared out. He's a tough one." Catherine winked at Elijah who held up his thumb in the 'it's-all-good' sign.

"Have you eaten anything?"

Elijah shook his head.

His cousins, Aunt Dawn and Uncle River filled the doorway then partway into Elijah's room. The children had been briefed on their cousin's advanced abilities and sworn to a new family secret for everyone's security.

Joseph couldn't wait for Elijah to morph again into the huge bird with the giant wings. "What you did yesterday was so cool. I really thought that stuff was only in comic books or the movies!"

Elijah couldn't talk with the mask still on his face, so he only nodded wishing yesterday had been just an ordinary birthday with only the pink theme and Aunt Lucille's embarrassing flannel pajamas.

"See you all later." Uncle River began to herd his family out. Then he looked from his father-in-law to Lucille. "Call if you need anything – anytime."

Later the three of them drove back to Grandpa's farm in silence. Aunt Lucille moved into her brother's bedroom on the main floor until the repairs to her house were finished, while Grandpa moved his clothes and personal items up to the loft with Elijah.

After lunch Aunt Lucille set up her sewing machine by the front room window to finish more family birthday presents.

Grandpa made some changes to the drawing of the bathroom addition. With his sister sharing the house for at least a full month maybe two, he and his son-in-law decided to start the new bathroom - immediately.

Elijah tried to read, but his lungs were still affected by the smoke. His sporadic coughing made his chest too sore to sit up and too sore to lie flat, and too sore to do much of anything so he tried reclining on one side.

While he breathed easier with help of a portable bronchodilator they borrowed from the hospital - Elijah sorted through more family photos.

Monday came and went with none of the members of Rock Clearwater's family, riding the school bus or resuming work. Elijah wasn't coughing as much. Aunt Dawn had phoned in to one of her staff to open her Hallmark Store in town, but Uncle River didn't open his carpentry shop. Instead he and Grandpa and James went to the lumber yard to pick up plywood and two-by-fours.

Tuesday morning Elijah awoke late to the sound of hammering and sawing. Downstairs he watched out the kitchen window as clouds of sawdust flew away with the wind. "Wish I could do that."

Aunt Lucille boiled water for a pot of herb tea for them both. "You'd like to be a carpenter like your dad was and your uncle?"

Elijah sneezed which started coughing spasms again. He made it to the kitchen table and dropped down onto one of the chair seats.

Aunt Lucille found his Podhaler then waited.

He took a deep breath with his inhaler then a sip of hot tea. "Maybe not, but *I'd* like the *choice*. James can choose anything so can my other cousins. Cystic Fibrosis was chosen for me and so it seems was this bird thing now."

"*The Crow Child.*" Aunt Lucille stirred honey in her tea.

"Yeah, I'm *The Crow Child.* Guess it means I can put out fires. Is that like a career?"

"According to the legend it's more like a calling."

150

"What's a *calling*?"

"Oh, a purpose or a mission, I guess. I don't understand it all, but you can ask your grandfather. He and the Council know much more than anyone else."

After lunch Elijah tried to read more of his book assignment and Aunt Lucille attempted to sew, but work on the addition was noisy. Very noisy.

"Do you feel up to going into town with me?" She turned away from her sewing machine. "I'll be thrilled not to need to pee down a hole a week from now, but in the meantime I can't hear myself think."

Elijah grinned and cheerfully closed the book again.

"Well, look at that!" As Aunt Lucille pulled into a parking place outside the yarn store, they saw Sergeant Wojuc escorting Larry Swallowtail into the RCMP Detachment across the street.

Then ten minutes later while Elijah waited in the truck for his aunt – Larry burst from the front door of the police detachment running with a handgun. On the corner a woman pushing a stroller had stopped to wait for the light to change when suddenly Larry pushed her down and grabbed her toddler from the stroller.

Sergeant Wojuc and two constables had rushed out after Larry, but in the five seconds it took for the officers to discover the direction their suspect went Larry had his hostage. They ran in the direction of the sound of a crying child and hysterical woman.

From his vantage point across the opposite corner what Elijah witnessed took no more time than a deep breath, but as he got out of his aunt's truck Elijah's reaction took even less.

In a rush of energy now familiar *The Crow Child* rose. His entire being expanded.

Cars crashed into one another. Pedestrians carrying briefcases, bags of groceries or tools dropped them from their hands then ran.

A flash of white light surrounded *The Crow Child* and transformed his physical form to that of a giant black crow with a wing span that touched the roof of City Hall.

Black Crow's form filled the open space.

With one sweeping flurry *Black Crow* stepped into the air, rising higher filling the town square with his light.

In rapid succession Larry shot at the giant menacing bird that again had appeared from nowhere. As the bullets were fired toward the hovering dark essence of *Black Crow* they exploded into dust before they reached him.

With the wave of his left wing the handgun was yanked from Larry's hand. With the wave of his right wing the terrified child was plucked from Larry's arms and returned her mother.

No one around them moved.

Black Crow became brighter more vivid growing even greater in size.

Aunt Lucille came out of the yarn store and dropped everything she carried. "Oh, you precious boy." Her words were almost a whisper.

When Larry tried to get his bearings to run, *Black Crow* swept him into the air then dropped him at the feet of Sergeant Wojuc. Larry tried to curse, but still no sound came from his throat.

Black Crow went higher then vanished descending two blocks away in an alley.

When Elijah reemerged he was coughing. Sweat dripped from his forehead and he reached in his pocket for his inhaler.

He made his way down the block then ducked into the back of the yarn store and emerged from the front door behind his aunt. He coughed again and Aunt Lucille jumped.

People rushed by them toward the intersection of accidents not paying any attention to an older woman standing beside a thin youth.

She hugged him tightly. "Well, I guess you can do a lot more than put out fires." She took out a hankie to wipe away the sweat. "Let's get you home."

"You can let me out here, please Aunt Lucille." Elijah took another puff from his inhaler. "I'm feeling better and I want to feed Arrow and Dart."

As he hurried away, Aunt Lucille was worried about the expression she saw on her nephew's face.

At the house, framing for the addition was finished for the day. Inside Lucille related what had happened in town to Rock.

Her brother was stunned. "Wow, and you think no one saw him? No one saw 'who' *Black Crow* is?"

Lucille shook her head. "No, no one recognized that the massive crow had transformed from the boy they know as Elijah. Larry Swallowtail can't speak and even if he could, who'd believe him? Elijah's with the horses."

Rock quickly changed his clothes and hurried to check on his grandson. His mare Dart met him at the gate. She nuzzled him and he gave her a hug around her neck, but he had walked only part way across the coral when he spotted his grandson.

Through the open door of the barn Elijah stood sobbing into the shoulder of his horse Arrow. The horse did not shift or move, but remained perfectly still with his regal head resting against Elijah's back.

He watched the touching scene for a minute impressed by the bond between the large horse and small youth. And it was Arrow who gave Rock's presence away.

When he walked to the barn Dart followed him inside. He gave Elijah his handkerchief then grandson and grandfather sat side by side on a bale of hay. "What's up buddy?" His arm went around Elijah's shoulder.

Elijah blew his nose then let out a deep sigh.

"If I can save people, if I can move the wind, if I can put out fires and other stuff – how come I still have CF? How come?"

The horses stood side by side with their heads down listening, sensing the turmoil of another being for whom they had an attachment.

"You'll need to become accustomed to your gift Elijah. You'll need to understand the legend. *Crow-power* will protect you and all those *you* protect."

"But everyone has something in the form of a limitation Elijah – it's meant to bring balance.

Prince Albert, Duke of York became the United Kingdom's sixth King George - but he still had to deal with his debilitating stuttering."

"Franklin Delano Roosevelt became a three term President of the United States - but he still had to deal with his polio."

"Everyone has something that makes them powerful and something else that makes them fragile and learning to deal with balancing our strength with our weakness is really what gives *everyone's* life its' purpose…

With our cries heard above the roar of fire

Comes *one* who hears those cries....

With

Outstretched wings

this *one* who walks as man

Sends wind to protect those who cry

and silence

To punish those who take...

PART TWO

Thanksgiving

In

St. Louis

CHAPTER...16

One year later - April/2017

Elijah Clearwater looked discouraged, stabbing his spoon into his hot oatmeal.

"I kind'a thought something would happen again, at least by my fourteenth birthday, but nothing else has happened Grandpa. No bank robbers, no kidnappers or even bullies at school. Why d'you think that is?"

Rock Clearwater smiled, spreading honey on his toast. "Just because you have the ability to deal with trouble doesn't mean you need to go looking for trouble. When *Crow Child* is needed, I'm sure the next challenge will find you..."

****

September/2017

"I have an Aunt Mary?"

Mystified, Elijah read then reread the note inside a bent birthday card. He held the card in one hand and the envelope with a return address that was creased and smudged, in the other.

Grandpa Clearwater looked over his grandson's shoulder more curious than surprised. "It would appear so."

As the decades drifted by Rock Clearwater had discovered that less and less surprised him. He realized he had seen or experienced a great deal while growing up on a First Nations Reservation. Then even more years later working his, own small animal farm. By the time he reached the age of sixty-two so many previous experiences had actually begun to repeat.

At the end of a long narrow driveway, where the school bus had stopped to let Elijah off, grandfather and grandson stood by their open mail box.

"Gosh my birthday was back in April." Elijah counted on his fingers. "Labor Day was a week ago. I wonder where this could have been for the last five months?"

A late afternoon breeze, crisp and cool hinted that fall would be short and winter would be early.

Grandpa closed the mail box and together they walked up the graveled driveway toward their A-frame log house.

The return address was slightly smudged. "This came from Alexandria, VA." Elijah was able to read most of the information except the last two numbers of the American zip code. "What's VA?"

"You mean where, is VA?" Grandpa corrected, wrinkling his nose at his collection of junk mail brochures, and utility bills.

"VA is postal shorthand for the State of Virginia. You know, one of America's original thirteen colonies."

Elijah grinned. "Yeah, yeah I remember. We learned about the first thirteen colonies at the same time we studied Upper and Lower Canada. They were all fighting with each other about the same time."

"That stuff was actually kind'a cool. But Mr. Booth is so b-o-r-i-n-g. He's more boring than watching Aunt Lucille give all of us haircuts every six weeks."

Half way up the driveway Elijah began to cough. They stopped by the horse corral and waited. In about half a minute he had caught his breath again, spitting several times.

"Where's your inhaler?" Grandpa was relieved that Elijah's cough sounded loose and less intense than the day before.

"In my backpack." He leaned against the middle fence rail. "Honest Grandpa this is the first time today I've coughed."

On the other side of the fence Elijah's gelding Arrow, and Grandpa's mare Dart, came to greet them with a snort and a loud whinny.

"Let's skip their brushing for today, we'll just feed them." Grandpa put his arm around Elijah's shoulder as they walked through the wide stock gate.

Inside the barn, Elijah climbed the ladder to the hayloft above the horse stalls. After taking another deep puff from his inhaler he waited a full minute then cut the binder twine holding the hay in bales. With the twine cut he kicked large chunks of hay through the open loft door to his grandfather on the ground below.

While grandpa spread the hay around in smaller loose piles Elijah topped up the water trough. "What are *we* having for diner?"

Grandpa hung up the rake without looking at his grandson, "Hay and oats." Then he opened the gate and waited for Elijah.

They walked the rest of the distance to the farm house Rock built in 1970 when he and his late wife Rose were newlyweds.

Inside, the vaulted ceiling extended twenty feet from floor to peak with a grey slate stone fireplace at one end of the living room. A divided bedroom loft was over the kitchen area that his son Glen and daughter Dawn shared growing up. The wall had been removed after Elijah moved in and he enjoyed the entire space to himself.

On the main floor was a second bedroom off of the large open living room, and a kitchen heated by a vintage cast iron stove. Just off the back of the kitchen was the new and only bathroom that Grandpa and Uncle River finished the year before. Along the front of the house ran a narrow deck that faced western sunsets over the Rocky Mountains.

Leading to the back door was a wider rear deck warmed by sunrises from the east, looking out over the chicken coop and beyond that to the pig barn.

Inside the back door the aroma of his grandfather's meatloaf filled the mudroom even before Elijah opened the door to the kitchen. "Seriously! Great *hay* Grandpa."

"I'll make you some hot cinnamon and strawberry tea right away, but get your vest, chest thumper going first."

"Ugh. I'm starving! I could eat our table leg."

"Well you'll need to eat it raw I don't cook table leg." Grandpa winked. But the fact that Elijah was hungry was a good sign. Monitoring the effects of cystic fibrosis required daily vigilance.

Elijah felt the first of several rhythmic thumps from his left side and then to his right side and then back. When he began to cough again he knew he'd need to keep his small spit bucket close by. Some days Elijah had more patience for his routine than others.

"It would be so amazing if kids grew out of CF like they do some allergies. Sasha Deerling can eat strawberries now *and* bread with wheat in it. How awesome is that?"

The kettle whistled and Grandpa poured steaming water over a single teabag in Elijah's *Hulk* mug. "Here this'll keep you from starving completely while I mash the sweet potatoes."

"And don't you dare snitch. You do five more minutes on that now, then another ten after we're done eating."

"My lungs will collapse!" Elijah made face.

"Gosh that's too bad there pal, you're in rough shape." Grandpa drained the water from the pot of sweet potatoes. "The medical examiner will list your cause of death as - *collapsed lungs due to starvation*!"

162

"Grandpa!"

But Rock Clearwater was grateful. Cystic fibrosis was not easy to treat, but for a full twelve months after his thirteenth birthday Elijah had only needed one trip to Alberta's Children's Hospital. And then, not at all since his fourteenth birthday last April.

Rock set a platter of thick sliced meatloaf on the pine kitchen table beside their salad, steamed green beans and mashed sweet potatoes.

"Man, I'm so ready for this." Elijah closed his eyes and hummed savoring one of his favorite ways to eat ground beef.

"Speaking of aunts," Grandpa chewed then swallowed. "Your Aunt Lucille stopped by with a batch of brownies."

"It's Friday, with meatloaf *and* brownies – so now I think I'll live." Elijah stabbed several green beans with his fork.

"Brownies tend to have that effect on most people." Grandpa winked again.

"You never told me what your *new* aunt had to say? That envelope looked like it was dragged behind a mail truck all the way from the east coast of the United States."

"That's because I never finished reading it." Elijah put down his fork and retrieved the card from his backpack.

"Aunt Mary said…" Elijah started to read the note inside. "Here, this is her phone number." He handed his grandfather a separate business card.

"A-l-l r-i-g-h-t! If I can visit - my birthday gift is a plane ticket from Calgary, Alberta to Alexandria, Virginia for American Thanksgiving at her house!"

Elijah looked from the late arriving birthday card to his grandfather. "American Thanksgiving is in November right?"

CHAPTER...17

"I find this very odd."

Early Saturday, the following morning, Rock Clearwater's widowed sister Lucille had made an unannounced stop at their house.

When Elijah and his grandfather returned from feeding the pigs and chickens, Great Aunt Lucille was sitting at the kitchen table. She was eating one of her own brownies and sipping a mug of coffee.

She had left the door between the kitchen and the mudroom open. "You can't really be considering this?" Lucille pointed to the card on the table.

Elijah made a face, cringing at his grandfather keeping his back to the open doorway.

Rock wasn't so lucky. All he could do was shake his head. "Did you forget something Lucille? Did you tell me you were coming by..."

"No." His older sister interrupted him.

"I stopped by to see if Elijah could go with me into Canmore. I only need him for a couple of hours to pick out fabric."

Surprise showed on both faces of grandson and grandfather.

Aunt Lucille rushed to explain. "This year, instead of pajamas for my four older nephews I decided to make each of them a quilt for Christmas."

Silently, Elijah was relieved. No more homemade pajamas in exactly the same flannel pattern that matched those of his six cousins, two of whom were girls. 'Yahoo.' He thought.

Out loud he said, "I'm not fussy, Aunt Lucille. I like any fabric in any shade of green, in any pattern except flowers."

Elijah filled the kettle with water to boil to make his orange and nutmeg tea.

Rock poured coffee into his own mug then joined his sister at the kitchen table. He sat in a chair across from her. "Actually, I *was* considering the trip. But with his card arriving so late we'll need to order our passports and fast."

"As you can see from her note, Elijah's ticket will be paid for as his birthday gift. All I need to do is check Air Canada ticket prices for me."

"You're going too!"

"Well none of this is chiseled in stone yet Lucille, but I'm certainly not letting him go alone. His health issues aside, Elijah has never been on a plane before, let alone out of the country."

"I haven't called…" Grandpa Clearwater pulled the business card from between the salt and pepper shakers, "Mrs. Mary Margaret O'Day Trent, as yet. However *dearest, nosey, interfering* sister of mine, I planned to do that later this morning."

Elijah kept his head down. He stirred a little honey into his tea mug so his aunt wouldn't see him smile. Listening to the aging brother and sister as they bantered, he had a pretty good idea how their childhood together had played out.

Whenever his grandfather teased his great aunt it was always entertaining - at least for Elijah.

Great Aunt Lucille opened her mouth to say something else about the pending trip then seemed to change her mind - for the moment.

With a deep sigh she finished her coffee. "Okay Elijah, a quilt in shades and patterns of green for you, it is then."

A warm breeze drifted in through the open kitchen window, bringing the sweet scent of poplar leaves morphing from emerald to gold. The early fall day had grown slightly warmer as the sun rose higher.

She stood and folded her knitted poncho. "Any color suggestions for your cousins James, Joseph and Jayson?"

"Jayson really likes blue. Joseph likes all those camouflage patterns." Then he shrugged, "but I don't have a clue about James since he got his driver's license."

Elijah suddenly grinned. "But if you can sew a car together instead of a quilt he'd probably take any color."

CHAPTER...18

"Teachers, must take a special class in university called *How To Annoy Kids*."

Elijah pulled out one of the pine kitchen chairs and dropped his back pack on the seat with a thump.

Behind Elijah stood his cousin Jayson, nodding.

Grandpa Clearwater studied two of his seven grandchildren. He finished chopping onion for the beef stew then added it to the large pot simmering on his wood burning stove.

"How are you Grandpa?" Rock started in a high squeaky voice. "How was your day?"

Jayson began to laugh reaching out to hug his grandfather. "How was your day Grandpa?"

Elijah rolled his eyes and hugged Rock too. "Sorry Grandpa."

"This weekend is Canadian Thanksgiving. You guys have three days off. How could that possibly be annoying?"

"Mr. Booth gave us a history paper assignment. We have to write the outline." Jayson grinned, elbowing Elijah.

Standing together Elijah had grown, but Jayson was still two inches taller than Elijah though the boys were only a few months apart in age.

"So over this weekend we have to pick a history topic and then finish an outline to turn in Tuesday morning. *But* after first period bell he overheard Jayson and I talking about me getting two thanksgiving dinners in two countries this fall."

"Naturally, Mr. Booth asked Elijah why he was going to have two thanksgiving dinners and we told him about Elijah's Aunt Mary."

"So I don't get to choose." Elijah lit a fire under the kettle plate to boil water for tea. "*My* assignment is to write on the history of Canada's Thanksgiving and why it is the first Monday in October *and* the history of America's Thanksgiving and why it is the last Thursday in November."

Grandpa set the cookie jar in the center of the table. "Pardon my confusion, but how is that annoying – I'd like to know some of that history too. What did you originally want to write about?"

"Ireland's history." Elijah set out a pitcher of orange juice for Jayson.

Grandpa burst out laughing. "You phony. You only wanted to write about Ireland because you still have the research we finished last year just before your thirteenth birthday - and you thought you could use it again."

"Hey, that's not fair!" Jayson bit into a chocolate chip cookie.

Elijah just scowled chewing on an oatmeal and raisin cookie.

That night the boys got to bed late with valuable property still unclaimed in their ongoing game of Monopoly.

Elijah had been restless, and had to get up to the bathroom twice. Grandpa made him drink more tea, because he hadn't had enough saltwater for the past two days and mild cramps had started. The tea had helped to settle his cramps, but then his bladder was full.

Jayson was sound asleep on the left side of Elijah's king-size bed. Elijah decided to take a melatonin so he could fall asleep too.

****

There was no light anywhere.

He blinked several times but everything was still dark. There was no form, no sound no smell – nothing. Elijah sat up and put his right arm out in front of him then to his side then extended his left arm out from his left side, but there was only air – he felt nothing.

The floor beneath him was cold.

Cautiously Elijah stood. He had only socks on his feet, his shoes were gone. He stuck his right leg out in front of him with his right arm straight in front too and his left arm feeling around above his head. Each step that moved him forward was slow and deliberate.

After twelve careful steps his toes hit something firm and his hand touched a cement wall as cold as the floor had been.

Elijah took a slow deep breath to calm his panic.

With his hand on the wall he kept moving along, but cautiously. He had moved only a few more steps when Elijah came to a corner, turned and then kept walking along the next wall until his foot bumped something soft.

When he knelt down, he felt a human shoulder then the person's head and upper chest...

****

Elijah's body snapped to a sitting position. His breathing was labored and perspiration ran down his forehead and around his eyebrows. It dripped from his chin like drops of rain.

When he reached for his inhaler, his hand was unsteady.

His cousin Jayson stirred in his sleep rolling over from his left side to his right.

Elijah slid from the edge of his bed to sit on the braided rug on the floor with his head resting against the box-spring and mattress. He took two puffs then waited for his breathing to return to normal.

When he could stand, he folded the afghan blanket his late Grandma Rose knitted for him the Christmas before he turned five.

At the half wall he looked out over the living room below. A bright fall moon peaked in through the tall west facing windows casting silver-blue light over everything in the room below him.

Treading the wide spiral metal stairs down from his loft bedroom to the living room, he tiptoed by his grandfather's open door to curl up on the sofa in front of the fireplace.

His chest felt heavy and he took another puff. He hadn't had any dreams since before his thirteenth birthday. But this one was entirely different.

This dream was not about events in his past.

This dream made him shiver, because *Crow Child knew* that this dream was about events in his future.

His eye lids became heavy and soon again, he was asleep.

CHAPTER...19

Late November travel weather in Alberta could be more of a gamble than spinning a roulette wheel.

After two months of numerous emails and Skype calls between the Clearwater log farm house west of Calgary, and Mary Trent's brick split-level in Alexandria - each generation in both families were excited to meet.

However, four days before American Thanksgiving snow started falling in the Canadian Rockies.

And when snow continued falling from the mountains along the foothills late Sunday afternoon, Canmore County brought out road graders and snow ploughs. Equipment worked from Sunday night and all through Monday so the yellow school busses that took students to school in the morning, could return them home after classes ended in the afternoon.

Graders and ploughs cleared steadily falling snow during Monday night and again all day Tuesday.

Then early Wednesday morning the home phones of students began to ring. A rare weather *snow-day* was declared for all rural areas. The recording advised that schools would be closed for Wednesday and Thursday west to the foothills - and north, all the way to Didsbury - and south of Calgary, all the way to High River.

Rock Clearwater stood in front of his twelve foot picture window searching for a break in the clouds. To feed and water the horses, their pigs and chickens he and Elijah had to strap on snowshoes to reach them.

He made sure that Elijah spent extra time with his chest clapper and drank even more fluids, to avoid developing bronchitis or severe gut cramps.

With three feet of snow in forty-eight hours only a snowmobile would have allowed them access to the county road then the Trans Canada Highway, if they had needed to get to the hospital.

"Grandpa?" Elijah finished his morning ten minutes then left his chest and back thumping vest in the kitchen. "How are we going to get to the airport tomorrow?"

Rock Clearwater didn't move away from the window. "I thought you might do that 'wing-thing' you do and fly us there."

Elijah laughed. Standing beside his grandfather he watched large fat flakes continue to cover the front deck.

"About that wing-thing..." Elijah's voice faded as he changed his mind.

He still hadn't mentioned either the first dream in early October or the second one he had a week later, to either his grandfather or his cousin Jayson

After a minute of silence Rock Clearwater reached over and messed up his grandson's hair. "Add another log to the fire then get out those giant marshmallows we bought Saturday. I'll brew us some hot chocolate."

Elijah had grown just over four inches since his thirteenth birthday. The extra height changed his stature from one of the shortest kids in grade seven to about the middle of the pack when he started grade eight.

The growth spurt had been a boon for Elijah, who had avoided most of the girls he had to look up at in his class and a relief for his grandfather who had no idea how to explain how people grew. Or didn't.

But fortunately it had less to do with having CF and more to do with having short parents and even shorter grandparents.

With chocolate squares melted completely into hot milk Grandpa Clearwater carried two steaming mugs to the living room hearth. "Why, are you using one of your arrows to roast that marshmallow?"

"It's an old one. Some of the feathers are missing, see. I got the long barbeque fork for you."

"Try not to set fire to the house." Grandpa frowned as Elijah's marshmallow turned black on one side.

They roasted and ate two marshmallows each, before Rock prodded his grandson. "You started to ask something about your wings, what was it?"

Elijah shrugged. "Well, nothing more has happened. I mean, I don't even know if I could do what I did last year. Last year doesn't even seem real anymore."

"*Black Crow* power doesn't emerge unless there is a reason. I thought you understood that. You're not in trouble and either is anyone else."

"But don't I need to *practice* or something?"

Grandpa smiled swirling some of the darker settled chocolate from the bottom of his mug. "It's not practice that you need Elijah – it is maturity. The ability that has come to you was not there until you turned thirteen. As you age and circumstances change you may very well be called upon again."

"Larry's at a reform school in Nova Scotia." Elijah reached for a third marshmallow. "Everyone else at school is great even my cousin James."

"You may not always live on this small farm between Canmore and Calgary. You may not even stay in Alberta." Rock stood and returned to the kitchen to refill their mugs.

Elijah watched the flames dance then glanced at his grandfather. Through the wide door opening between the living room and the kitchen Grandpa poured more hot chocolate into their mugs.

Elijah suddenly wondered where his future would be. 'Where did he want it to be?'

"If you try to eat that burning marshmallow, I'll need to stuff your mouth with snow."

The fire snapped and spit sap from the bark of aged pine logs.

Startled Elijah looked up to see his marshmallow charred to ash at the end of his arrow. "Oops."

Grandpa put down their mugs reaching for a marshmallow from the bowl. "Like I said don't burn down the house." Rock bit into a soft gooey unroasted marshmallow.

"I have no idea what the forecast is," he said dislodging white spongy goo from his teeth, "but I think we need a plan 'B' to get to the airport for our flight tomorrow morning."

"Does it involve our snowshoes – cause those things are s-l-o-w?"

When Rock checked, amazingly flights were still taking off with blue skies reported above 20,000 feet. By noon Grandpa had reserved a room at the Airport Hotel and two seats on the Greyhound Bus from Canmore to Calgary.

All they needed after Grandpa got off the phone was a means of getting to the Canmore Hotel and that need presented itself, an hour later.

"Good thing we're packed cause Uncle River and Cousin James are heading this way on their snowmobiles."

They tramped through the snow to get extra water and rations to their chickens, the pigs and horses incase their neighbor couldn't get to the animals until Friday.

Leaving Canmore they couldn't see anything out of the bus windows except a wall of snow. A four lane highway had been reduced to a two lane tunnel on that section of the Trans Canada highway all the way into Calgary.

By the following morning as they lined up for their 6AM flight it was no longer snowing in Calgary, it was only overcast.

Settled in their seats with their seatbelts fastened, Elijah watched out through the tiny portal window as the ground crew loaded luggage.

Rock happened to look up as he was unfolding the plane's flight brochure. His sharp intake of breath was so sudden and so loud Elijah thought his grandfather was having a stroke.

When he followed the direction of his grandfather's shocked expression, he saw his Great Aunt Lucille.

Six rows ahead she was making room for her carryon case in one of the overhead bins. People waited in a long line behind her.

When she was finished the passenger in the aisle seat of her row stood to let her in. She smiled and then waved at her astonished brother just before she settled into a middle seat.

CHAPTER...20

Elijah's grandfather sat silent for several seconds staring at, but not truly seeing the flight brochure he clutched with both hands. Nor, did Rock notice other passengers shuffling along the narrow aisle searching for their rows and seat numbers.

"Grandpa?"

Rock Clearwater looked up as a man about the same age as his son-in-law, Elijah's Uncle River, sat in the aisle seat to his left next to him.

"That sister of mine is something else. She must have invited herself. Was there any mention of your Aunt Lucille when you emailed or talked to your Aunt Mary? Mary sure didn't say anything to me last Saturday."

Elijah shook his head, deciding to stay neutral with this latest bit of family excitement. He thought about his late mother and decided the Clearwater family must have been a major culture shift for her after she moved from Ruan, Ireland to Canmore, Alberta.

He knew some of his mother's story. Margaret O'Day, kindergarten teacher - met Glen Clearwater, accountant and part-time farmer. The last of that branch of the O'Day clan, she fell in love immediately with the only remaining son of the Clearwater line of the Sarsi Tsuu T'ina tribe.

Elijah didn't remember his parents well anymore. Eleven years had dulled most of his early memories, but he kept several framed photos around his loft bedroom. And he savored the stories his grandparents told of his dad as a boy, his Aunt Dawn as a child and his mother's short time with them.

His Grandma Rose he remembered more clearly, though some of *her* was fading too. She had died suddenly three months after his fifth birthday.

Watching the ground crew finish deicing the plane, Elijah wondered about his Great Aunt Mary. She was funny and sounded like a happy person when they talked on the phone. His mother had been named after Mary Margaret O'Day who was his Irish grandmother's younger sister.

He thought about all of the family he had lost that he could never meet and then about all of the family he still had. Elijah was excited about this trip. He wanted to learn about the early years of his mother's life growing up in Ireland as he had about his father's life growing up in southern Alberta.

The plane jerked then slowly moved back up and then away from the passenger gate ramp. Elijah didn't want to miss any of this new experience.

Over the speaker the pilot announced, "You'll be relieved to know the snow has tapered off along the Rockies. Above the clouds over Southern Alberta the sky will be a clear blue at our cruising altitude of 25,000 feet. Chicago is an hour ahead, which makes it now 7AM in Illinois, so you can reset your watches. Our arrival at O'Hare Airport will be 10:10AM local, Central Time."

"Virginia is two hours ahead of Alberta, right Grandpa?"

Rock Clearwater nodded, folding back the cover of his *Time* magazine.

"That's so cool. It's 8AM at Aunt Mary's house. Right now she's having her coffee and getting her turkey ready for us. Then seven hours from now, we'll be on the other side of North America eating her dinner! That's seriously amazing Grandpa."

The passenger seated beside Rock overheard Elijah and smiled. "Is this your first flight?"

Elijah nodded.

"First flight for me *and* my grandson. I'm Rock Clearwater and this window hog is Elijah." Grandpa let go of the right side of his magazine to extend his hand.

"Nice to meet you both. I'm Eric Wheeler."

The man looked to be in his late thirties like his Uncle River. He had friendly hazel eyes and though his head was shaved the dark morning stubble on his face made Elijah think his hair was also dark.

"This is not my first trip by air." Mr. Wheeler continued. "But I do remember my first flight so this should be pretty exciting for you both and especially you Elijah."

Their plane reached the runway and the pilot revved the jet engines for takeoff. Elijah held his breath as the massive machine sped faster, faster and faster then lifted off the ground as if it was weightless.

Quickly the runway shrunk smaller and smaller becoming a thin pencil line in the packed snow as the pilot banked steeply to the left already five thousand feet over Calgary's rooftops.

Abruptly there was nothing, no view. A thick grey wall of cloud blocked Elijah's vision then just as abruptly he saw a slice of light just as the plane broke through, to level off.

"We have reached our cruising altitude," the pilot announced. "Enjoy your morning sunshine and our complimentary Tim Horton coffee."

"Grandpa, look," Elijah pointed. "It's like we're riding on whipped cream that goes forever."

"You can see many interesting cloud formations at this altitude," offered Mr. Wheeler, "and, some amazing sunrises and sunsets when it's clear."

"I'll bet." Elijah turned back to study the clumps of rolling clouds of pale grey mixed with white.

An aroma of strong coffee filled the passenger cabin as Air Canada flight-attendants started down the narrow aisle with a cart.

"Tea, coffee or juice?" A young man, who didn't look any older than Elijah's sixteen-year-old cousin James, stopped next to their row.

"I'll have coffee with cream, please," Rock spoke up, "and just hot water for my grandson, he has his own tea, thank you."

"Coffee black for me please." Mr. Wheeler passed a cup of hot water to Elijah and Rock's coffee then took his own, letting down his tray table.

"Would any of you care for a croissant, a cinnamon roll or, a doughnut with your beverage?" The flight attendant offered.

"Grandpa we got'ta fly more often! I'll have a doughnut please."

"Chocolate iced or glazed?"

"No way! Chocolate for sure." Then Elijah counted out several digestive enzymes and swallowed them before biting into his early morning treat.

Grandpa chose a cinnamon roll, but Mr. Wheeler shook his head.

"I've never flown with anyone who brought their own tea with them."

"My grandson has cystic fibrosis Eric. Besides adding salt to his bottled water, I've found three particularly strong herbal tea combinations that are good for his sticky digestive system."

"Grandpa! Good thing Mr. Wheeler isn't eating."

"That's okay Elijah," Eric smiled. "I grew up in a large family, so something 'sticky' is nothing."

After the flight attendants returned to gather all paper napkins and empty cups Mr. Wheeler plugged an ear piece into his right ear. Grandpa returned to his magazine and Elijah returned to cloud gazing.

Twenty minutes later, everything began to change.

"Ladies and gentlemen this is your captain speaking. Due to the down grading of a weather system over Chicago from falling-snow to blizzard-conditions we have been diverted to Denver International Airport."

"As soon as I have more information for those who must catch connecting flights to other US destinations I will pass that on to the attendants so they can update you. That is all I have for now. We are truly sorry for this inconvenience."

CHAPTER...21

"What does this mean, do you know Mr. Wheeler?" Elijah leaned forward still buckled in his seat.

Mr. Wheeler didn't answer until he had finished sending a text. "Don't worry Elijah." He looked directly at both Rock Clearwater and his grandson. "Everyone will just need to arrange connecting flights from Denver instead of Chicago."

"I've had to do this before. We maybe a little late, but we'll still get there." He smiled. "Where are you…"

Several layers of Aunt Lucille's new perfume arrived just before she did.

She leaned on the back of the seat facing Mr. Wheeler. "I just asked one of the flight attendants and this diversion could easily push our arrival to the DC Regan Airport back three to four hours. But then the woman sitting next to me said that a loss of a few hours would only happen if we were seriously *lucky*! One time she had to spend the night in an airport! "

Rock looked up at his sister. "Guess then, we'll get there when we get there." Then his tone changed. "It's not as if we can ask our *driver* to stop at the side of the road, so we can get out and take alternate transportation…"

"I don't appreciate your sarcasm," Lucille interrupted her brother, "thank you very much." Then she pulled back and disappeared behind the lavatory door, leaving one layer of her perfume behind.

Grandpa Clearwater checked his watch, returning the setting to Mountain Standard Time.

"What time is it in Denver, Grandpa?"

"The State of Colorado is in the same time zone as Alberta. But with several weather issues causing delays and diversions, there's no point in texting your Aunt Mary until we reach Denver and find out what time zone we fly to next. Hopefully we can still go direct to DC."

Lucille reappeared. "We may not get to Mary Trent's house today at all."

Rock shook his head. "Not that we don't love you," he whispered, "but how is it that you are on this flight at all dearest sister of mine?"

Aunt Lucille hesitated for a few seconds.

"Well?"

"I telephoned her. I copied Mary's phone number from the business card she sent then about a week after Elijah received his late birthday card I called to check her out. Sometimes you don't always ask all of the right questions."

"And sometimes you ask far too many." Her brother shot back. "You still didn't answer my question."

Mr. Wheeler looked uncomfortable sitting between the sparing brother and sister, but Elijah caught his attention and winked.

"I was invited too." Aunt Lucille was defensive. "Mary generously invited me, so we could meet in person. And I've invited her to stay with me if she comes to Alberta."

Lucille had to move into their row a few inches to make room in the aisle for another passenger to reach the lavatory.

"Fine, but why didn't you say something to me? Why the secrecy?"

"Because I was sure you would object, or try to talk me out of going."

"Okay. However, since *you* decided to come along for this visit, I don't want to hear one more complaint from…"

"Excuse me ma'am." A flight attendant approached Aunt Lucille. "Please take your seat."

"For safety reasons the aisle must remain clear unless we're serving. All passengers should remain in their seats with their seatbelt securely fastened."

He smiled and nodded as Lucille squeezed by, returning to her seat. Rock was relieved though from his perspective the topic wasn't closed.

After a minute Rock tried to return to the article he had been reading, but instead he looked up and over the tops of the heads of everyone in the rows between them and the front of the plane.

"Where was your connecting flight from Chicago headed?" Eric Wheeler opened a pack of gum, offering to share with his row mates.

Rock laid his *Time* magazine down on the tray table. "Well, originally we scheduled a flight - Calgary to Chicago - Chicago to Regan International Airport/DC. Elijah's great aunt just lives across the Potomac River in an older area of Alexandria."

Mr. Wheeler nodded. "American Thanksgiving is a tricky time of year to travel, though yesterday would have been worse."

"Where were you going, for Thanksgiving Mr. Wheeler?" Elijah had instantly liked the quiet man who shared their row of three seats.

"My connecting flight from Chicago was to St. Louis, but not for Thanksgiving. I'm going to St. Louis for business." He smiled.

CHAPTER...22

Since Mr. Wheeler didn't volunteer details of his business, grandpa cleared his throat as a signal to Elijah then picked up his magazine again.

Elijah smiled back at Mr. Wheeler and then tried to concentrate on writing notes for his school assignment. Their trip so far had been noteworthy, but after doodling clouds all around the edge of his page for several minutes he gave up.

Out of the portal window the sky was no longer blue, but grey with thick darker clouds replacing the earlier whipped cream colored ones.

The 'fasten seatbelt' sign came on then the captain spoke again over the cabin speakers. "We have started our descent into DIA. We hope this diversion doesn't interfere with too many of your thanksgiving plans."

"The weather in Denver is overcast, 40F and dry with a 10MPH southeasterly wind. We'll be on the ground in about twenty minutes."

For Elijah, coming in for a landing was even more thrilling than experiencing a takeoff.

When the passenger jet broke through the clouds, the southern section of the same mountain chain that graced the western edge of Alberta rose up several thousand feet along the western front range of Colorado.

But the city of Denver was significantly closer to the Rocky Mountains than the city of Calgary by forty miles.

"You know Grandpa, except for missing the Bow and Elbow rivers, I think, the skyline of Denver looks a lot like Calgary's.

"That shouldn't be too surprising, Elijah." Mr. Wheeler locked his tray table in place. "Since much of the history of both metropolitan centers is oil, cattle and farming, with some mining."

"Really? That's awesome."

When the distinctive roof peaks of DIA came into view, Elijah was astounded. "Grandpa! Can you see? Look at that, it's like an entire Indian village down there."

He pushed himself as far into the back of his seat as he could. "Mr. Wheeler can you see?"

"I've been to Denver before, but thank you Elijah. Actually the airport terminal was designed to mirror both the tops of Indian teepees and the peaks of Colorado's section of the Rocky Mountains."

"So cool."

However, the serene sight of DIA's exterior was soon replaced by the crowned chaos of DIA's interior.

Under the architecturally unique roof, every passenger gate at concourses A, B and C was packed with additional passengers. Some had been diverted due to stormy weather from west to east along the Canadian-US border, while others couldn't leave due to the same weather system.

Regularly scheduled passengers sat waiting at their designated gates with those who needed to be reshuffled to their original destinations. Long lines of people waited to talk to an airline representative – *any* airline representative.

"Okay," Rock returned to where his sister and grandson stood by a support post near a moving pedestrian walkway. "I have some good news and some not so good news."

"Well, tell me the *news* when I return from the ladies room." Aunt Lucille headed toward the woman's lavatory sign. She excused herself several times as she threaded her way between the packed crowds of people around them. Fortunately her new perfume was fading.

"Speaking of lavatory how many bottles of saltwater have you finished today so far?"

"Three Grandpa not including my tea. I already went before you got back."

"Good. How are you feeling?"

"Great. What's your news?"

"We change from Air Canada to United Airlines. The United planes have seats for us, but we'll be split up. They have one available seat to St Louis leaving in forty-five minutes. It connects with another flight to DC."

"There are two seats on a flight to Dallas that connects with a third flight to DC. It leaves in ninety-five minutes. I put Aunt Lucille on the flight to St. Louis with you and me on the flight to Dallas."

But Elijah hadn't heard anything his grandfather said after the words *St. Louis*. A cool swirl of energy swept over Elijah that moved from his feet to his head.

"Grandpa? You need to give United Airlines my name for that seat to St. Louis. I *know* I must fly to St. Louis."

Then Rock Clearwater felt a chill. "Why do you need to be in St. Louis Elijah?"

Elijah shook his head. "I don't know exactly yet. I just know that's where I am supposed to go first."

Without another word or doubting *Crow Child*, Rock turned and worked his way back to the ticket counter. Twenty minutes later, after he amended the name of the passenger taking the seat to St. Louis, he sent another text to Mary Trent.

As Grandpa Clearwater and Aunt Lucille watched Elijah line up behind Mr. Wheeler and other passengers to St. Louis, Lucille still questioned her brother's decision.

"For all you know, if you had waited perhaps that *feeling* Elijah had might have left."

With a hand wave goodbye, Elijah disappeared through the doorway of the United Airlines gate, and Rock looked up to check their Dallas departure gate number.

"It wasn't an Elijah feeling Lucille, it was *Crow Child*. Elijah Clearwater gets a-feeling and the rest of us get a-feeling, but *Crow Child* 'knows'.

"Another phase of his special abilities has obviously emerged. *Crow Child*'s skills are completely different and we need to trust when Elijah tells us he is certain."

"I don't like it he's only fourteen." The walkway was so crowded Aunt Lucille pushed her carryon suitcase at a snail's pace in front of her. "You realize that he could be flying right into danger and we won't be there."

They walked toward their departure gate talking with their voices low. When they reached the flight gate with *Dallas-Fort Worth* written in bold print across the sign they stopped, and lingered off to one side.

"I know what you're saying, but now we need to separate the boy Elijah from the being *Black Crow* and the more powerful being *Crow Child*. Elijah Clearwater is only fourteen, but *Crow Child* is six-thousand."

Grandpa Clearwater looked around them. "We will definitely need to be there for Elijah Clearwater, but *Crow Child* can take care of *us*!"

CHAPTER...23

From the very second Elijah stepped onto the plane bound for St. Louis a suffocating veil of foreboding surrounded him like a heavy, wet wool coat.

As he took his assigned aisle seat, three rows behind Mr. Wheeler, Elijah remembered his grandfather's words after his thirteenth birthday... *"You'll need to become accustomed to the duty you owe your gift Elijah. You'll need to understand the legend. Crow-power will protect you and all those 'you' protect."*

'I certainly hope so Grandpa,' he thought.

And - with his grandfather's words still playing in his head Elijah *knew* there was another challenge in some form waiting for *Crow Child* in St. Louis, Missouri. A city he had only seen in photographs.

In the middle seat next to Elijah sat a woman he *knew* was the same age as his Aunt Dawn, his late father's younger sister. Sitting beside the woman was a young girl he *knew* was her niece, who was the same age as his Cousin Spring.

'How,' he suddenly wondered, 'did I *know* the woman's age, that she was unmarried and the eleven-year-old girl was her niece?'

Then Elijah realized *he* didn't *know*, but *Crow Child* did.

As *Crow Child*, Elijah was developing other abilities within him that he hadn't expected. To himself he recited the first lines of The Legend. '*With our cries heard above the roar of fire... Comes one who hears those cries.*'

Then he realized that *Crow Child* was able to *hear* by other means besides the human ear.

He looked around at the other passengers who were seated nearby. It didn't appear that he could pick up on anyone's thoughts, nor information on anyone who was further away than his arm's reach.

The woman in the seat in front of him was a widow, who had just retired. The man in the seat to his left across the aisle was married with three daughters and hated his insurance job.

Elijah closed his eyes while he tried to settle the turmoil in his mind from the sudden onset of this newfound ability.

'I'll never be normal again!' Elijah panicked when in a blink he realized the true weight of responsibility that *Crow Child* carried.

The 'fasten-seatbelt' sign came on and two flight attendants went through their preflight safety program. He heard it before, but paid even closer attention this time to distract his churning thoughts.

The plane backed away from the last gate of Concourse C. With several passenger planes ahead of his flight their plane inched forward slowly.

Looking beyond the woman and her niece next to her, Elijah saw tiny dry snowflakes begin to fall through the portal style window. The snow wasn't accumulating on any of the runways that he could see, but he wasn't concerned *knowing* that the incoming weather would not prevent this plane from taking off.

Abruptly - from two different directions inside the passenger compartment *Crow Child* picked up a disturbing energy.

He couldn't get specific details like he could from people sitting closer to him, but he *knew* – somewhere on this plane there were two men who both travelled with a gun.

****

Standing at the window next to their gate great aunt and grandfather watched Elijah's plane gain speed on the far eastern runway then smoothly lift off. In less than a minute the plane was out of sight, swallowed by low hanging cloud.

"I'm not complaining," Aunt Lucille began to complain, "but since it's started to snow here too we may find ourselves stuck in Denver, Colorado."

Rock took a deep breath. "Only, if the weather along Colorado's Front Range dumps six feet of snow in the next twenty minutes. Otherwise I think we'll be fine."

He tapped a small square on his new cell phone. "Apparently our plane is arriving from Tampa, Florida - it's not snowing in Tampa. It had a stop in Dallas, Texas where it's only raining. Our plane drops off and picks up people here then returns to Dallas, dropping off and picking up some more folks before it returns to Tampa."

"Well if it's not snowing in Florida or Texas then that's about the only place it's not snowing this week in North America!" Lucille's left hip bothered her and she looked for a place to sit.

"No, southern Arizona and California look good too."

"Swell, what's the weather like in St. Louis?"

"Aw, Elijah is flying into light rain."

But where Elijah was concerned Grandpa Clearwater wasn't worried about the weather or the power of *Crow Child* – he worried about the triggering effects of his grandson's cystic fibrosis.

After a long forty-three minutes the plane from Florida, via Texas pulled up to their gate. Eight minutes after that the first passengers to disembark came through the door into Concourse C. Sixteen minutes later Aunt Lucille and Grandpa Clearwater lined up with other passengers for their flight to Dallas-Fort Worth.

"What time is it where Mary is?" Lucille checked her new seat assignment again.

Rocked walked down the connecting corridor beside his sister, grateful they were not seated anywhere near each other. "It's just

1:12PM. Mary asked me to text her again when we got on our flight from Dallas to DC."

Lucille looked her watch. "It's only 11:12AM, why does it seem like we've been traveling for days?"

They reached the open door to the plane. "We're so fortunate to have a flight out of Denver at all. The traveling families who couldn't, or who weren't willing to split up are still waiting to find a flight with enough seats."

Lucille's assignment was a middle seat two rows from the front of the plane. Rock's seat was on the aisle two rows behind the right wing.

When he was settled, he closed his eyes, relieved his sister could not natter in his ear for the next eighty-six minutes.

He thought of Elijah and for the first time saw the value in a cell phone for both of them. Before this trip and before *Crow Child* there didn't seem to be a reason for a phone other than their landline, but Rock was rethinking many changes.

Then Grandpa Clearwater prayed that his precious grandson would be able to rise to the tasks required of *Crow Child*. He knew there was a great deal more involved than the power behind sweeping wings.

CHAPTER...24

Elijah decided to test his sudden ability to *know* information from spontaneous thoughts that came to him from some new hidden place.

Flight attendants had just begun a mid morning beverage service, so Elijah pulled out his small lined note book and pen. He flipped the latch that held up his tray table and let it drop.

When the woman in the middle seat smiled at him, he took a chance. "Excuse me, my name is Elijah. I have a school assignment to write about my thanksgiving experiences. Would you mind telling me where you plan to spend thanksgiving with your daughter?"

"Oh, no, not at all." The woman was enthusiastic then frowned. "But how nasty, that your teacher gave you homework over our Thanksgiving holiday weekend though."

Elijah decided not to explain that *his* holiday Thanksgiving was six weeks before. Instead he just shrugged, wrinkling up his nose.

"I'm Karen and this is my niece Ella."

Elijah suddenly felt light headed. He had been correct and struggled to concentrate on what the lady was telling him.

"We're flying to have Thanksgiving with my brother in North Carolina. Ella's mom and my brother divorced just this past spring, so this will be Ella's first Thanksgiving without her mom."

Ella turned her brown curly head away from looking out the airplane window. The thick glasses she wore reminded him of his school bus driver's daughter, Sasha.

"Where is your family Elijah? Are you flying alone?" Ella's face had no expression.

"Yes and no," he answered. "Our flight to Chicago was diverted to Denver because of a blizzard."

"To make it to my Aunt Mary's house - she's in Virginia - my grandfather got me a seat on this flight and then two seats on another flight for him and my Aunt Lucille."

The snack cart made it to their row. "I can offer soda, juice, tea, coffee or water?" The flight attendant's eyes almost disappeared when she smiled.

"I'll have water, please." Elijah moved his notebook over to one side on his tray.

"Coffee, black, please. Karen smiled up at the flight attendant."

"And for you miss?" The flight attendant handed out a small bottle of water then a cup of coffee.

Ella looked uncertain. "My stomach's a little funny."

The flight attendant spoke softly. "May I suggest a ginger ale with some soda crackers?"

Ella nodded, still unsmiling, or showing emotion. "Thank you." She accepted the soda and a small packet of crackers.

"For the two of you I obviously have soda crackers too," she smiled again, "or packaged mini Oreo cookies, or mini pretzels."

Elijah chose the pretzels, because with CF he needed the extra salt, and because pretzels didn't contain fat he wouldn't need to take any digestive enzymes before eating them.

Ella's Aunt Karen chose a package of pretzels too, but stowed them into her bag under the seat in front of her.

General conversation on the plane was subdued as Elijah emptied a tiny travel packet of salt into his water bottle. And while Elijah ate his snack he tried again to locate from where the energy of the two guns was coming, but there was nothing.

'Odd,' he wondered. 'What good, is *knowing* only part of something, or not being able to *know* more when a person tries to focus for a really good reason?'

Eric Wheeler stood up and walked to the back of the plane. He smiled approaching Elijah. "How'you doing?"

When Mr. Wheeler stopped, Elijah suddenly *knew* where one of the guns was located and who carried it. He had difficulty getting his words out and pretended to choke on some of his salted water.

"Sorry, Mr. Wheeler. I'm fine sir, thank you." He managed finally and noticed that Mr. Wheeler was taller than average and looked quite muscular, even under his shirt. Then he *knew* that Eric Wheeler was an RCMP officer working undercover in the US.

Mr. Wheeler looked around the plane. "I don't see your grandfather or your aunt."

Elijah fought a jumble of emotions to remain outwardly calm. He looked down at his watch to collect himself. "They should be boarding a plane for a short flight to Dallas, about now."

"That winter storm that hit Chicago really messed up thousands of travel plans. I'm lucky." He smiled again. "When was your Aunt Mary supposed to meet all of you?

"Our original flight was supposed to be six hours with a forty-minute stop in Chicago to change planes from Air Canada to United Airlines. We were scheduled to arrive at 3PM Eastern Time."

'Not bad, not bad at all," Mr. Wheeler nodded. "By the time this flight lands it will be 1:35PM in St. Louis, and 2:35PM in Virginia. You might only be a few hours late if you can get another flight out quickly."

When the lavatory door opened Mr. Wheeler took his turn. And then – Elijah *knew* instantly there wouldn't be a quick flight out of St. Louis – not for him. Not for either him or Mr. Wheeler.

****

Aunt Lucille had deplaned first. She and thankfully, her subdued perfume waited for Rock just beyond the gate door at the Dallas airport. "I was thinking on this flight."

Rock cringed inside bracing to hear what she had been thinking, but he hoped to distract her. "Can you wait until I've eaten? My stomach is so empty it's shaking hands with my back bone. And besides that, we need to check on seat availability from here to DC."

Rock got in another line to the ticket counter with his diverted-flight paperwork. This time Aunt Lucille and Grandpa were separated again, but not just by seats in different rows. By accepting a seat on two different flights Rock could leave Dallas in fifty-five minutes with Lucille's flight departing only ten minutes ahead of his, on a separate carrier.

"Here's your new boarding pass, you have forty-five minutes." Next he looked around for some sort of food, fast and nearby.

Lucille hurried to keep up with Rock as he searched for a place to eat. "Thank you."

"Rock, we may be able to separate Elijah from *Crow Child*, but if he walks into some sort of trouble in St. Louis how does the US media separate the *huge being* he becomes - from the young teen we're trying to keep anonymous?"

Rock stopped in front of a deli style vendor. His booth looked smaller than Lucille's walk-in closet. Studying the variety of prepackaged sandwich choices, two cheddar cheese and lettuce sandwiches with two bottles of water seemed like a safe purchase. "I don't know."

CHAPTER...25

"Ladies and gentlemen we have started our descent into St. Louis," announced the captain.

Elijah finished the last of his saltwater then just before putting both empty plastic bottles in his backpack, he added more salt planning to refill them at the nearest water fountain.

Glancing out of the window next to Ella, Elijah couldn't see anything beyond solid grey. As the plane made a wide sweeping turn to the left it broke through low clouds and Elijah caught a brief glimpse of the St. Louis Arch.

The plane landed on a wet runway. Thick clouds dropped a steady light drizzle over the city that even in late November still displayed green grass around the airport and a few orange colored leaves clinging to several tree branches.

"As soon as you can, Elijah come see me at the ticket counter after you leave the plane." The supervising flight attendant smiled then moved to the front of the plane.

When the plane came to a complete stop, the light behind the 'fasten seatbelt' sign went off. Elijah as well as other passengers along the aisle could stand. Some reached up to retrieve belongings from the overhead bins.

Elijah was surprised to notice that just before the plane had even stopped, Eric Wheeler was out of his seat and talking to the same flight attendant who had offered to assist Elijah with his next boarding pass. But as more people crowded in front of him he lost sight of Mr. Wheeler.

One by one peopled filed out from their rows then down the narrow aisle and out the plane's front side door. When Elijah walked by a row of seats at the front of the passenger section he noticed a tall elderly woman waiting in the center seat. Close by was a wheelchair folded and leaning against the wall.

When Elijah turned his head their eyes met and he *knew* the perfectly groomed hair was a wig. And–the disguise was for this person, who was a man carrying the second gun.

Shaken and confused, Elijah stumbled across the plane's exit door threshold.

He moved to one side as other passengers hurried by him from the adjoining hallway between the parked plane and the terminal.

Emerging into the terminal, Elijah was thrilled to spot Eric Wheeler. But then, surprised, Mr. Wheeler appeared to be using a vendor's cart packed with souvenirs, newspapers, magazines and snacks to remain partially hidden.

'Why had Mr. Wheeler rushed to leave the plane only to remain so close to the gate door?' Elijah wondered.

But the question was no sooner asked, than *Crow Child knew* the answer. 'Mr. Wheeler was watching each of the other passengers leave that newly arrived plane.'

Then just as Elijah turned to look back at the doorway to the gate the man posing as an elderly woman appeared in the wheelchair. The wheelchair was pushed by a dark-skin younger man with deep brown eyes and bleached blonde hair.

Elijah's attention returned to the vendor's cart where it was obvious to him that Mr. Wheeler was also interested in the disguised *woman* in the wheelchair.

He didn't see the flight attendant who offered to help him at the ticket desk yet, so Elijah gave into a strong urge to follow.

Eric Wheeler didn't notice Elijah who fell into step five people behind him, as Mr. Wheeler followed the passenger disguised as an elderly woman pushed in the wheelchair.

The young man with the bleached blonde hair wore overalls with a Lambert-St. Louis Airport crest on the upper left side of his chest and sleeve. He stopped outside of the ladies restroom to assist his wheelchair passenger, who boldly walked into the ladies lavatory.

Eric Wheeler kept walking, but turned into the doorway to the men's restroom. Elijah pulled out one of his empty plastic bottles from his backpack. Darting his attention between both doorways he took off the lid then filled it at the water fountain across from the men's and ladies lavatories.

His heart raced. 'This surveillance stuff is hard on a person's nerves.' He thought. Then stalling for time he filled water into his second empty bottle.

When, the bogus *elderly woman* reappeared, Elijah moved away from the fountain. He was able to remain from view behind a mother who stopped to adjust a bag on her toddler's stroller. Then he quickly, turned away a second time after Eric Wheeler reappeared from the men's room doorway.

Fortunately for Elijah Mr. Wheeler was more focused on the imposter in the wheelchair and only glanced quickly in the direction they had just come.

But as Mr. Wheeler began walking, searching the crowd for the *grey haired lady* – the wheelchair followed Eric Wheeler.

Elijah looked at his watch again. He needed to check in with the ticket desk, but was reluctant to let Mr. Wheeler out of his sight. 'Five more minutes,' he thought. 'Just five more minutes shouldn't hurt anything.'

Mr. Wheeler came to the end of the concourse where three hallways funneled passengers in the direction of baggage claim and passenger pickup, or toward two other concourses.

Realizing he may have lost the *grey haired lady* in the wheelchair, Elijah watched as Mr. Wheeler struggled with an important decision.

Then abruptly, the attendant pushing the *grey haired lady* veered, hurrying for a side door with a sign that said: *Employees Only*.

The sudden change in direction appeared to Elijah as if it had been a deliberate attempt to attract Mr. Wheeler's attention. And it worked.

The rush across a wide corridor in the opposite direction of dispersing travelers was caught in Eric Wheeler's line of sight. The man dressed as an airport attendant turned his head quickly looking over his left then his right shoulder, pretending not to see where Mr. Wheeler stood.

But *Crow Child knew* the attendant was well aware of the man who followed them because Eric Wheeler was *their* prey.

And in that instant Elijah forgot about the flight to DC and Thanksgiving at Great Aunt Mary's house - and *knew* the reason *Crow Child* was in St. Louis was to save the life of RCMP undercover officer, Eric Wheeler.

Predictably Mr. Wheeler waited a full minute looking cautiously around as he walked to another small cart vendor. He bought a package of gum then crossed the width of the corridor to stand by the closed door marked: *Employees Only.*

Eric opened the gum packaging, dropping the torn cellophane into the trash bin then slipped through the door, almost unnoticed. Except that is for Elijah Clearwater.

Elijah had watched Mr. Wheeler closely and hoped he could open then slip through the restricted doorway as smoothly as the undercover officer had.

Mirroring Mr. Wheeler, Elijah stepped up to the small vendor cart and bought a package of gum.

With his heart punching at his chest like a dozen elbows he could barely breathe. Elijah removed his backpack carrying it on one arm toward the trash bin as he removed the gum wrapper.

When a family of six stopped, Elijah was shielded from other passengers while the dad re-tied the shoes of their youngest child.

Calming his pulse, Elijah opened the side door and slipped through the narrow opening, reclosing the door as if he had perfected this move many times before.

He slid both arms through his backpack straps and turned to check where he was. He could hear the muffled chatter of passing travelers as they walked by on the other side of the closed door.

Before him was a brightly lit hallway, five feet wide but only twenty feet to a corner where the hall made a ninety degree turn.

At the corner Elijah looked down a much longer hall that ran several hundred feet, with an adjoining hall to his left just fifty feet beyond where he stood.

As he waited listening, he was surprised there was so little sound. He could still hear the muffled voices of travelers beyond the closed door to his right, but no new sounds seemed to be coming from anywhere along the empty hallway.

Staying close to the wall to his left Elijah cautiously moved down the hall to the second corner. This time he was stumped. There was no indication which direction either the airport attendant or Mr. Wheeler had gone.

Since he could see to the end of the shorter hallway on his left he decided to check that direction first then double back if he had to.

As he walked further down the hall he could hear the sound of machinery growing louder and louder. Then in a three foot alcove at the end of the hall he saw a set of wide double metal doors and a second posted sign: *Maintenance Personnel Only.*

Warm air was pushed through a vent just above the floor on the wall behind him and he could hear machinery cycling behind the closed doors.

When Elijah reached for the door handle he was expecting the doors to be locked, but they weren't. Inside, the sound of motors running and fans turning was too loud to have carried on a conversation with anyone else.

With the maintenance doors closed behind him – the vast, high walled area was dimly lit. A network of crisscrossing steel beams supported a wavy aluminum ceiling.

From where he stood Elijah couldn't see around a tall wide boiler without squeezing between a panel of gauges and a cement wall. He realized that a wheelchair certainly couldn't have been pushed through the narrow space either, though the fake old-lady could walk.

Elijah didn't think anyone came this way, so he closed his eyes and tried to let *Crow Child* get a sense of what to do next... But when his eyes opened, his head jerked to the left just in time to feel a sharp needle sting on the side of his neck.

CHAPTER...26

There was no light anywhere.

He blinked several times, but everything was still dark.

There was no form, no sound, no smell – nothing. Elijah sat up and put his right arm out in front of him then to his right side - then extended his left arm out from his left side. But there was only air – he felt nothing.

The floor beneath him was cold.

Cautiously Elijah stood. He had only socks on his feet – his shoes were gone. He extended his right leg out in front of him with his right arm straight in front and his left arm feeling above his head. Each step that moved him forward was slow and deliberate.

After twelve careful steps his right toes hit something firm and his hand touched a cement wall as cold as the floor had been.

Elijah took a deep breath to dissolve his panic. He worked to remember he was *Crow Child* with an inner wisdom that could protect his direction…

Calmer Elijah moved his hand along the wall until he came to a corner then kept walking along the wall until his foot bumped something soft. Kneeling down, he felt a human shoulder then the upper chest but *knew* the person lying on the floor was Eric Wheeler.

On the side of Wheeler's neck Elijah felt a slight pulse. The man groaned in obvious pain then he *knew* the police officer had been severely wounded.

Without thinking Elijah raised both of his hands holding them over the man's body. In the dark he realized Mr. Wheeler had been shot in his lower side just below his left ribs.

Unzipping the officer's jacket, he unbuttoned his shirt peeling the cotton fabric away from the bleeding tissue. Then leaning over him a blue light shone from his hands over the wound. *Crow Child* took a deep breath then sent pure oxygen into the wound.

The tingling of healing tissue brought Eric Wheeler back to consciousness, startled that someone else was with him in the cold, coal-black space.

"Who's there!" Eric sat up abruptly, pulling back with both of his hands doubled up in fists.

"It's just me Mr. Wheeler, Elijah Clearwater."

The boy's voice was familiar, but Eric was confused thinking he was being tricked. Then he realized his shirt was unbuttoned and his jacket was open. He remembered being shot, but when he grabbed his left side there was no bleeding wound. His side only felt tender, bruised and sore to his touch.

"Who's really there?" The officer's voice sounded annoyed. "It's not possible that you're the young teen from the plane."

Elijah let out a deep sigh, searching for the right words to account for how he came to be with this man and in this place void of any light. The very place he remembered from his dreams.

"Yes sir it is. I followed you, while you followed the old-lady in the wheelchair."

"What, the…"

"It's not that easy for me to explain, Mr. Wheeler, but I *know* you're a Royal Canadian Mounted Police officer working undercover."

Elijah wished Eric Wheeler could actually see him and he wished he could see the expression on Eric Wheeler's face.

Much had happened in just a few short minutes and Elijah was still trying to process the discovery of *Crow Child's* latest remarkable ability. He could heal gunshot wounds!

"What are you, some sort of super kid with psychic skills?"

"Yeah," Elijah felt some relief. That explanation could work. "I'm kinda like that. I just *know* things, sometimes."

"Then do you know where we are *and* how we can get out of here?"

And just like that he did *know*.

"I think so. It's a solid cement storage-hold for barrels containing used airplane motor oil. Some of it is underground. If we find the door, we can get out if it's still day time, cause it is kept open during work hours."

"Are you hurt Elijah?"

"No sir. I have a small swelling in the side of my neck, from something that obviously knocked me out. How do you feel? I found you lying on the floor.

"Guess I'm okay. I thought I was shot, but maybe not though my side sure is sore."

Elijah said nothing.

Eric Wheeler stood slowly, still wobbly. He stumbled backwards and was stopped from falling when he bumped into the cement wall behind him.

Elijah stood too, but didn't try to move. "Are you okay?"

"Yeah, I'll just lean against this wall for a minute. But we gotta get outta here son and quick! That old lady in the wheel chair was in disguise and a pretty good one too, but *she* is a *he*! A US Marshal turned traitor to be exact."

The officer was silent for several seconds then spoke again. "Since you're already here, I might as well tell you, that I'm working undercover for American Homeland Security."

"Since the AHS Director wasn't sure how deep this breach in security went he contacted the Ottawa RCMP Bureau to send in someone the Homeland Director was sure couldn't be recognized."

"The US Marshal in the wheelchair, Lad Swanson, had supposedly been under surveillance for months by both FBI and NSA. But none of the agents in either of those agencies had been able to pin down Marshal Swanson's plan."

"All they confirmed was that he met regularly with former members of the US military, most dishonorably discharged, who at first emailed derogatory comments back and forth about their service disappointment. Then it changed to actively considering a major threat, but nothing too concrete."

"If you followed me then you came into the same hallway I did. I watched Lad Swanson and one of his partners, Al Farez, go into the mechanical room from the doors at the end of the longest section of hall. But I knew from studying airport plans that there was a second door, airport maintenance used to quickly check pressure and flow gauges."

Elijah spoke up. "That's the same doorway I used, but that's all I remember."

"Your magical powers let you down, huh?"

"It seems to come and go." Elijah scowled in the dark.

"Isn't there some medicine you need to take?" Eric Wheeler fought back his own sense of panic.

"No, just my inhaler if I start to cough too hard. And a bunch of digestive enzymes, but only if I eat fatty foods. I do need to drink lots of salted water though. Because of the gunk in my system my body sweats and I lose salt so I get dehydrated easily. But if we stumble over my back pack, everything I need is in it."

"If we split up and you follow the wall on one side and I follow the wall on the other, maybe we can find a door or opening out of here." Eric buttoned his shirt in the dark and then zipped up his jacket.

Elijah heard the zipper and moved toward the sound. He stood beside Eric Wheeler at the wall. "Okay, I'll go back this way. I was somewhere on the floor next to the wall around a corner that's only about four meters from where we are now. Do you think you can walk Mr. Wheeler?"

Elijah started to move away from Officer Wheeler, following the wall.

"I feel a little weak, but I'll be fine. I have to be fine Elijah!" Eric Wheeler's tone became desperate. "I know what they intend! Before, I was discovered I overheard them finalize the eight targets of their plot!"

Reaching the corner in less than a minute, Elijah listened in horror to the plot Mr. Wheeler uncovered. He tried to move as quickly as he could, following the second wall.

"There's much less security with cargo planes." Eric explained walking in the opposite direction. With his left hand on the cement wall he leaned forward slightly, feeling ahead with his right hand.

"Lad Swanson and Al Farez are being paid millions to assemble disgruntled ex-military pilots to stowaway with cargo on Federal Express airplanes."

"Once the eight planes are in the air they'll hijack each of the eight Fed-Ex cargo planes, allowing them to fly to their regular destinations using the flight plans that are already registered."

"But instead of landing the planes at the airports of cities with Fed-Ex deliveries, they'll use each plane as an airborne torpedo – just like 9/11 and take out each of those eight major airports."

"These ex-pilots don't mind dying?" The chill Elijah felt wasn't only due to the unheated cement space.

"They don't think they will die Elijah. They think that after they set the plane on a dive course they can bail out. Lad and Al handed out parachutes to each of the twenty ex-military traitors, but just before everyone arrived for their final briefing I saw Al cut and knot the ripcords then reclose each pack. None of those parachutes will open."

Eric Wheeler's voice grew fainter as he talked. Elijah worried they were in a space too vast to find their way around, but after three more steps he came to another corner. "I'm turning a corner and following a wall that parallels the one you're following." Elijah called out.

"Perfect."

Elijah was getting thirsty and Mr. Wheeler was tired.

CHAPTER...27

"That was fast. You got us a seat out of Dallas already?"

Rock held yet another pair of boarding passes, one for his sister and one for himself. "Yes." He gave Lucille her boarding pass.

"However, I had to allow for a slight modification in our travel plans."

"Don't tell me, let me guess." Her voice had an edge sharp with sarcasm. "We fly to Cuba first!"

From somewhere to his left, Grandpa Clearwater caught a whiff of freshly brewed coffee and he decided to follow his nose.

"Rock?" Lucille had no choice, but to follow her brother.

At a quaint looking faux outdoor style café, Rock ordered a cappuccino and a slice of pumpkin pie.

"Why did you order that, I'm sure Mary will have pumpkin pie ready..." She stopped talking and decided to order tea and a cranberry muffin.

"We are going to get to Virginia today aren't we?"

He looked directly at his sister – savoring a moment that didn't include standing in line again. "Yes. At least we're scheduled to get to the Regan, DC Airport yet sometime late afternoon-early evening."

"Only now your plane leaves before mine does, but not for another," Rock checked the time, "fifty-eight minutes."

Their order arrived.

"So, please enjoy your tea." He took a long sip of his hot coffee and felt the liquid all the way down through his esophagus.

"Are you sending Mary another text?"

"Yes, but not quite yet. I'll wait until your plane has taken off." He thought of Elijah and wondered if he would be able to get a seat for a flight out of St. Louis that afternoon.

****

Elijah hurried walking close to the longer wall, as quickly as he dared. It went on and on. He kept his right hand on the wall as he walked and his left hand extended out in front of him.

He started to take longer strides when is right toe hit something that made a muted vibrating sound. "Ohhh!"

"Elijah?"

"Mr. Wheeler I bumped into a barrel. No a whole row of barrels." Feeling his way next to a row of large oil barrels that

219

extended away from the cement wall, Elijah realized he was walking toward the center of the storage space."

"Oooff. I just hit a barrel with my knee." The thump Officer Wheeler made echoed. "I'll follow it from the wall too. Wait, there are only two rows of barrels."

"Then can you go around them. Is there more than just those two?"

Mr. Wheeler's voice sounded as if he was several feet behind Elijah. "No. It feels like the barrels are lined up along the wall, but only two deep. You're just ahead of me right?"

"Yeah, I think so."

"Damn, I wish we could see something – anything."

And then just beyond the next barrel on Elijah's side of the storage space he felt a railing made from steel pipe. "Wait a minute Mr. Wheeler, stop walking. I just found a railing of some kind."

"Okay." Eric was grateful to be able to rest, leaning over one of the barrels.

Elijah slid his sock feet along the floor below the last rung of the railing. He discovered the floor dropped off. Walking even slower, holding tight to the metal pipe he slid his feet on the smooth, cold cement. After changing direction for a short distance the cement floor stopped at the top of a step.

He sat and then extended his legs out in front. "I found some stairs Mr. wheeler. We must be on some kind of upper level."

Eric Wheeler rose up from resting on his barrel. "Keep talking, I'll follow the sound of your voice. Are you very far from the end of your last barrel?"

"I came only about five, maybe six meters."

Then Eric reached the last barrel on his side, only a short distance behind Elijah. When he spoke he was so close it made Elijah jump.

Eric sat down on the floor and slid himself up beside Elijah. They both were at the top step. Eric stretched his arm behind Elijah grasping the bottom railing.

"There's no railing to our left."

"I know and no railing that goes down these steps."

"Let me scoot down first." Eric slid down two steps beyond the top one. "Keep one hand on the right edge of these stairs so we don't get to the lower floor the hard way."

They reached a short landing, where the steps turned sharply to the right. At the bottom of the steep descent of cement stairs, they discovered more barrels they needed to navigate between, in the darkness.

"I found a narrow open space." Eric was weary.

Elijah knew his body was getting too dehydrated.

Eric felt around, but there were barrels crammed everywhere, not just single rows on the floor, but barrels stacked high above their heads.

"Feels like there's only one direction we can go. Grab a hold of the back of my jacket and let's see where this takes us. *Seeing* – being a figure of speech that is."

Eric took one step and hit something lumpy with his foot. Keeping one hand touching the barrels beside him he crouched down, pulling Elijah with him. "I think we just found your back pack."

Elijah felt the canvas bag Eric handed him. "Yup this is it." Relieved he unzipped the upper section and took out both water bottles. "Here," he nudged Mr. Wheeler in the dark then Elijah drank the entire contents of one bottle completely.

"That was a lucky break, in a string of breaks that have been everything except *lucky*. My watch was taken. You don't happen to have one in your backpack do you?"

"No, my watch is gone too."

"Ugh! Thanks for your water, but I can't drink this – its' way too salty. Here."

They walked in the narrow alley of stacked oil barrels for a full six hundred meters then came to a metal wall.

Eric tapped on the metal. "It feels fairly thin."

Listening to the sound *Crow Child knew* what the metal was. "That's an oversized garage style door, it lifts up and there's an access ramp for loading and unloading on the other side."

"Then let's hope we can find a way to open it."

Walking the forty-foot length of the metal door they came to the edge and felt concrete again. Just a few feet from the end of the large garage door was a standard metal entrance door, securely locked.

Sliding his hand along the cement wall high above his head, Eric reached a metal box with a large round knob set in the center. He pushed the knob and a motor started, but the door stopped just barely off the floor. They still couldn't see very well, but something blocked the shipping and receiving door from going up any further.

Fresh air rushed in under the door with the first slice of light they had seen for over an hour. Elijah lay flat on the cement floor looking out under the door.

Fortunately planes taking off and coming in for a landing had been louder than the sound of the garage door motor. "We need to rethink this way out." Elijah looked up at Eric.

"There's a guy sitting in a black van at the edge of the parking lot and he's holding a nasty looking rifle."

Their eyes had adjusted to the dim light quickly, that seemed bright compared to the blackness of the last hour.

Eric leaned his head against the door frame. "I'm sure they expected me to die, but just in case you managed to find your way out obviously US Marshal Swanson posted a guard outside the only door that could open. However, it isn't opening."

Looking around, stacked barrels almost reached the twenty-foot ceiling. Then he looked up to the side of the garage door. A large bolt was pushed through the holes in the metal door frame to the door edge.

"If I can pull out that bolt – I can likely get the door open, but then our *friend* with the gun will see the door opening."

"If you could just open it high enough so we could crawl under he might not even notice the door was partially opened at the bottom."

"Well there's a red stop button, so let's give it a try."

Eric hit the white *Close* knob, slid back the bolt then hit the green *Open* knob then the red *Stop* button.

"Is that enough?"

"It's enough for me." Elijah rolled out of sight keeping watch on the van and the armed man.

Eric had to take off his jacket to fit. He pushed it through the opening then flattened himself on the floor. Turning his head to one side, he inched himself out from under the bottom of the door.

On the loading dock outside both Eric and Elijah stayed flat with their heads down. The man inside the van seemed to be dozing wearing head phones.

"Not much of a guard." Elijah rolled to the edge of the loading dock then jumped down.

Eric followed him.

On the ground they were out of sight behind a low cement block wall. It wasn't raining, but the sky was still heavily overcast.

"We still have daylight, but with such thick cloud cover it's too difficult to guess the time."

Eric put on his jacket. When he looked down to zip the front closed he saw his blood stained shirt for the first time. "Holly…!"

He looked over at Elijah shock and disbelief on his face. Quickly he lifted his shirt. On his lower left side was a large purple bruise the size of a pancake. "If all I have is a bruise, whose blood is this?"

Then Eric spotted the hole in his shirt and jacket too. "Who *are* you?" The tall muscular man began to shake.

"It's kind of long story, sir." Elijah cringed. "I don't think we have time right now."

Mr. Wheeler stared at Elijah, completely mystified.

Elijah looked around quickly, noticing it was obvious that the long wide loading door was open if the guard woke up to check. "Sir?"

"Mr. Wheeler? What do we do about the guard? If, or when he wakes up – he's gonna see that gap."

Eric was still breathing heavily, but rallied. He scanned the loading dock. "There might be - aw, yes there is - up there above the door. There's an exterior button, but you'll need to stand on my shoulders to reach it, unless you have some other trick up your sleeve."

Elijah only shrugged looking slightly sheepish.

A cement support post blocked them from view while Elijah, hit the *Close* button set thirteen feet from the floor of the loading platform.

****

In line to board his plane from Dallas to DC, Rock sent a text to Mary Trent. BOARDING DALLAS FLIGHT #1622 - LUCILLE LEFT ON FLIGHT #886 – DO NOT KNOW ELIJAH'S FLIGHT NUMBER HE LEFT FROM ST.LOUIS – I HOPE...

Then something *told* Rock that Elijah still hadn't left St. Louis. 'Keep that boy safe, please,' he prayed.

CHAPTER...28

"Sure wish I knew what time it was." Eric Wheeler looked up at the darkening overcast sky again. "But it must be getting late."

Mr. Wheeler and Elijah had spotted the Fed-Ex cargo hangars from the loading dock of the used oil storage depot.

"Can't you call for backup, or something?"

Taking advantage of the guard napping in the black van, they kept low crossing an open field of tall damp grass between the depot and the Federal Express taxiway.

"If I still had my burner phone I could call the US Secretary of Defense, the Director of Homeland Security and my boss in Ottawa, International Division."

"Oh yeah, sorry. That Swanson guy would have taken all your stuff." Elijah tried to hold back a rising cough, but without success.

"That didn't sound good. And with this wet ground and no shoes, we'll both get sick."

Pulling up his backpack Elijah fished out his inhaler.

The officer watched Elijah take several puffs and then attempt to take deep breaths - concerned. "I don't know how you do what you do, but does your breathing sometimes interfere?"

"Not so far. If I can wear my chest-thumper-vest a couple times a day that sure helps, but I have terrible gut cramps if I don't stay hydrated. Then my intestines can get blocked. "

"Sounds complicated?" Eric Wheeler frowned.

Elijah felt his chest muscles relax. "You have *no* idea."

As much of a surprise, and as valuable as Elijah had proven to be the officer worried that the young teen carried a heavier load of stress than was outwardly obvious.

"But a better answer to your question Elijah would be, yes. We could crawl away right now and sound the alarm, but there's no physical evidence for charges, nothing except my word."

"Lad Swanson, Al Farez and the hostile ex-military pilots could be arrested under suspicion to commit a terrorist act, but likely only get a little jail time. Swanson would be pensioned off early and the others might have a good scare because they were caught, but later just move any future plans underground."

They managed to crawl under a twelve foot chain link fence where the ground had sunk from water runoff. Staying behind thick clumps of tall wild grass, they watched as a Boeing 727 moved from the side of a warehouse loading dock to park on the taxiway a thousand feet directly in front of them.

"The timing here is tricky. I've got to confirm their target cities, and witness one or more of the terrorist suspects sneaking onto one of the Fed-Ex planes *then* call it in - somehow."

A second 727 moved into place behind the first plane, then a third smaller cargo plane, a Cessna Caravan.

"But Elijah, I can't endanger you, no matter what unique abilities you may have. If you keep low and follow this fence, you'll reach the UPS hangars. Tell them you got lost, or something. Someone from UPS can get you to the main terminal where you can still get on a flight out to meet up with your aunts and grandfather."

The first three planes moved further up on the taxiway several hundred feet, making way for a fourth, larger cargo plane a Boeing 767.

"Sir, I'll be fine and you need back up *now*. You need another pair of eyes and another witness for sure. I can stay out of the way and safe, don't worry about me."

"I can't let you do that." Eric Wheeler went into police officer mode. "This is my job, my assignment, my risk, not yours. By now your family could be trying to trace you through the airlines, and they'll be frantic."

****

Nervously Aunt Lucille stood with the other passengers waiting for her turn to leave the plane. She was relieved to have arrived in DC. She had a photograph of her counterpart Mary Trent, but no idea how to get to baggage claim.

Following her fellow passengers Aunt Lucille kept up, hoping they knew where they were going and that Mary Trent was somewhere at Regan International Airport.

The signs above her head were easy to read from a distance and the further along she went the calmer she became.

Keeping sight of several of the passengers she recognized from her most recent flight Lucille waited by an empty, dormant looking baggage carrousel.

"Are you Lucille Lilley?"

The baggage claim carrousel sprang to life, as Aunt Lucille turned her head toward the voice. To her left, stood, a small boned lady about her age with short curly grey hair dyed a pale blonde.

She recognized Mary Trent immediately. "Yes I am, and so glad to see you."

The two women who had only exchanged emails, cards and phone calls – hugged.

"This fine young man with me is my neighbor's son Jordan Roberts. I brought him along for suitcase-muscle and to meet Elijah, he's only a year older and just discovering chess as Elijah has. His parents are back at my house babysitting our turkey."

"So nice to meet you, Jordan."

The teen almost as thin as Elijah was four inches taller and as fair, as Elijah was dark. His red hair was stick-straight, his skin was the color of chalk.

"Nice to meet you too ma'am. What does your suitcase look like?"

As she described her luggage they turned toward the carousel just in time to see Aunt Lucille's new red and navy striped suitcase disappearing on the moving ramp, around to the other side.

"That's pretty distinctive Mrs. Lilley. Wait here I can get it when it returns to this side."

****

Rock smiled, relieved when he read the text sent to his phone by Mary Trent. Aunt Mary had pushed their American Thanksgiving meal back to 7PM Virginia time. He changed his watch from 3:42 Mountain Time to 5:42 Eastern – amazingly it looked like they just might make it and only about four hours late.

The captain had just announced their descent into DC. If Lucille's luggage made it from Denver to their final destination then there was hope for his and Elijah's.

When he thought of Elijah in St. Louis, it was 4:42 Central Time. Rock wondered where his amazing grandson was and dared to expect that their ancestors were watching over him.

****

Elijah waved good bye to Mr. Wheeler, pretending to comply. He crawled only a short distance dragging his backpack with his body flattened from sight. It was easy enough to do in the darkening day.

Crow Child knew the late fall sun was setting, so it was just before 5PM.

CHAPTER...29

Crow Child watched Officer Wheeler sprint in stocking feet across the runway, stopping by the tires of the Fed-Ex cargo plane that waited first in line. He knew he'd need to get closer to each of the planes to know which one if any, carried a second, terrorist crew.

From his backpack, Elijah put his inhaler inside one of his jacket pockets. He quickly ate the last two pieces of a sliced apple and then downed what was left of the saltwater from the bottle Mr. Wheeler didn't finish.

Leaving the backpack hidden in the grass, *Crow Child* waited. His feet were cold inside his wet socks.

When he saw Eric Wheeler run from his hiding place behind the wheels of the first plane, *Crow Child* ran to the same spot. He watched the undercover officer slip into the nearest of two maintenance hangars on the opposite side of the cargo taxiway.

The engines of all four planes were idling as they waited to move to the runway for takeoff.

Crow Child had no sense of negative energy from the first plane. When the pilot of the second waiting plane left his seat in the cockpit, he ran to the wheels below for cover. Under the second 727 there was no telltale negative energy.

But under the belly of the third smaller Fed-Ex cargo plane, the *Crow Child* sensed the destructive intentions of two stowaways hidden well behind the wings in the rear section of the Cessna Caravan.

Still out of sight behind the landing gear of the Cessna *Crow Child* watched the pilot and copilot in the last and largest of the four planes. The overhead light was on in the cockpit of the Boeing 767 and the man and woman, both wearing a Fed-Ex uniform, were conferring over an iPad.

Since they were distracted, *Crow Child* checked activity around the other buildings then ran for cover by the massive plane's four and a half foot tires. Immediately after he stopped by the landing gear he felt a harmful energy from three sources, two on the left side of the plane's cargo hold and one on the right.

The destination of these planes didn't matter. *Crow Child* needed to devise a plan to expose the stowaways. Neither cargo plane should be allowed to take off.

****

"We only have about twenty minutes to wait before your brother will likely arrive at luggage claim, so we can have a coffee, to pass the time." Mary Trent mistook Aunt Lucille's nervous pacing for worry. "I'm sure Rock's flight and Elijah's will be uneventful, the vast majority usually are."

The pixie of a woman, wore cotton slacks with a pattern of large red roses on a black background. Under her grey wool jacket was a red pullover style sweater with snowmen knitted around the border along the front and back edge.

The trio found a café style deli in clear view of a 'Flight Arrivals' board and settled in with two coffees and a soda.

"You told me in one of your emails this was going to be your first flight." Aunt Mary stirred cream into her cup. "But at this time of year and certainly later it can be so unpredictable. I'm thrilled all of you could come, but so very sorry the weather has made your first experience such a difficult one."

Aunt Lucille patted Mary's hand across the small bistro style table. "It's been a long day, but we'll be fine, none of us got lost or crashed. Rock managed to get us seats for other connecting flights fairly quickly - and we have travel vouchers that are good for two years. Though my next venture out won't be during any winter months." She smiled behind her raised coffee cup.

****

Grandpa Clearwater couldn't relax. He followed the progress of the Dallas to DC flight on the small monitor set behind the seat in front of him. When the tiny plane illustrated on the screen map flew just south of the dot marked St. Louis, Grandpa remembered holding Elijah and rocking him to sleep the night his parents died.

Now, eleven years later he could sit on Elijah's lap. And he wondered, how his precious grandson with the weight of an amazing destiny - was going to do with whatever it was he needed to do - without attracting national attention.

Exhausted, he thought he'd close his eyes for a few minutes they felt dry from the air vents above his head. Twenty minutes later he awoke abruptly, surprised he had been able to sleep so soundly.

"This is your captain speaking. For those anticipating a late thanksgiving meal we have begun our descent into DC, Regan International Airport."

"We should be on the ground in eight minutes. Thank you for flying with us and Happy Thanksgiving from myself and my crew."

****

Crow Child heard the higher pitched sound of the jet engines revving louder from the first plane, as it began to move from its' place at the front of the line to the runway for takeoff.

Then *Crow Child* spotted Eric Wheeler. He appeared at the side of the vast opening of a hangar doorway, looking stressed. Somehow he needed to let the officer know that he hadn't gone to the main terminal.

He had no idea what Lad Swanson looked like, but he could easily recognize Al Farez with his bleached hair if he saw him. *Crow Child* studied what limited staff activity there was around the warehouses on that national holiday.

At the far end of a long narrow warehouse only two forklifts were operated by people who seemed like they belonged. A van with a Fed-Ex logo pulled away from a loading dock. But as would be expected, few people were working.

Taking another cautious look around and seeing nothing that caught his attention, he moved to the tail of the cargo plane then across the edge of the taxiway to the corner of the maintenance hangar.

But in the shadow of the parking lot to the east of the last row of warehouses a black van had just stopped to collect two passengers.

Al Farez closed the side sliding door as Lad Swanson got into the front passenger seat. When he looked out through the windshield a sudden movement one hundred-seventy yards away caught his attention.

In shock and disbelief Swanson watched the young teen they'd left unconscious in the oil storage depot run from behind the wheels of the last waiting plane then out of his line of sight. "You watched that loading dock door?" He yelled at the surprised driver.

"I just saw that same kid run from the back of the plane scheduled for Seattle to the other side of this building!"

Al Farez, unbuckled his seat belt leaning forward. "Can't be the same kid. Are you sure? Even if he woke up from the juice I shot in his neck that oil storage depot was completely black. Finding anything in the dark for a kid would be like winning a lottery."

"Well guess what? *That* kid won the lottery! I recognized the jacket, it was him! Damn, damn…"

"Let's get…" Farez reached for the back passenger door handle.

"Shut up! Damn it and let me think!"

"The kid can't *do* much of anything." Farez persisted, he can't even identify us."

Lad Swanson wasn't listening. He reached over and grabbed the jacket shoulder of the van driver jerking him roughly. "Listen very carefully and follow my instructions."

"We're going to find out where that kid went then take care of him permanently. You drive to that café at the last turn into the airport, order a cup of coffee and wait there. Got it?"

The driver nodded.

Swanson looked at Farez. "We'll only need our hand guns to deal with the kid, but we'll take our silencers. You go around that way," he pointed south and I'll head around this warehouse in the other direction." He pointed toward the taxiway-side of the warehouse.

The traitors with silencers in place, didn't watch the black van leave the east parking lot, they were concentrating on the new task at hand.

"Elijah! Why are you here? Now I must worry about you too."

Eric Wheeler pulled Elijah away from the northeast corner of the maintenance hangar, just as Lad Swanson checked around the northwest corner of the warehouse.

"I can't explain it all right now Mr. Wheeler, but you don't need to worry about me at all. Let me help, because I can, sir."

"Well it may be too late for that plane anyway it's heading for the runway, and three others took off twelve minutes, eighteen minutes and twenty-one minutes ago." He rubbed both hands across his shaved head in frustration.

Crow Child reached out patting the sleeve of the officer's jacket. "I don't know about those other cargo planes that already took off, but that first one we saw and the second plane there getting ready to go didn't have any stowaways."

Eric Wheeler dropped his arms by his side astounded.

"But that third smaller plane has two guys way in the back, and the fourth giant sized plane has three guys hiding, two on the right side of the plane and one on the left."

CHAPTER...30

Elijah was all Grandpa Clearwater could think of, as he stood behind yet another line of other passengers waiting to deplane.

He followed dozens of other weary travelers he hoped would lead him to the baggage carrousel. With any luck, *Crow Child*'s test in St. Louis had been a quick one easily completed and Elijah was on his way.

As Rock approached the baggage claim carrousels, he spotted Lucille standing beside a fine boned woman of a similar age, slightly shorter and certainly more festively dressed. With them was a thin youth about Elijah's age slightly taller, with a pale complexion and dark red hair.

His sister nearly knocked over two airport staffers in her rush to reach him. The young man with Mary extended his right hand and Mary Trent, simply blew him a kiss waiting for her turn to greet him.

"I'm Jordan sir. What does your suitcase look like?"

"Like nearly everyone else's, it's black."

"But, remember?" She looked at her brother. "I tied a bright green ribbon on the handle."

"That should help you, Jordan." Aunt Lucille offered.

Jordan nodded silently then disappeared into the crowd assembling around the baggage carrousel.

Mary Trent gave Rock a wink then stepped forward to give her latest guest a hug. "After so many phone calls and emails I feel like all of us have known each other for decades."

Aunt Mary had a slight Irish lilt to her speech and an endearing impish grin that Grandpa Clearwater knew Elijah would find amusing.

"We've been watching the Arrivals Board." Aunt Mary pointed to a wall beyond the café where they had waited for Rock's flight. "There are three flights heading this way from St. Louis. Hopefully on one of them dear Elijah was able to get a seat."

"How would we know?" Aunt Lucille's brief moment of relaxation - with a single cup of coffee - evaporated.

"We can just check at the airline desk." Mary was as cheerful as a pixie sprite.

"But how do we do that?" Grandpa Clearwater's gut felt like a hive of angry bees. "Lucille and I flew here on two different carriers. This morning we all started out on Air Canada. Then from Denver she and I took United to Dallas while Elijah flew to St. Louis. Then Lucille flew on Delta and I got a seat on American."

****

The undercover officer took another three seconds to mentally process what the young teen beside him had just told him. Then he decided to believe Elijah.

"There's a maintenance log book on a tool bench at the back of this hangar. Because of the Thanksgiving holiday only sixteen cargo flights were scheduled today. The northern storm was also a factor, so of the three that were grounded only two took off just before I was shot."

"Since I hadn't heard anything from Ottawa, I'm assuming those two cargo flights, one to Charlotte, North Carolina and one to Albuquerque, New Mexico made it safely."

"But the Fed-Ex cargo planes bound for Denver and Phoenix took off just before the one we saw at the front of the line. That one is taking packages to Spokane, Washington and the plane behind it according to the log book has a flight plan to Portland, Oregon."

Crow Child suddenly *knew* the undercover officer had been compromised. "Sir, who was your contact in Ottawa?"

Elijah had no sooner asked the question than Eric Wheeler realized he hadn't been *discovered* by Lad Swanson and his traitors, they had been expecting him. He had actually followed the wheelchair into an ambush.

The expression on the face of the officer was painful for Elijah to witness. "I also think, sir we can assume that since the terrorists planned to use the Fed-Ex planes from the facility here in St. Louis there could be some local police officers in on this too."

"Then authorities in Denver and Phoenix could be compromised as well and there's only one way to handle that possibility?" He looked beyond Elijah through the glass window of the office door."

"After I call the Denver police, the Phoenix police, the Colorado FBI and Arizona FBI office – then I call the media."

They heard the crackle of conversation from the cockpit of the plane scheduled for Spokane, Washington. The pilot received his clearance then it sped down the runway, lifting smoothly into the air.

The plane scheduled for Portland, Oregon moved from the front of the taxi line to the runway to wait its' turn for clearance.

"I gotta get to the phone in that office."

"Guess you can't just tell the Fed-Ex guys that you're with the RCMP, huh?"

Officer Wheeler shook his head. "Everything was taken. I'm lucky I still have my life, thanks to you. Right now my only advantage is that Swanson thinks I'm dead, and you're still locked up in the dark with my lifeless body."

Over the radio in the maintenance hangar they heard the pilot of the plane to Oregon receive clearance for takeoff.

"If I can sabotage the Cessna where it is - then that will block the way for the 767 behind it. And that will also block the two remaining 727 cargo planes coming up to wait now."

Crow Child smiled at the undercover officer, who looked weary and so alone. "I can do that sir, while you make your phone calls."

The officer's jaw dropped then just as quickly he closed his mouth and nodded. Something told him to believe this unusual kid – yet again.

He let out a deep sigh. "I'm not even going to ask your plan. But there are two Fed-Ex staffers I'll need to convince or subdue quickly before I can call."

The Cessna cargo plane bound for Houston began to move from the taxiway toward the runway. The massive 767 behind it moved forward followed by the two additional smaller Boeing 727 Fed-Ex planes.

As *Crow Child* stepped across the threshold of the maintenance hangar door he *felt* the presence of imminent danger. And from his right came the swift, hot breath of two bullets that passed before his face.

Officer Wheeler stopped with one hand on the office door knob. He had recognized the barely audible sound of a silencer and turned instinctively to protect Elijah.

…In a rush of energy he hadn't experienced for over a year *Crow Child* rose. His entire being expanded.

Time stopped.

A flash of white light surrounded *Crow Child* and transformed his physical form to that of a giant black crow with a wing span that touched the roof of the maintenance hangar.

Black Crow's form filled the open space.

With one sweeping flurry *Black Crow* stepped into the air, rising higher filling the space with his light.

In rapid succession Lad Swanson fired at the giant menacing bird that had appeared from nowhere. As the bullets shot toward the hovering dark essence of *Black Crow* they exploded into dust before they reached him.

With the wave of his right wing the handgun was yanked from Lad Swanson's grip.

Black Crow became brighter and more vivid growing even greater in size.

With the wave of his left wing *Black Crow* lifted Lad Swanson into the air then dropped him at the feet of Officer Wheeler.

Swanson looked up stunned to see Eric Wheeler. He tried to call out for help to the two Fed-Ex office staff who came running to check out the commotion, but no sound came from Lad's throat.

The RCMP officer grabbed an extension cord and bound Lad Swanson's hands behind his back.

Wheeler and the Fed-Ex staffers took Swanson into the office as *Black Crow*'s light became a blinding white.

In a blink *Black Crow* was in front of the Cessna. His wings snuffed all air from the engines – they stopped immediately.

From the cargo hold at the back of the Cessna and from all three cargo holds in the bellies of the other Boeing planes came eleven armed terrorists. They shot directly at the giant ball of bright white light shading their eyes from the glare.

The white light around *Black Crow* altered to violet – sending a second massive wave of wind that sucked the air from the lungs of each and every armed traitor.

From the shadows of the east corner of the Fed-Ex warehouse, a shaken Al Farez, fumbled to find his phone he dropped in the dark.

CHAPTER...31

Elijah's coughing spasm was so violent he almost passed out from lack of air.

He couldn't crawl to reach the edge of the taxiway so he rolled to the cover of the grass. With more will than energy Elijah managed to reach his discarded backpack and a second full inhaler.

It was several minutes before his cough became less severe, but it was the sound of his cough that led Eric to where Elijah lay.

Gently Eric sat Elijah up supporting his weakened body.

"Thump my back..." Elijah coughed, "hard - please..." he gasped for another breath, "Mr. Wheeler..." Elijah closed his eyes.

****

On the Arrivals Board there were three flights from St. Louis to DC listed. But each flight was with three separate airlines, so they split up to check on passengers from those incoming flights.

Aunt Lucille and Jordan waited for a representative at the Delta Airlines desk. Aunt Mary waited at American Airlines and Rock waited to speak with someone at the United Airlines customer service desk.

Abruptly, as each of them stood waiting a siren sounded. The siren triggered all overhead lights to cycle on and off then on and off.

Suddenly from numerous closed doors came dozens of armed agents in uniform swarming from everywhere in tight groups of six, as if conjured by a magician.

Over a loudspeaker - an authoritative voice boomed out to surprised travelers. "This airport has been placed on immediate lockdown. Please remain calm and remain exactly where you are."

At the customer service ticket counters airline employees took charge of those in line. "Please, everyone - if you are able to then sit on the floor right where you are. If you are unable to sit on the floor please raise your hand and someone will provide a folding chair or wheelchair for you."

****

With energy returning to Elijah Clearwater – *Crow Child* opened his eyes.

Eric Wheeler was stunned by the transformation. When they stood, unconscious traitors lay on the ground below all four cargo planes.

Shocked Fed-Ex pilots huddled together, confused.

The sound of sirens grew louder blaring with lights that rotated on the roofs of Homeland Security vans. Five vans screeched to a halt on either side of the parked planes, doors opened, and agents flooded out rushing to the prone suspects.

Agents secured their recovering suspects, the Fed-Ex office staff, and took Fed-Ex pilots into custody as well.

Though Officer Wheeler had discovered his identification in Lad Swanson's jacket pockets, he remained on the grass side of the Fed-Ex taxiway. His hand gun was still missing and he suspected that Al Farez, wherever he was had kept the undercover officer's sidearm.

The driver of the first van spotted the lone man standing with a youth. When the driver left the van his handgun was drawn held high in his left hand with a wide flashlight held in his right hand. "Agent Hank Thomas, Homeland Security - identify yourself."

Officer Wheeler immediately put his hands on his head.

Elijah followed Mr. Wheeler's lead. *Crow Child*, whispered, "He's okay, sir."

"I'm Staff Sergeant Eric Wheeler of the Royal Canadian Mounted police, undercover. Agent Thomas, my shield and identification are inside my left jacket pocket. Beside me is Elijah Clearwater. He's a civilian passenger Lad Swanson and Al Farez took him hostage with me."

Agent Thomas checked the shield and ID card. "You're the one who called this in?" The agent still held the RCMP shield and ID card.

Officer Wheeler nodded. "Assignment code number; STLM181821."

Still holding his gun and flashlight, the agent made a call. Whoever answered on the other end of the call was given Eric Wheeler's badge number, name and ID number, with Wheeler's assignment code.

When Agent Thomas ended his call he handed Wheeler back his ID and badge, lowered his hand gun then pointed toward the stopped Fed-Ex planes. "So what's going on?"

Officer Wheeler dropped his arms. "This," he pointed with a broad sweep of his left arm, is only half of our problem. I managed to confirm that U.S. Marshal Lad Swanson put a plan in motion to use Fed-Ex cargo planes as 9/11 style airborne torpedoes."

The agent stared for a full three seconds. "How? Any change in flight plans would automatically send out immediate alarms."

"But that's the beauty of his plan, they weren't going to change any of the cargo plane's flight plans – just crash them into the terminal buildings of their destination airports at the last minute – making a pretty impressive and devastating statement."

Agent Thomas frowned and dropped his head as if most of the air had left his body.

"But three for sure perhaps four other Fed-Ex planes have been boarded by other armed members of Lad Swanson's organization and they're already in the air."

"The stowaways may not have shown themselves to the flight crew yet. They may wait until the planes are closer to each of the major airport destinations."

Agent Thomas looked up as complete awareness hit him. "Come on then." He led the way running toward the office in the Fed-Ex maintenance hangar.

Inside the office the freed Fed-Ex maintenance manager pulled up their flight-schedule screen. "Like I told the Canadian police officer before your guys arrived, originally for today we had sixteen cargo flights scheduled. But the three bound for Boston, Chicago and Cleveland were grounded because of the snow storm."

"You got the Cessna to Houston, the Boeing 767 to San Diego, the 727 to Oklahoma City and 727 to Seattle stopped out there." The man waved his hand in the direction of the wall to his left without taking his eyes from the screen.

"We had a 727 to Spokane leave twelve minutes ago, and another 727 to Portland that left eight minutes ago."

"An earlier flight, our Cessna to Charlotte, North Carolina landed safely four hours ago and our other Cessna Caravan landed safely in Albuquerque, New Mexico two hours ago."

"By my count," the Homeland Security agent rubbed the back of his neck, "that leaves four others you say have been boarded by terrorists." He looked at RCMP Staff Sergeant Wheeler, who nodded.

Agent Thomas checked back to the computer screen. "Where are those four cargo planes now?"

The maintenance manager typed in the PM flight schedule for the American Thanksgiving holiday. "The 727 to Phoenix left two hours ago." He looked up and behind him to the two officers. "That's only a three hour flight."

Wheeler asked. "About where would that plane be now?"

Without hesitating the manager answered, "Somewhere between Carrizo Mountains and the Painted Desert."

Agent Thomas made a call. "We got just enough time to scramble fighter jets from Tucson. That's open territory over a lot of nothing if we must shoot down the plane."

The Fed-Ex maintenance manager looked stricken. "We got two of our pilots on that plane!"

"I know…" When Agent Thomas walked away to make his call, his face was ashen.

"Where are the other three planes?" Officer Wheeler focused the maintenance manager back to the screen.

The Fed-Ex manager took a deep breath and scrolled down to the next flight record. "We had a Cessna that took off to Colorado Springs, forty-six minutes ago and that's only a two hour flight. Right behind it by eight minutes was a 727 to Denver. The flight to Denver is only two hours too. Then eleven minutes after that cargo plane took off, another 767 left - bound for Dulles, Virginia. That's another two hour flight from here."

Agent Thomas returned and Eric Wheeler got him caught up. "We've got seventy-four minutes before the Colorado Springs plane takes that airport and eighty-two minutes before the plane heading for Denver takes out the Denver International Airport."

"But we gotta divert or destroy them well before that!" Agent Thomas was barely breathing. "What's open east of Denver and Colorado Springs?"

The Fed-Ex maintenance manager pulled up a second screen. Tiny airplane symbols popped up on a screen over locations on a miniature map showing states west of the Mississippi.

"Our plane to Colorado Springs can be intercepted here before Cheyenne Wells. A-n-d the best place to approach the plane to Denver is between Ray, Colorado and Burlington."

"We got just enough time to get jets from the Air Force Academy!" Agent Thomas was on his phone again.

Officer Wheeler leaned over the shoulder of the maintenance manager. "Now we need to see a screen for the Dulles flight across the states east of the Mississippi."

The maintenance manager moved the computer mouse and clicked on the East-Routes box. But the second screen was almost blank except for one tiny plane symbol heading toward Atlanta, Georgia. Each of the states east of the Mississippi River glowed in slightly different shades of orange, green and blue.

"Go back to the West-Routes screen." Wheeler was frowning.

The west screen showed tiny planes approaching their destinations of Spokane, Portland, Phoenix, Denver and Colorado Springs, Houston and San Diego.

"What do these screens tell us?" Wheeler tried not to panic.

"Well the small star indicates a plane has landed, like here in Albuquerque. All of the other flights are still active so they still look like planes."

"Okay, so where's the fourth cargo plane - the one heading for the Dulles airport in Virginia?"

CHAPTER...32

The ringing alarm throughout the District of Columbia, Regan International Airport was dialed down, but only slightly.

Overhead - arriving travelers, travelers on their way to another destination, and people who came to meet incoming visitors - heard the unmistakable sound of military helicopters and jet fighters overhead.

When armed soldiers appeared at each airline's customer service desk, people were allowed to stand and continue, but the lines moved slower as the soldiers questioned everyone and checked all identification.

Rock reached the customer service representative for United. Aunt Mary still waited behind two customers for American Airlines while his sister waited behind a large family and two couples at the Delta Airlines customer counter.

Grandpa Clearwater showed his passport, his eTicket and separate boarding passes to the attendant, as a soldier looked on listening. "I'm enquiring about my grandson."

"His name is Elijah O'Day Clearwater. We were originally scheduled to fly from Calgary, Alberta to Chicago, Illinois then to here. However due to the severe weather along the border we were diverted to Denver, Colorado."

"My sister, my grandson and I took whatever seats we could get on other airlines that unfortunately stopped in other cities first. My grandson flew from Denver to St. Louis while we flew from Denver to Dallas. We recently arrived on a flight from Dallas to DC and we expected that Elijah would be able to get a flight from St. Louis to DC."

"Was the District of Columbia, your final destination sir?" The soldier was blunt, but his tone was not threatening.

"Yes."

"The purpose of your trip sir?"

"We came to visit relatives for American Thanksgiving."

"Your relative's name sir?"

"Mary O'Day Trent. Aunt Mary lives across the Potomac River in Alexandria, Virginia. We weren't sure on which carrier Elijah was able to get a seat, so Mary is in a line for American Airlines over there," Rock pointed, feeling worried and faint. "And my sister Lucille is in a line to check with someone at Delta."

The soldier nodded. "Proceed."

"Is it possible for you to check your incoming passenger list for the flight from St. Louis to DC for Elijah O'Day Clearwater? Clearwater is one word."

The exhausted looking United ticket agent smiled despite the stress of the chaos around them. She typed in the St. Louis,

United flight number with Elijah's full name, date of birth and country of origin.

"I'm so sorry sir, but no passenger named Elijah Clearwater was assigned a United Airlines seat. Perhaps your grandson was able to get a seat on one of the other two outbound flights."

But as Rock nodded to the ticket agent and the soldier, he had his doubts that Mary or Lucille would have any better luck. District of Columbia local time was 6:47 PM. Grandpa Clearwater had forgotten to take his new cell phone off Airplane-mode.

$$*********$$

The Fed-Ex manager frowned looking at the East-Route screen. "There's only one reason why the cargo plane to Dulles isn't showing up and that's the transponder. Either its' not working or it was turned off."

"Could the plane have crashed?" Wheeler asked.

"Sure. But if any of our planes crash then a circle with an 'X' in the circle shows up on our screen map."

Agent Thomas returned. "Okay so let's deal with the Dulles plane. "Where is it located now and how much time do we have?"

Staff Sergeant Wheeler brought a second glass of water for Elijah from the Fed-Ex staff break room. "We have less than eighty minutes. Local time in Virginia is 6:47 and the maintenance manager believes we can't see that cargo plane on their screen because the transponder on that Fed-Ex 767 was likely turned off."

"You can't be serious! Damn!"

Wheeler had an idea. "Does anyone know where Al Farez might be? If he was hidden here or someone he paid works here, and saw Homeland arrive then my guess is that somehow the traitors in the Dulles plane have been tipped off."

Agent Thomas shook his head. "For some reason Lad Swanson can't talk or isn't talking. He wrote a note that he wanted a deal, but he won't get a deal until he starts talking. So, we're at an impasse."

"As for the others they don't seem to be able to talk either. We have a doctor examining them. So, that makes the answer to your question a no."

"Okay. Is the flight plan for each shipment to the same cities, day after day, week after week exactly the same?" Wheeler hoped that Fed-Ex technology would fit his idea.

The manager nodded.

"Then what you're saying is the airspeed and altitude of that cargo plane now about sixty miles out from the Dulles airport tonight would be the same as it was last Thursday?"

"But last Thursday, our pilots didn't have terrorists threatening them on their flight." The manager was tired and annoyed that terrorists were causing him to miss his favorite meal.

"Good point." Officer Wheeler looked at Agent Thomas. "But given that each flight's typical airspeed and altitude is usually known, could you order jet fighters to fan out and scan for say thirty miles out from Dulles? They might just spot the plane."

"We got nothing else so that's worth a try." Agent Thomas picked up his phone again. "And precious minutes are ticking away!"

Officer Wheeler looked over at the second desk. Elijah sat quietly in a desk-chair looking pale, but breathing evenly. "How are you feeling now?" He joined him sitting on one corner of the desk.

"I'm good, thanks Mr. Wheeler, but I could eat an entire turkey myself right now." He grinned.

"And I wish I could reach my grandpa, though I'm not sure where he is. He may still be in Dallas if he didn't get a flight out to DC."

"This your first time in St. Louis, kid?" The manager rocked back on his office chair.

"Yeah, my first time out of Alberta, or out of Canada or out of anywhere really."

"Well not much of a thanksgiving for you here in St. Louis, not much for me either and I live here." The manager stood up. "I'm making a fresh pot of coffee, if any of you are interested."

With the manager in the office break room and Agent Thomas on the phone, Elijah felt freer to ask Wheeler his question.

"So until the snow storm, Boston and Chicago and Cleveland were also on the U.S. Marshal's list?"

"No *because* of the snow storm they had to alter their plans and pick three other destinations for their list." Then Eric looked at Elijah and back to the map on the screen.

Elijah stood and walked over to the chair in front of the computer. "If that Al Farez guy did see what happened here earlier - I think you can assume that he did - then might he have altered the plan again for the fourth plane?"

"That makes sense." Eric pressed the palms of his hands over his face. "If I was Al Farez, and saw half my plan blocked here, I'd expect some kind of resistance at all the other airports. But the Fed-Ex cargo plane to Dulles gives him more time to make a change."

"What's another airport close to Dulles?"

The question was no sooner asked out loud than *Crow Child knew* the planned flight path of the 767 cargo plane *had* been altered.

And simultaneously they both said "DC!"

Agent Thomas returned to join Eric and Elijah at the Fed-Ex computer screen. "I just ordered two dozen fighter jets to patrol the airspace over the entire state of Virginia."

Staff Sergeant Wheeler realized that was a huge area with several thousand feet of air. "Would that include all of the airspace over DC's Regan Airport?"

"Not yet, but it will."

Wheeler nodded. "Elijah asked me a question about the three original destinations that were altered due to the northern snow storm. That got me thinking, if Lad Swanson was still here an hour ago then likely Al Farez was with him."

"Following that thought then it would be logical Al Farez saw the planes stopped and Homeland arrive. He may not have been able to redirect the planes heading to Phoenix, Denver and Colorado Springs – but the fact that the cargo plane to Dulles isn't showing up on the screen makes me think the flight path of that plane may have been changed."

"The original plan was for eight planes to take out eight major US airports. Due to weather, they had to pick three alternate destinations – but their plan was discovered."

"With seven of the eight blocked or identified, the biggest impact they could hope to make now with only one plane is the DC Regan Airport – or more likely a crash landing down Pennsylvania Avenue."

Agent Thomas looked at Wheeler then at Elijah and then back to Wheeler. "Well as a precaution your earlier call caused the Director to launch Red-Code. Both Dulles and the DC passenger terminals were put on lockdown twelve minutes ago.'

"Now I need to order all outgoing planes grounded and incoming planes redirected! It's 7PM there."

"Wait. I don't think that will help us. We can be sure the stowaways are monitoring communication frequencies. So halting all takeoffs and landings of any planes we can clearly follow, won't allow us to find one dark plane in a huge dark sky."

"Damn, you're right. As it is now if that Fed-Ex plane is spotted by one of the fighter jets it'll be pure dumb luck."

The manager came into the office from the staff break room. "Coffee's ready. The kid can have soda, or water from the fridge."

Elijah tapped Officer Wheeler's elbow. "I suddenly feel very tired sir…"

The manager pulled out his desk chair. "We got a leather sofa in our break room. There are no blankets or anything, but you can rest there."

Elijah's color was good, but Wheeler worried that Elijah should see a doctor. "How are you feeling? I can call an ambulance."

"I'm fine, really – don't know why, but just feel like I should lie down all of a sudden."

"Drink more water before you rest."

Elijah grinned. "Now you sound like my grandfather."

"Shouldn't we have called someone?" Agent Thomas was on the verge of overload. "Was he hurt? Where are his parents?"

"I tried his grandfather's cell phone, but got no response. Due to the northern snow storm Elijah and his family were separated on different standby flights. Not sure where they are now. He wasn't hurt, but he hasn't had much to eat and Elijah has cystic fibrosis."

"That's a worry." The manager started toward the break room again. "I got an apple in the fridge he can have."

Agent Thomas was quiet then shared, "I have a niece who has CF. Lacey's in and out of the hospital about every other month. That kid looks pretty good, but we need to watch him."

Hank Thomas stared at the closed break room door for a second then picked up his phone again. "I'll need to call the Pentagon on this one. We can't shoot down an *elephant* like a 767 filled with jet fuel and crates of cargo, over our densely populated capitol."

****

In a quiet corner of the Fed-Ex break room *Crow Child saw* the massive cargo plane shining in a moonlit sky.

All exterior lights were turned off before the hijacked cargo plane had entered West Virginia airspace. He *watched* with his mind as the plane descended to an altitude of five-thousand-two-hundred and eighty feet, only one mile above the ground.

With a distance of less than sixty miles, the plane would be directly over the Washington Monument in eight-teen minutes.

Even with the assistance of a thousand fighter jets there was no conventional way to bring down a plane that size without significant loss of life and property damage.

Crow Child left the sleeping body of Elijah Clearwater.

In the stroke of a heartbeat *Black Crow* landed on the branch of a cherry tree growing on the north lawn of the White House.

Holiday traffic on Pennsylvania Avenue was sparse. No horns blared, no sirens screeched – and *Black Crow* waited.

Night lights twinkled like July sparklers reflecting off the Potomac River. Then *Black Crow* felt the air vibration of the speeding cargo plane swiftly approaching the city.

Black Crow took flight from the branches of the cherry tree climbing high.

The plane pierced the air dropping farther - flying faster.

A flash of bright white light surrounded *Black Crow* expanding the reach of his wings beyond the side streets of Pennsylvania Avenue.

Cars crashed into each other. Pedestrians ran for cover.

Rising higher *Black Crow* filled the open space with his light sending a giant wave of wind with his left wing.

The sudden powerful rush of air slowed the oncoming plane to just above stall speed.

Black Crow became brighter – more vivid – even greater in size.

White light altered to violet.

A second massive wave of wind lifted then flipped the fifteen thousand pound plane and cargo over on its roof into the Potomac River. Snap! *Black Crow*'s light merged with the swiftly moving water and was gone.

Three jets swooped down from dark skies and circled as two military helicopters landed on the banks of the river.

CHAPTER...33

When the Homeland Security helicopter carrying Elijah, Staff Sergeant Wheeler, and Agent Thomas landed at the Pentagon - Grandpa, Aunt Lucille and Aunt Mary, were waiting.

Jordan and their luggage had been taken to Mary's house by the Capitol Hill police.

Aunt Lucille, heavier than Elijah, but certainly no taller ran to him and lifted him off the ground. She cried and talked at the same time. "Never been, so relieved to see anyone in my entire sixty-four years."

Grandpa Clearwater said nothing, just held his grandson close for a full minute then introduced Elijah to his Aunt Mary.

The slim little lady smiled with her hands on her hips. "Well I don't know what was going on with our airport, but you can't say that traveling is dull." Then she opened her arms to hug Elijah, laughing out loud.

Technically it was still Thanksgiving.

At 10PM the drive from the Pentagon to Aunt Mary's 1953 split-level on Richenbacher Avenue, took less than twenty minutes.

But then Mary Trent liked to drive a little faster than the posted speed limit.

As she parked in her driveway, Elijah could see that lights were on in every room that faced the street.

The sound of slamming car doors brought Mr. and Mrs. Roberts and their son Jordan out the front door to the wide slate stone steps.

After a round of introductions the women hugged, the men shook hands and the boys nodded to each other. Inside everyone was greeted by the familiar smells of sage and pumpkin.

Mr. and Mrs. Roberts had converted the long since over-roasted bird into a stack of sliced turkey, dressing and sweet potato sandwiches.

All seven people were well beyond hungry. Elijah swallowed a handful of digestive enzymes as saliva filled his mouth. Both boys held a thick turkey sandwich in one hand while they tackled a slice of pie with a fork held in the other.

Soon after the meal, Elijah's cough returned.

With Elijah's chest-vest still in his suitcase and his suitcase still in St. Louis, he and Grandpa Clearwater went upstairs to the guestroom they shared. Thumping Elijah's chest and back by hand his coughing got worse before it got better.

It was midnight in Virginia – 2AM in Alberta – when Elijah's breathing returned to normal. He closed his eyes and slept the sleep of complete exhaustion.

****

When Elijah awoke the following morning the other twin bed in Aunt Mary's guestroom was empty and remade. As he looked around, the wall clock that hung above a tall dresser clicked over to 9AM. It was 7AM in Alberta – he'd actually slept in.

Beyond the closed bedroom door he heard the muffled sounds of clinking dishes and voices from the floor below.

He was rested, but his chest felt heavy. Immediately when he sat up a coughing spell began. Shaking Elijah reached for his inhaler.

As if on cue Grandpa opened the bedroom door. "Let's get those lungs clearer."

It was difficult to talk with Grandpa pounding his back and chest so he waited. In his memory he relived the day that had been his first American Thanksgiving.

Twenty minutes later he could breathe with deeper less congested breaths again.

"Here," Grandpa held out a ten ounce glass of salted water. "Drink all of this then take your shower. I think Aunt Mary told me you had ten minutes." He gave his grandson a long hug.

Eight minutes later he was dressed in his rewashed travel clothes. Breathing easier, Elijah followed the smell of bacon, fresh coffee and cinnamon along the second floor hall and down the stairs to Aunt Mary's kitchen.

Five plates with cutlery were set out on a small round table by a long low window. The blinds were open partway and Elijah could see the eighty-foot magnolia tree Mary had described in her emails. The tiny photo attachment hadn't done justice to the tree with long broad leaves half the size of dinner plates.

"How are you dear boy?" Mary carried a platter of scrambled eggs and bacon. She placed the platter in the center of the table then gave Elijah a hug.

"I'm good. Hungry again, but really not tired."

Aunt Lucille set down a basket of freshly baked cinnamon rolls. "You look surprisingly well for someone who spent a couple of hours stopping cargo planes."

She placed a hand on each shoulder and looked into Elijah's dark rimmed eyes. "What you were able to do was amazing you know." She leaned in and kissed his cheek.

"No one has any true idea what actually happened. But every media network has gone berserk." She pulled back smiling.

Grandpa put a pot of coffee down on a hot mat. "Yeah," he chuckled. "The plane you flipped over into the Potomac, according to one news report – was caused by a sudden updraft and wind shear conditions."

"And of course no one who witnessed what happened in St. Louis is talking, literally. As is *Black Crow*'s standard method, all of the traitors taken into custody no longer have the ability to speak. When they requested lawyers they had to write everything down." Grandpa winked.

Elijah glanced again at the plates. "There are five settings. Is Jordan joining us for breakfast?"

Mary Trent's front doorbell sounded.

Aunt Mary pulled a chair out for herself. "Would you get that for me please, Elijah?"

On, the front steps, stood RCMP Staff Sergeant Eric Wheeler. "Good morning partner." The officer smiled.

In Mary Trent's sun filled breakfast room, the police officer, the grandfather, grandson and two great aunts settled into a traditional morning meal.

"You'll be relieved to know that none of the other Fed-Ex cargo planes needed to be shot down." Eric Wheeler poured coffee into his mug. "When each plane was surrounded by fighter jets, the stowaways wisely surrendered to the Fed-Ex pilots."

"A-n-d everyone was rescued from the plane that mysteriously landed on its' roof in the Potomac River."

He took a sip of coffee. "As for the rest of yesterday's events, I have no idea, how to explain what, I actually did see – nor what I heard happened later."

The experienced officer looked around the table from Elijah, to Lucille, to Rock then to Mary. "Elijah Clearwater is obviously a courageous and gifted young chap."

Elijah looked at his partially eaten breakfast.

Aunt Mary put down her mug and patted the hand of the police officer. "There are energies in our universe mere mortals can't

269

even imagine. Please just believe me when I tell you that *Crow Child* is fulfilling an ancient Irish legend."

"That is also a First Nations legend." Rock added.

Raising his head again, Elijah looked directly into the eyes of the ethical man *Crow Child knew* could be trusted. "I can do things sir that are quite unusual."

"But what I am able to do only started on my thirteenth birthday - just eighteen months ago."

Elijah looked at his grandfather then his Aunt Mary. "But yesterday was kind'a different. I mean it was sort'a the same, but with more - so much more."

"Out'ta nowhere I knew stuff about the people standing or sitting close to me. Then I was able to stop the bleeding of Mr. Wheeler's wound. Then I was able to *see* things - be me and *Black Crow* too!"

Everyone seated at the small round table in the sunny morning room were silent for a full minute.

Mary Trent poured cream into her mug then more coffee for herself. "As Elijah Clearwater matures then so expands the abilities of *Crow Child* to use *Black Crow* energy."

"This was your second *trial* Elijah, another test of your resolve and courage. And when the time is right there will be a third trial that tests you..."

PART THREE ...

The
Sound
Of Rain

CHAPTER...34

April 2018

As Elijah slept, Crow Child energy swirled around him and through him - unsettled...

******

"I'm so sorry Mr. Clearwater, but if your grandson's blockage doesn't show signs of clearing in the next four hours, he'll need surgery."

The pediatric specialist folded a stethoscope into the hip pocket of her white lab coat. Stray strands of her straight black hair had slipped away from the single thick braid down her back.

Rock Clearwater took in a deep breath striving to remain calm. He brushed back strands of graying black hair from his forehead. "Elijah's birthday is tomorrow, pretty grim way for a kid to turn fifteen here."

Dr. Sinha who had first met Elijah Clearwater when he was two days old didn't hide her concern. "I agree. I see far too many stressful birthdays in these rooms every day. It happens to CF kids and so many others with diabetes, cancer, weak hearts and many, many other health issues."

"Keeping Elijah well hydrated, and giving him two enemas with a round of Klean Prep hasn't cleared the blockage in his large intestine."

Keta Sinha checked the wall clock behind the desk of the fourth floor nurses' station then her own wrist watch. "It's just after nine now. I'm going to reserve an operating room for 2PM."

"We'll run another quick MRI to check for any movement at one forty-five then if we need to we can prep Elijah quickly if there's no change."

Rock Clearwater nodded, he understood. His brown eyes almost disappeared behind weathered brown skin, tanned by years in the sun and his Sarsi-T'suu T'ina heritage. "I'll call my sister and my daughter. Do you want me to tell Elijah?"

"No need I've kept him lightly sedated. The abdominal cramps would be too painful for him if I didn't, but you can certainly sit by his bed," She smiled.

"And perhaps you can read to him. Headlines from the daily newspaper are always exciting for teens." She made a face pulling out another patient's chart.

Grandpa Clearwater phoned his daughter Dawn cowardly asking her to call his older sister, also her Aunt Lucille. He then slid a chair closer to Elijah.

Many nights and days he kept vigil by his grandson's bed over the years. He sighed.

Watching him now, again Rock was amazed by how much Elijah had grown and yet how young he still looked while he slept.

His unruly mop of dark brown curly hair was a mix of his Irish mother's red curls and his Sarsi father's straight black hair. Elijah's hazel eyes were also a blend of his father's brown eyes and his mother's pale blue.

****

There was a disturbance that Crow Child sensed - something malicious was gathering momentum with an unavoidable looming force toward a mammoth calamity.

****

Spring in Morristown, New York, U.S.A. - population 13,000 had been mostly overcast and mostly windy. Due north across the Saint Lawrence River to Brockville, Ontario, Canada – population 22,000 the residents had faired about the same.

So the multiple explosions came as multiple shocks to the citizens of both towns, as had the foreboding, simulated sound that had preceded them. That tiny clue had also gone unnoticed.

Simultaneously at 11AM Eastern Time three upper floor windows of Morristown's main courthouse and city hall - and Brockville's historic courthouse and city hall addition were pierced, followed immediately by a high pitched sizzle then twelve fiery explosions.

Shattered glass, debris and flames shot out from the window openings of all four buildings on three sides. People who weren't immediately hurt were trapped by fires in several locations, falling walls and ceiling plaster.

Outside - vehicles collided in the streets while pedestrians who weren't injured by flying glass and debris ran for cover.

People living in both towns could actually see the mirrored unfolding tragedies from opposite banks of the major river and shared seaway.

Immediately local Morristown and Brockville police, ambulance and fire firefighters responded. But it was chillingly clear to Canadian RCMP in Ottawa, Ontario and American FBI agents in Washington, DC what had just happened.

And worse, what had just happened was likely only a test - only the beginning.

To the authorities on both sides of the US-Canadian border this was another well planned, well coordinated, terrorist attack on North American soil.

When the phone rang on the desk of the newly promoted Inspector Eric Wheeler, he was immediately sorry he had answered it – though he had no other options.

"No way!" He listened to the emergency caller at the other end.

"It just happened?" He looked at his watch, listening again.

"How is that possible?" He scribbled notes as the voice continued with preliminary information. If he had had hair to pull, this would have been the time. But all he could do was slap one side of his shaved head.

"Okay thanks, I'm on my way. I'll take the 416 and be there in an hour."

Inspector Weller had hesitated exactly one second, squinting at his wall map despite remembering to wear new contacts over his grey-green eyes.

He could have arranged for a police helicopter. However, by the time he'd driven to the heliport then flew out – he'd use up over twenty minutes only to arrive at Brockville about the same time – then he'd still need a car.

The mid morning traffic on Ontario Highway 416 was mostly transport trucks. Their size made it easy for him to weave between them maintaining a high speed with only his lights flashing.

Just 12 miles from the city limits of Brockville, the officer could clearly see thick dark grey smoke. It rose to the low ceiling of overcast cloud then spread east toward the St. Lawrence River. Just beyond the Hwy 29 sign he took the off ramp.

Barricades were already set up across all major roads in and out of the small city. He slowed then stopped showing his badge and ID card to one of three officers posted to monitor traffic.

"Thank you Sergeant." Wheeler clipped his badge to the outer collar of his jacket.

She smiled. "You're welcome sir. The courthouse and city hall are on King Street, but I don't think you'll need directions. Just follow the smoke plum."

He nodded and did just that. Passing through two more barricaded check points he parked one block away from the burning city hall then stood on the roof of his RCMP patrol car with his binoculars raised.

One water truck remained at the courthouse. It looked like the fire there was under control.

However, at city hall three water trucks were parked on three sides as close to the building has was safely possible. Stubborn flames continued to punch through blackened windows on the north side.

Then with a sudden thunderous roar, the top floor of city hall collapsed onto the floor below, igniting fresh fuel of more varnished wood, furniture and interior walls.

Immediately, two water trucks began to spray through the lower floor windows to keep the ceiling and ground floor cooler. A fourth truck raced from the court house to assist the other water trucks fighting a renewed fire.

He panned his attention across the river to Morristown, with its struggling volunteer fire department losing the battle to save either one of their historic buildings.

"Inspector Wheeler?"

Eric looked down to see, a short muscular, grey haired man with a thin moustache and glasses standing beside a much younger woman about the same height with coffee colored skin and short cut curly black hair.

"I'm Brockville's police Captain Rex Treadway, and this is FBI Agent Opal Thane."

Eric Wheeler slid from the car roof to the sidewalk, extending his hand first to Agent Thane, then to the local police captain.

"We've already met with RCMP Staff Sergeant Zenas who told us he had called you." Agent Thane spoke first.

"The last time we saw Officer Zenas he was walking around the court house with a Brockville fire inspector and two FBI arson experts."

Inspector Wheeler locked his car. "Looks like everyone we need is here."

The trio headed east, taking a wide route to the north of the burning city hall toward the blackened and smoldering courthouse.

"Where's your office Agent Thane? You and your team got here fast enough. It's only a few minutes to one."

They stopped walking as a traffic officer waved another ambulance through the intersection.

"Please call me Opal. Ironically we were already *here* sort of. Three weeks ago we set up a monitoring station at Ogdenburg only eleven miles farther east. It's the next community beyond Morristown on the U.S. shore side."

"We've been monitoring terrorist chatter that first began to mention the St. Lawrence Seaway five months ago."

They reached the middle of King Street then crossed over to a stand of oak trees that once shaded a corner of the court house's front park. Now the grass and the brick walkways were ridged with tracks from the tires of ambulances and heavy fire trucks.

Agent Thane looked up at Inspector Wheeler. "We've been sending duplicate updates directly to your RCMP Commissioner at Federal and International Operations, in Ottawa. I'm surprised you weren't briefed."

"My promotion has only been effective for the last three days. I didn't have an office until eight o'clock this morning."

Eric searched the crowd of police, rescue and fire personnel for RCMP Staff Sergeant Doug Zenas, but Doug Zenas, spotted him first.

"Inspector!" The officer broke away from his group of local police. He rushed over and acknowledged the other two superior officers. "Agent Thane, Captain Treadway," he nodded.

"Hell of a mess sir. I regret to report this, but the Brockville mayor has been confirmed dead and so were two judges. Other confirmed dead from the latest hospital report is eighteen, with forty-two serious injuries."

Wheeler looked beyond the courthouse across the river to Morristown. "What about casualties over there?"

Zenas pulled out his phone and scrolled to a third screen. "They've only been able to get tug boats in position to help with water on their fire about thirty minutes ago, so all Morristown could report were injuries. So far there have been twenty-seven, five serious."

"As far as casualties or any rescue attempts that hasn't been possible, yet. It's still way too hot and dangerous for rescue."

Inspector Wheeler nodded absently watching the hurried activity between the two historic buildings on the Canadian side of the border then the same heroic attempts across the shared St. Lawrence River to the American side.

He looked at Agent Thane. "What do we know?" Around them under the grouping of oak trees sirens echoed and voices called out.

"Both municipality locations were hit simultaneously at 11AM." Opal Thane responded from memory. "The targets were the top floors of each town's courthouse and city hall with incendiary devices programmed to penetrate each window on three sides of all four buildings. We haven't ruled out small long range rockets with GPS capability, but so far the actual delivery system of this attack hasn't been determined."

CHAPTER...35

"Mr. Clearwater?" Dr. Sinha gently tapped Rock Clearwater's shoulder. He had dozed off in the chair by his grandson's hospital bed.

"I haven't cancelled the operating room, but the tests came back looking like we can use another option for Elijah."

The bed Elijah had been sleeping in was empty.

"Option?" Grandpa Clearwater became fully awake. "What might that be?"

"We got excellent pictures that showed the blockage is breaking up, so that's a relief. Now I can go in using a laparoscope with just a couple of band-aid sized incisions which is much less invasive."

"I feel certain I can massage the blockage further down the large intestine and into slightly smaller segments."

"Sounds good to me." His new cell phone buzzed.

Rock looked up at Dr. Sinha. "My daughter Dawn is heading for the elevators. She's brought her son Jayson, Elijah's cousin and my sister Lucile. Will that be too many for his room?"

Keta Sinah shook her head smiling. "That's just fine, you need the company and so does Elijah. "I'll see you in about two hours."

The doctor was gone less than three minutes when Aunt Lucile swept through the door of Elijah's hospital room. A typical Calgary wind had loosened wisps of hair from her usual pin neat braided bun.

As usual she peppered her weary and worried brother with questions. "Do they need to do surgery? How extensive? Will they cut out some of his intestine? What are the risks of infection? How do they contain all, that gunk? What do you want to do about Elijah's birthday?"

Rock stood and greeted his daughter Dawn with a hug then his other grandson Jayson. Still ignoring his sister, he put his arm around Jayson's shoulders.

"I haven't had any lunch yet, how about joining me in the cafeteria for some apple pie and ice cream?"

Grandfather and grandson headed for the door.

"Dad!" Dawn followed her father and son.

"Rock Clearwater, you didn't answer any of my questions." Aunt Lucile was compelled to tag along or remain in the room alone. She decided that her questions could just as easily be answered over pie and coffee.

A line for a second seating of the lunch crowd had formed by the salad bar and hot buffet, but there was no line anywhere near the desserts.

"Dad, you're not setting a good example..."

Rock placed a loving hand on his daughter's shoulder. "Sweetheart sometimes what we really need is pie."

Jayson ran to get his grandfather a tray and the two loaded up. "Besides apples are fruit and ice cream is dairy – right Grandpa?"

Dawn gave in and filled mugs of hot water for tea for each of them.

Aunt Lucile waved from an empty table she had found in a far corner.

With everyone settled, about two bites in – Aunt Lucile once again pressed her brother for Elijah's condition.

"Dr. Sinha will cut just a couple of tiny incisions to," Rock swallowed, "as she explained – *massage* the blockage into smaller segments. Then the medication can be more effective. She's pretty hopeful."

After that, everyone finished their pie and drank their tea in silence.

****

Rushing to gather as much information as possible as fast as possible all RCMP and FBI fact gathering expertise were ordered to send *any* findings no matter how preliminary to Inspector Wheeler and Agent Thane.

By midnight initial lab testing results began to trickle in along with dozens of eye witness interviews conducted by members of both the Canadian and American joint investigative teams.

"Birds?" Wheeler looked at Agent Thane.

They were the only investigators still working in the temporary FBI office set up in the basement of the Ogdenburg police station.

"In the statements from fifty-six pre-explosion eyewitnesses they claim to have seen what looked like a flock of grayish colored birds, resembling seagulls."

"That doesn't describe any known type of rocket to me," Opal rolled her shoulders to work out tense shoulder muscles. "But that *could* describe a type of drone."

"I thought so too. If these stylized bird shapes were drones we don't know where they originated, but the *flock* was first spotted circling over highway 29 on the Canadian side."

"Two couples out in separate sail boats stated the *birds* appeared to split up into two groups just north of Brockville's courthouse with the second group *flying* across the river to Morristown."

"Witnesses next realized the odd shaped birds were no longer visible, but then they heard multiple explosions and saw flames from the upper floor windows of the four public buildings."

Opal was adding data to their evidence board. "Besides the explosions did any of the witnesses remember hearing anything distinctive? Did the *birds* make any bird like sounds?"

Wheeler shook his head. "No not really. Six witness statements mentioned checking the sky then looking at the street and holding out their hands to check for rain drops. Because the sky was overcast it sounded like it was raining."

Agent Thane rested her key board on a stack of early lab findings. "Several drones shaped like a flock of seagulls make a sound like it was raining?"

"Apparently so."

****

Lena Nicolas was released from the Brockville emergency room a full hour before her husband Nicos with the superficial cut on her left arm cleaned and bandaged.

"Excuse please me," she asked the woman at the Information Desk. "My husband Nicos Nicolas also come to here with ambulance."

Lena spoke fluent Greek, but had perfected her broken English style of Greek for cover purposes. She also spoke fluent English, French and Arabic.

"And your name ma'am?" The information clerk asked, checking the computer data base for Nicolas, Nicos.

"So many injured have been brought in for treatment, he may not be in our system yet ma'am."

"Lena, Lena Nicolas." She showed her forged Greek passport to the woman.

"I found him. He's being treated on the second floor in orthopedics."

Lena frowned pretending not to understand.

"Orthopedics - bones ma'am. He may have a broken arm or leg? Just take that elevator there and press the number two button beside the door." She smiled.

Lena nodded.

Outside Mario Vito the third member of the terrorist organizers waited in a van in the parking lot. When a uniformed RCMP Constable knocked on the driver's window, he was prepared.

"Your name and reason for being here sir?"

Mario nodded retrieving his phony Italian passport with a smile. "My friends injured. I wait for them to take home."

The officer checked each page of the passport. "The name of your friends Mr. Vito?"

"Nicos Nicolas, his wife Lena."

The constable handed Mario's passport back to him. "I hope your friends weren't too badly hurt, sir. Drive home safely. Good night."

Mario watched the constable as he continued to check each parked vehicle in the rows behind him.

He spotted Lena and Nicos outside the emergency room doors and flicked his headlights then turned the key in the ignition moving the van under the patient carport.

He opened the side door and his partners climbed in without comment. Nicos' self-inflicted dislocated shoulder was taped.

The small basement apartment they had rented to share was less than six blocks from the attack site. Their elderly landlady had been only too eager to help the recent *Canadian immigrants* settle in.

With three new tenants the widow felt much safer than living alone…

CHAPTER...36

"Elijah. Elijah, wake up son."

The following morning Grandpa Clearwater awoke just after sunrise. He got himself going, shaved and brushed his teeth then returned to Elijah's bed.

He rubbed the back of his grandson's hand. Elijah stirred but didn't open his eyes.

His nurse Catherine came in to remove the empty glucose and saline IV bag. "He isn't going to need his drip now, fortunately."

"I'm sure when he wakes up he'll be hungry." She smiled. Pink cheeks contrasted with her long thick brown hair twisted into a bun high on her head.

"Go easy at first, but you can take him to the cafeteria for some scrambled eggs or soup if he feels up to it. I'll get you a wheelchair."

Then she leaned forward and lowered her voice, her clear brown eyes twinkled with mischief. "Maybe even a bite of cupcake for his birthday?"

Catherine took Elijah's temperature and blood pressure then finished unhooking several cords. She studied her patient's devoted grandfather, concerned. "Mr. Clearwater, how are you doing?"

Rock shook his head. "You'd think I'd be used to this by now. But for some reason this time his condition felt more urgent."

"I know. We feel helpless too sometimes." She tossed the empty IV bag into the designated trash bin then pushed the IV pole with one hand carrying the cords with the other out into the hall.

Rock Clearwater thought of his ancestors. They had been farmers as he was and hunters, warriors, scouts and ranchers.

But more than anything, living close to *Mother Earth*, he as much as any other member of Canada's First Nations people, understood the cycle of life.

They understood that life offered the 'easy' and the 'not-so-easy' and understood at an even deeper level that the 'not-so-easy' was just as much of a *gift* as the 'easy'.

He tried to remember that *truth* as he let tension and worry of the last three days dissolve on the wings of his Hawk-guide. This too had been another life-test.

Elijah opened his eyes. "Hi Grandpa. I'm starving, did you sneak in any of your cornbread?"

He gave his grandson a long hug. "How do you feel?" Then Grandpa sat back in the hospital recliner.

"A little dizzy, but my cramps are gone. Guess the enema and the medicine worked."

"Not quite. Lift your sheet and gown then take a peek at your belly."

"Oh." Elijah's voice came from under the lifted sheet. "What did Dr. Sinha do?"

"Let's just say you got an unusual *massage* unique only to people with cystic fibrosis. Happy Birthday." Grandpa grinned finally feeling relaxed again.

Elijah let his sheet drop. "Not funny. I get three, one centimeter incisions? Who gets that for their birthday?"

"Well besides those cool band-aids taped over your stitches, your Aunt Dawn and I decided that you and Jayson can write for your learner's driving permits."

"Yes!" He sat up then winced and fell back. "Ouch!"

"Would you rather wait for breakfast here or try for the cafeteria?"

"I'd like to try for the cafeteria. When can I go home?"

Grandpa Clearwater pressed for the nurse and as if reading their minds, Catherine appeared with a wheelchair. "Your *limo* sir," she giggled. "But first I need to check your stitches."

"Looking good Master Elijah. Take my arm," she helped him sit. "I'll drive this chair. I'm heading for the cafeteria anyway."

With Elijah settled at a small round table, Catherine offered to help Rock Clearwater gather food and beverages.

"What would you like Elijah?"

He spotted a thick waffle on the plate of another patient one table over. "Four of those!"

His nurse made a face. "That's a little too ambitious for your digestive system at the moment. How about half a grapefruit and some scrambled eggs?"

"Rats!"

****

A joint team of RCMP and FBI investigators, forensic and explosive experts gathered around a crowded conference table, in the borrowed basement office.

Neither the Ogdensburg sheriff nor any state police were present. The special terrorist investigation unit was deliberately kept to a minimum number of experts for maximum security.

It was just after sunrise, and none of the seasoned officers had had any more than four hours of sleep.

Agent Thane was back at the evidence board using her handheld pad to input that day's date with new data.

"As yet no group has claimed responsibility for the devastation of yesterday." She sipped a double cappuccino from a tall travel mug.

"Of the fifty-six eyewitness statements collected, so far, Inspector Wheeler and I have six couples claiming they saw several grayish colored birds that looked like large seagulls near all four buildings."

Opal took another gulp of her coffee. "We're not sure yet if there is a connection or what the significance might be, but several people besides the couples who saw the birds claim they thought it was raining. They heard what sounded like rain, but the streets were dry."

"We both agreed that the possibility of an explosive device delivered by a GPS guided drone may be more likely than a type of small arms missile. The sound of rain may be connected to the mechanics of what propelled the disguised drones, if that's what we're dealing with."

She looked at her team's FBI explosives expert seated at the far end of the table, chewing his way through a large cranberry scone. "Roger? Anything yet, or are the buildings still too hot?"

He swallowed and took a sip of black coffee laced with three sugars. Roger looked to Allen his RCMP counterpart and waved for him to give the report.

"The explosions may very well have been delivered by some type of drone, we couldn't tell because everything eighty feet from impact was almost vaporized. And you're not gonna like what we suspect we're dealing with."

"After midnight we were able to tramp around in several spots wearing asbestos boots. Nearly everything around the outer edges was still super warm but we found *hot-spots* that mean more than only fire."

"We immediately put up the wide orange tape and all firefighters, ambulance personnel and volunteers were sent to be tested for possible radiation poisoning."

Opal Thane stopped in mid bite with icing from her cinnamon roll on one side of her mouth.

Eric Wheeler felt sick. He knew exactly what the explosives expert had just told them. "You're saying that whatever went through the windows of each building had nuclear explosive devices, correct?"

"Correct. Small, but deadly."

****

At dawn all three of the elderly widow's tenants had quietly departed their temporary apartment through a side door.

Their rent had been paid for six months in advance. In the four weeks they lived in the basement suite, they came and went without question claiming to have found simple, unskilled jobs that required working odd hours.

Deliberately acquiring minor injuries allowed Lena and Nicos inside the hospital emergency to listen to medical staff and to be interviewed by police. In turn they could ask questions that wouldn't arouse suspicion. But they hadn't learned as much as they had hoped, it was too soon in the investigation.

However the terrorists suspected that soon enough authorities would discover the residue of radiation and then they'd certainly pay attention to any of their future demands.

And their mission would remain several steps ahead of any authorities in all targeted locations. On-the-heels of their first attack in Brockville and Morristown their next assault would make an even greater impact.

Nicos, Lena and Mario left Brockville driving east toward the town of Verdun, five miles south of Montreal. The 127 miles took two hours putting them at their second temporary apartment on the Rue Dupuis in time for morning prayers.

Then some much needed rest – for the night ahead would be a busy one, this time after dark…

CHAPTER...37

Simultaneously at 11PM Eastern Time multiple explosions were targeted to the upper floor libraries of Ecole Parkdale Elementary in Montreal, Quebec and Channing Elementary in Boston, Massachusetts.

In Boston a man had been walking his dog a block from the explosion site. Later he stated to local police that he saw what looked to him like a flock of sea gulls, but street lights made accurate identification difficult. And just before he saw the birds, he thought it was starting to rain because above him that's what is sounded like to him.

At once RCMP Inspector Wheeler was roused from an exhaustive sleep by his emergency cell phone. In turn he called FBI Agent Thane.

Immediately Wheeler was on a military helicopter with half of his team to Montreal, while Thane with her expertise support, headed to Boston.

Immediate orders went out to all Montreal and Boston firefighters to remain a minimum of 600 yards away from the burning schools.

Firefighters were hindered using only high powered, long distance hoses. They complied with the distance restrictions until it could be determined if these fires were also ignited by a mini nuclear explosion.

Eric Wheeler's helicopter landed at the outer edge of the school's playground. Montreal police were already placing cement barricades creating a wider perimeter around the severely damaged school in case of radiation contamination.

The building was still smoldering and the night darkness made any entry into the lower floors too dangerous due to structural damage, but Allen was out of the helicopter already wearing his protective clothing.

And the closer he got to the darkened seventy year-old school illuminated only by the headlights of fire and rescue trucks - the higher the radioactive reading went.

"Inspector Wheeler," Allen was on his cell phone, walking the perimeter and watching the readings change. "The radiation levels are even higher here than they were in Brockville or Morristown. We need to evacuate everyone for a full two blocks around this school, sir."

"If you recommend it – that's what we'll do, at once." When Eric turned around a woman and the Mayor of Montreal stood right behind him.

Eric recognized the mayor, but not the woman with him. "I'm Inspector Eric Wheeler. Please excuse me for a moment ma'am."

"Mayor this is urgent. First, I need to arrange for the immediate evacuation of homes, and apartments for two blocks around this school."

"My explosives expert has detected a radiation level that is unsafe from only cement barricades set where they are now. He began to move by them. "Then, I can bring you up to date on my last twenty-four hours."

Mayor Charles Ponce and Ecole Parkside Principal Yvonne Blanc watched the inspector rush toward a car marked with a fire captain's crest.

As he ran across the grass, a short procession of three black SUVs stopped parallel to the helicopter.

The mayor and the principal were soon joined by the RCMP Commissioner Quinn Fuller and Zacharie Platt the Premier of Quebec.

With the evacuation underway, Inspector Wheeler called Agent Thane. "It's a mess here Opal. We got an elementary school with radiation readings higher than any of the buildings that were attacked yesterday. What d'you have?"

"I'm at an elementary school too. What's that about? Anyway, Roger got high readings here as well before he was even close. We've had to evacuate all adjacent buildings for a full two block perimeter around the school grounds."

Wheeler thought out loud with his phone line still open. "There must be some connection to these two schools."

Opal attempted to find a connection. "Channing Elementary is an old school, like eighty or ninety years. Where's your school?"

"Ecole Parkdale's in Ville Saint Laurent, Montreal – it's age is about seventy."

He stopped for a moment. "Okay we have two old elementary schools attacked after dark, thankfully. Or was that the point? Is the message in the fact that two historic schools normally filled with young children, were attacked simultaneously?"

"There's a pattern of sorts emerging, I think." This time Opal was theorizing aloud.

"Courthouse and city hall in Canadian Brockville attacked across the river from courthouse and town hall in American Morristown at exactly the same time, 11AM. Now we have a Canadian elementary school in Montreal attacked at the same time as an American elementary school in Boston, this time 11PM."

"If it's the same terrorist group, and we have every reason to believe it is and the delivery method was the same, some type of missiles or drones – the GPS system is pretty sophisticated. I just looked up the distance between Montreal and Boston and its 307 miles."

Crowded between two of the black SVUs, Inspector Wheeler brought the mayor, the principal, the commissioner and the premier current with the investigation.

"There are more details behind the simple news headlines of the explosions and fire in Brockville and Morristown."

"The official press release to the media was that it was too soon to determine a cause for the explosions and resulting fires. We didn't want the media to create a major panic that generated speculation, but RCMP experts and FBI experts detected low level radiation within a few hours."

"And unfortunately the readings appear to be higher this time. I spoke with FBI Agent Opal Thane only minutes ago and her site is also an elementary school, with radiation readings that have forced them to evacuate further back for safety precautions."

RCMP Commissioner Fuller had developed a knot in his gut. "You believe it's the work of the same terrorists who sent some type of explosive carrying drones, into both courthouses and city halls?" He believed this was going to get far worse, with the perpetrators staying well ahead of investigators.

Inspector Wheeler nodded.

****

"Elijah, listen to this." Grandpa Clearwater spread the front page of the Calgary Herald out on the kitchen table.

"There's been some sort of fire caused by an undetermined explosion on both the Canadian and US side in the resort towns of Brockville and Morristown on the St. Laurence River."

"Our old friend Staff Sergeant Wheeler was quoted, though he's now an Inspector. Good for him."

Elijah looked up from his breakfast bowl of sliced fresh fruit. "Is there a picture?"

"Of Eric Wheeler? No, just a small map of that section of the river with dots showing the location of Brockville and Morristown."

The kitchen door was open to a warm Alberta morning sun. Elijah was relieved to be home again and feeling his energy returning.

All the windows of their 'A' frame log cabin faced east for sunrises or west for sunsets. Light flooded into Elijah's upper bedroom loft and filled the main floor rooms even on cloudy days.

He could hear the chickens clucking and chicks chirping in their enclosure outside and the new baby pigs squealing as they played in their pens beyond the chicken coop.

Robins returning from their winter in the south sang a shrill song hidden in the branches of tall evergreens that grew around the house like protective sentries.

"How many chicks did we get this year?" Elijah really didn't care he just liked to play with the new hatchlings.

"Your Uncle River counted fifty in the warming shed. And so far the piglets number almost the same. Those five young sows we bought two years ago are productive mothers. They've had anywhere from eight to ten each. You can't walk into the pig barn without stepping very carefully."

"Where do ya hav'ta step carefully?" The screen door opened and Elijah's cousin Jayson walked in. He kicked off his boots then slid across to the pine table on the wood floor wearing his thick woolen socks.

"Not the doo-doo in your pastures from your dairy cows, dirt-ball."

Elijah thumped his cousin on the shoulder as Jayson sat in the chair beside him. "We have a bumper crop of new baby pigs."

"Cool."

"Tea Jason?"

"Yeah, what's *the-pig-king* here drinking?" He shouldered Elijah back.

"Cinnamon and raspberry." Rock Clearwater set the kettle back on the wood stove to reheat water for herbal tea.

"Sounds good Grandpa."

"I got the morning off and rode over on Storm," Jayson turned to Elijah. "Do ya feel like goin for a short ride, or is it too soon?"

"I been home almost two days and feel great." Elijah looked at his grandfather.

"Let me call Dr. Sinha first." The kettle whistled. He poured boiling water to steep Jayson's tea then called the doctor's direct hospital line.

"I hope we can go. There's a great fishing spot that my dad and Joseph found only a mile east of where we've been going all this time."

"The stream turns into a short water fall that drops into a pretty deep pond and the fish are so thick you can practically scoop'em out with your bare hands. If it doesn't freeze in the winter that's gonna be an even better bonus."

Grandpa Clearwater reappeared through the wide doorway from the front room. "Your doctor wants assurances that you'll not be jarring your insides. You can ride 'only' if your horse walks and just for no longer than forty minutes. Otherwise wait another three days."

"Rats!" Jayson swallowed a large gulp of his tea. "It's pretty hilly between here and the fishing spot I wanted to show Elijah."

"Well," Grandpa poured himself another mug of coffee. "You still have the morning off from chores and in a few days we can all take a ride to the new fishing spot."

Outside the cousins checked out the baby chicks then the baby pigs before heading down to the corral.

Grandpa Clearwater's farm had been a safe calm place to grow up. Elijah had been orphaned since he was three after both his parents died in a car accident. Then his grandmother had died two years later when Elijah was five.

Elijah didn't remember his parents or his grandmother, but he knew Grandpa Clearwater still missed his wife and mourned for his son and daughter-in-law.

Growing up with his grandfather had not been as lonely as other kids with siblings believed.

The turkey farm of his grandfather's sister, Great Aunt Lucille was three miles east. And the dairy farm of his grandfather's daughter Aunt Dawn and Uncle River was two miles south. His cousin and best friend Jayson was the third of six first cousins all born close to Elijah's age.

It was rare that Jayson got to leave his house without taking a younger sibling with him and even rarer that he didn't need to stay home for chores on a Saturday morning.

Jayson had tied his rust colored quarter horse Storm to an upper fence rail.

"You coulda just let him in with Arrow and Dart."

"I know, but I thought we might be riding out again soon." Jayson untied his horse and followed Elijah into the corral.

The horse barn and exercise corral was set on the northwest side of the house midway down the long narrow driveway that led to the main county road.

Elijah's grey colored gelding Arrow and Grandpa's black mare Dart, shared the barn with a small tractor and trailer, a small mower, other farming supplies and stored feed.

Surrounded on two sides by tall poplar and more evergreens, the wind swayed close growing trees back and forth. The trunks made a rubbing sound that echoed above their heads.

Jayson unsaddled Storm then began to brush his mane and back.

Elijah scooped oats for all three horses then started brushing Arrow. "Gosh, it's such a perfect morning Jayson. Maybe we could just ride down to the meadow…"

'*NO.*'

"What?" Elijah looked at his cousin.

"What, what?" Jayson frowned. "I heard you."

"But you said no"

"No I didn't, I didn't say anything."

Elijah looked at Arrow and wondered. From where had he heard the distinctive but clearly direct – *no*? Then instinctively *Crow Child* knew…

CHAPTER...38

Simultaneously at 11AM Eastern Time each of the upper floor windows in each of the historic public libraries in eight separate capital cities were pierced, followed immediately by a high pitched sizzle then sixteen fiery explosions.

News of a third series of multiple explosions produced a heightened level of demoralizing distress among the special joint RCMP and FBI investigative unit.

The RCMP office in Fredricton, New Brunswick had been the first to report, but by only two minutes. Within eight more minutes everyone in the joint investigative unit had heard from, Halifax, Nova Scotia and Charlottetown, Prince Edward Island, and St. John's Newfoundland followed by – Augusta, Maine and Montpelier, Vermont, and Concord, New Hampshire and Hartford, Connecticut.

The attack on this larger scale of target had caused even more deaths and hundreds more injuries. But this time there was no radiation readings.

The media could no longer be put off.

Every form of journalist from radio to print to network and web news had begun to put the pieces of events of the last forty-eight hours together and ran all-out with a major *terrorist invasion*.

The Canadian Prime Minister and Parliament joined with the U.S. President and Congress for an immediate call for military action. But against whom?

Leaders in France, Britain, Poland, Portugal and the rest of Europe called for a special emergency session of the UN to address what they feared could very easily become a synchronized series of multi-country attacks.

Canadian military assisted with rescuing trapped and injured people and guarding other library perimeters in the Maritime Provinces - while the U.S. military did the same in each of America's New England States.

Inspector Wheeler and Agent Thane were called to the Pentagon for an emergency meeting with the Canadian Deputy of Defense, the US Secretary of Defense and the CIA Director.

Besides the Chairman of the Joint Chiefs three key people invited to the Pentagon sat at one end of a twenty foot mahogany table surrounded by dark green leather chairs. The meeting room had no windows, no pictures, and no other furniture.

"It's clear," the CIA Director began, "that North America is under attack - again."

"We realize it's only been forty-eight hours since Montreal and Boston and another twenty-four before that since Brockville and Morristown, but what is known for sure? Do you have any theories, any hunches, speculation, guesses - anything?

Agent Thane began. "We know for sure that each of the first two attacks, were generated by a small nuclear explosion, via some type of miniaturized missile or drone."

"Interviewed witnesses from the first and second attack areas stated they saw what looked like a flock of large birds resembling seagulls. And before they saw the birds there was a familiar sound, but unusual, like it was raining."

"To accomplish each attack with the timing and precision required took an amazing GPS launch sophistication we haven't seen before."

"We don't know what the drones or missiles were made of, because everything around the explosion cores were almost vaporized. They could be plastic or a light metal, or glass, anything really."

"We don't know who to blame yet because no known terrorist group has claimed responsibility."

"After the first attack Inspector Wheeler thought we should keep what we discovered in Brockville and Morristown as quiet as possible, and I agreed. Keeping the media and the rest of the public only partially informed gave us greater uninterrupted time to collect witness reports and better forensic data."

"However while we were still assembling and sorting what we'd gathered the terrorists struck a second time. Now with this third and much broader attack – we're playing an unstable game of catch-up." Opal stopped to sip some water, nodding to Inspector Wheeler.

Eric stood. "For some reason and we're certainly grateful, but for this third attack no nuclear components were used on the targets in the Maritime Provinces or the U.S. New England States."

"However, we still need to source the nuclear components used for the delivery system, in the first two attacks regardless of whether its drones or small disguised missiles. From where did the nuclear devices originate and who bought them?"

"It's logical to speculate the drones or missiles were launched from within a few miles of their targets. It's also logical to speculate that the delivery system has been assembled at a location or locations on both Canadian and or American soil."

"But as much as this situation has escalated, and our joint unit could use additional intelligence–both Agent Thane and I believe we'll have a better chance of hunting individuals down quicker, if our original unit remains the only funnel through which all information flows."

The CIA Director nodded. "I agree with that. Your evaluation and turn-around-time will be faster with staff and departments from two countries reporting only to each of you. But from now on you'll be reporting to your RCMP Commissioner, Secretary of Defense and me directly."

"So if the emerging pattern of morning, then evening then morning stays true, do the two of you believe there could be another attack somewhere along the Canadian or U.S. border at 11PM tonight?"

They both nodded.

Inspector Wheeler checked his watch. "It's 1PM here now so that's ten hours. In the meantime, we assigned people in our unit to look for nuclear transactions no matter how insignificant going back at least a year or more if need be."

"We have other unit members combing through Canadian immigration records for the last eighteen months, flagging passports from countries other than Middle Eastern. Our theory was that terrorists travelling on fake or stolen passports arrive with less scrutiny from neighboring Mediterranean countries like Greece, Italy, Portugal or Spain."

"As for the next attack location, we believe it will be further south along the U.S. coast. The first three followed the Saint Laurence River moving further east with each attack."

Agent Thane stood. "I believe it makes sense for them to turn their attention and ours due south of Boston to New York and DC?"

The Deputy of Defense asked, "And the likely targets?"

Opal Thane spoke again. "Since they seem to like the number eleven, we've selected eleven high value targets in Manhattan and along Pennsylvania Avenue."

****

Elijah was part way through his second home-school year. Grandpa was relieved by Elijah's reduced hospital trips for bronchitis and intestinal blocks – that is until the latest scare.

After Jayson left to return home Elijah was supposed to rest between catching up on his missed week of school assignments. But every time he tried to concentrate his mind drifted...

Once again Crow Child sensed a malicious energy gaining more and more power.

His white light rose above the trees, the foothills and mountain peaks then several thousand feet above the clouds.

Crow Child understood the looming threat and that it had only just begun...

Elijah lifted his head from the kitchen table with a jerk – disturbing visions with flocks of giant grey birds were still vivid.

None of the visions made sense and either did struggling with his homework. Elijah gave up on his history essay and left the kitchen table.

When the kitchen phone rang Elijah was sitting on the raised fireplace hearth. He'd been lost in thought about the strange visions while staring out across the farm fields that surrounded the southern edge of the town of Canmore.

It was 11:23AM in Alberta, Canada and 1:23PM in DC, United States.

Grandpa came through the back door carrying a small bucket of freshly gathered eggs and answered the phone on the third ring.

"Sergeant, oh I mean Inspector. Good to hear from you again. Yes it has been. Oh we're fine. Elijah had a bit of a close call, but he's back home and recovering well."

"Yes, yes I did. I read about the explosions and fires in Brockville and Morristown in the Calgary Herald. I read the article to Elijah too. I'm homeschooling him this year as well."

"You're on your way? I don't understand, on your way where, here?" Grandpa set the bucket down on their kitchen table, beside the scattered pile of Elijah's history research for his homework.

Elijah had remained sitting on the fireplace hearth, but started paying closer attention to his grandfather's end of the phone conversation.

Rock walked slowly toward his grandson "I suppose so. Where did you want to meet that won't attract attention? Your jet will be landing about the time we reach the Northeast side of Calgary."

Elijah stood moving closer to his grandfather. He remembered waking from his vivid vision of odd shaped birds. He wondered if the Brockville and Morristown explosions were connected to what he 'saw' – then knew immediately that they were.

"That's okay. We'll listen Inspector, but that doesn't mean Elijah can help. The incident last year placed my grandson at risk – high risk." Grandpa waited. "Okay.

"There's a Tim Horton's in the Cove Meadow Shopping Centre off Deerfoot Trail and Country Hills Blvd." Then he set the cordless phone in its charger.

"There have been two more incidents since the news article I read to you. The details haven't hit all mainstream media yet, but major news networks are speculating. Apparently the east coast of Canada and the US are under a systematic, surgical terrorist attack."

"Inspector Wheeler will meet us at the Tim Horton's in the Cove Meadow Shopping Centre. He was already airborne in a military jet when he called."

"He might even beat us to the café." Grandpa returned to the kitchen to rinse the eggs then laid them on a cookie sheet covered by a paper towel.

"How do you feel about this? If you'd rather not meet with Inspector Wheeler, I can go alone and give him your regrets."

"I've been having odd visions Grandpa and I know they're for a reason. *Crow Child* needs to go. I mean, that's why I'm here, right?"

Rock Clearwater gave his grandson a hug. He put the egg filled cookie sheet in their fridge then they took the truck and headed east on Trans Canada Hwy #1 for Calgary.

****

After seven hours of driving from Montreal, Quebec to Philadelphia, Pennsylvania - Nicols, Lena and Mario reached their third temporary basement apartment, just north of Philadelphia in the town of Hazelton.

Mario smiled to himself as he prepared the internet press release written entirely in Arabic.

The strategy had been carefully calculated in meticulous detail since the *murder* of their revered leader Osama. The mission was unfolding as planned.

Creating the Islamic State had been a perfect distraction for western countries to *chase* while Al Qaeda quietly reorganized and prepared for its' ultimate global strike.

Al Qaeda would continue to hit their preprogrammed targets several hours, several days ahead of the tangled global intelligence agencies. No MI-6, no Interpol, no RCMP no CIA or FBI no Israel Masada or any policing authority could stop them.

Democratically elected leaders and their policing powers would continue to be ineffective. And they'd begin to live in terror with complete helplessness as thousands of their citizens died while their honored historical landmarks were destroyed.

And tonight would establish the continuation of Al Qaeda's far reaching, untouchable global-control abilities.

CHAPTER...39

Inspector Eric Wheeler was indeed sitting at a table inside the Tim Horton café when Grandpa Clearwater and Elijah arrived.

"Hey, how'd you do that? Grandpa said you might beat us here." Elijah held out his hand to the RCMP officer with whom he'd made such an impression only five months before.

Eric's drawn expression mixed with an alert intensity was not lost on either Elijah or his grandfather as they took chairs on the opposite side of the table.

Grandpa extended his hand. "At the risk of sounding like my sister, you don't look like you've slept in days, Inspector."

"That's likely because I haven't. I'm presently MIA from this latest mission only because I understand how critical it is to protect the identity of *Crow Child*."

The inspector opened a folder. He slid copies of the Associated Press news features of each attack, across the table to Rock and Elijah. "And this mission needs *Crow Child*."

"What can I get you, while you read my notes on these articles?"

"I'll have a coffee with cream. Elijah has his saltwater but he can also have a bran muffin. Thank you."

"Grandpa! Not even one doughnut?"

Wheeler returned in two minutes carrying a tray with a bran muffin and small box of Tim-bits. The 'bits' were iced doughnut holes for which the franchise was nationally known.

Eric's hand shook when he lifted his coffee mug to drink. "We're running completely blind on this with only weak guesses and hastily gathered assumptions. This systematic series of attacks caught every global agency by surprise."

"There was no communications through typical tech channels and no intelligence from any agents inserted in known neighborhoods or terrorist groups."

"We expect there'll be another bombing attack tonight 11PM Eastern Time," he checked his watch, "about six hours from now. My FBI counterpart believed the next targets would be New York City and the District of Columbia."

"We're organizing major resources in identified, high value areas of New York and DC, hopeful our guess is correct. If not then we can only dread what might happen as with each attack the target significance has escalated."

Grandpa felt a dread of his own. He understood the destiny of *Crow Child*, but was duty-bound to protect Elijah, the grandson.

"What do you expect that *Crow Child* can do, exactly?"

Inspector Wheeler took a long, slow swallow of his coffee and shrugged. "I really have no definite idea."

"In St. Louis *Crow Child* seemed to pick up on the unseen and the unknown and that's what we desperately need with this. We can't stop what we can't 'see' and don't 'know'. *After* - an attack makes all of us useless."

Elijah slid the papers back to Inspector Wheeler. "What else is there? What's not in the news articles?"

Wheeler hesitated. "Radiation. Each explosion was generated by a small nuclear blast. Not enough to spread much farther than a city block perimeter, but enough to send a chilling message. The terrorist group, as yet unidentified, appears to have some nuclear means."

Grandpa Clearwater cringed internally knowing the best he could do was guide Elijah's decision, but not interfere with *Crow Child*'s path.

"If you propose to return to New York and DC with Elijah how will you explain his presence?"

"My cover story is that Elijah's my nephew and I'm his legal guardian. It will explain why he may be seen around me, but not seen actively doing anything. I expect to keep that protected."

Elijah had gone quiet while *Crow Child* went to the Universe for greater insight. His head was slightly bent and his eyes were toward the floor. "New York City and Washington DC are not in danger tonight."

Instantly all attention was riveted on the youth.

Elijah's head came up. "Philadelphia is the next target. There are eleven major historical objectives in Philadelphia. There are no missiles, there are only drones and they receive a signal from a specific satellite."

Inspector Wheeler was silent for a second. "If three or four guided drones are programmed to hit eleven locations, that's a potential thirty to forty, or more separate impacts, in multiple locations. How do we stop something like that, especially if they're armed with the same nuclear capability?"

Crow Child was quiet again for a full minute then Elijah looked over at his grandfather and Eric Wheeler. "There's a small satellite hidden in a parallel orbit behind a French communications satellite. If the smaller satellite can be taken down then all the drones should drop from the sky harmless."

"At a preprogrammed time the satellite sends coded GPS messages to each drone. If *Black Crow* can interrupt the signal, that would sure jolt the terrorists, majorly."

Inspector Wheeler was stunned. "How did a primitive terrorist group get the capability to orbit their own satellite as well as nuclear capability?"

"They paid for it." *Crow Child* responded. "Watch North Korea more closely. They have aligned with false allies of Western democracies."

"And the terrorist group responsible is not primitive, it's Al Qaeda. Al Qaeda is well funded and well connected and protected by several countries governed by leaders who hope to gain a global advantage with the fall of Western Europe, and North America."

The air around them suddenly felt cold…

****

As they had with each of their previous attacks, Mario, Lena and Nicos positioned themselves in a key location to witness their success.

Photos of the two earlier attacks were already posted on the internet, striking the desired level of fear in the minds of all European and western governments.

Mario wanted to shout to the clouds in the sky, he was so happy. After twenty years of planning, their second time had finally arrived.

Soon unquestionable control would be in Al Qaeda hands. Those who did not follow the Koran would live a life of labor and servitude. All women would obey them and the Al Qaeda elite would prosper beyond measure.

Mario had chosen Independence Hall. The office window of his mock business looked down the length of an alley that gave him a perfect line of sight.

Lena had chosen City Hall and Nicos set himself up to watch the Franklin Institute. All they had to do was wait another three hours.

****

When Inspector Wheeler's plane landed at Saratoga Springs Naval Base, thirty-five miles north of Albany, Elijah did not descend the steps with the RCMP investigator.

Without questioning his orders the pilot, refueled then filed a new flight plan with coordinates for the airport at Reading, Pennsylvania - taking a single passenger.

In a safe room in a lower level at the naval base, Eric met with Agent Thane who had coordinated agencies in place to protect the identified New York targets.

Inspector Wheeler checked on the matching progress of operations in DC, but said nothing of *his* secret plan. He listened while Opal described the rush to complete final details in both cities.

To keep *Crow Child*'s identity protected, Grandpa Clearwater had suggested that the RCMP officer not alter any defensive plans for New York or the American capital.

"This may be difficult, but I think we need to trust that *Black Crow*'s distinctive abilities can protect Philadelphia."

"If *Black Crow* is there alone then what needs to be done can be done without hundreds of investigators from two major countries getting in the way."

CHAPTER...40

The covert, British four seat jet lifted straight up then shot south into the darkened night sky as the clock ticked over to seventy-three minutes before the expected fourth assault.

The military jet dissolved 235 miles of highway below them setting pilot and passenger back on the ground and parked in only sixteen minutes.

With fifty-eight minutes to the expected impact of eleven separate targets, Elijah wasn't entirely sure how *Crow Child* was to move across 63 miles from Reading to Philadelphia.

Immediately feeling the need to be alone Elijah hurried to the nearest men's lavatory and closed the door of the first stall. 'I need to be in Philadelphia,' he thought closing his eyes in prayer.

When he felt a slight wisp of air pass by his cheeks Elijah opened his eyes. He was standing on a slight rise.

Just below him was a baseball diamond. Further from the baseball diamond grew a stand of mature maple trees with the lit city skyline rising beyond.

Elijah stood for several seconds checking slowly and carefully around. His newly acquired form of transport had shaken even him.

Crow Child settled his mind.

He searched in the space between Earth and its' moon for the distinctive pulse he knew the hidden satellite would send just prior to transmitting the distinctive signal to the drones.

Every satellite cycled Earth at specific times. And he knew that to locate the key signal, at the exact time, it was a necessity for the terrorist satellite to be directly above the city of Philadelphia.

He waited patiently while another twenty-eight minutes elapsed.

The bells of St Mark's, chimed half past the hour, interrupting his concentration.

With the last chime silent, *Crow Child* refocused, looking up into a starless night sky.

A Russian satellite crossed over the city at twenty-three minutes to eleven.

A Chinese satellite followed at sixteen minutes to eleven.

A Canadian satellite past at nine minutes to eleven.

At two minutes to eleven, *Crow Child* felt a dual signal approaching from, the west.

In a rush of energy now familiar Crow Child rose.

His entire being expanded.

A flash of white fire light surrounded Crow Child transforming his physical form to that of an enormous black crow with a wingspan that surpassed the height of the park's mature trees.

Black Crow's vast form filled the open space.

And with one sweeping flurry Black Crow stepped into the air, rising higher and higher over the meadow of Fairmount Park below him with his light...

Spreading out just above the entire city of Philadelphia a protective shield of Black Crow's dense light blocked forty-six deadly radioactive drones from their eleven appointed targets.

The reversed signals overloaded the small satellite, disabling it.

From the ground - those still at restaurants or walking their dogs or making their way home - saw the night sky over the city appear as if all visible outdoor lights had had a power surge causing the sky to glow.

And then almost as quickly, the white sky that caused minor curiosity became less so with all night lights back to normal power.

Three homeless men and a stray dog had been the only witness to *Black Crow*'s appearance. The dog ran to hide under a nearby shrub, whimpering softly. The three men rushed away from their night camp by a park bench, vowing never to drink anything with alcohol again.

There were no explosions in Philadelphia.

There were no explosions in New York City or DC.

Black Crow's light diminished as did the great bird's presence.

Crow Child emerged from the center of a stand of sixty foot maples, into a clearing between the trees and second base. He had just enough energy to return to the jet plane hangar by the same means he'd arrived.

****

Nicos, Lena and Mario were appalled by the failure of their fourth planned assault.

Dismayed, they were troubled by the sudden brighter night sky over the city and worried it was linked to the interference of their armed drones.

Trying not to consider what might have happened they wondered if Western authorities managed to guess Philadelphia was the fourth target then used a new technology their secret mole hadn't known of?

Soon becoming alarmed they knew they needed to find out exactly what went wrong with the fourth scheduled assault and find out fast - before they launched the next planned attack.

Mario's cell phone rang breaking the first rule of each mission – no direct communication with each other for a full two hours after an event.

"Do we look for our birds?" Nicos disguised his voice, speaking in French.

Mario responded in Spanish. "No. We move on immediately and meet at our fourth apartment."

****

Agent Opal Thane had remained in New York to oversee the identified possible targets. At ten minutes after eleven, she was on the phone to Wheeler.

Inspector Eric Wheeler had flown on to DC to coordinate with three other agencies protecting the nation's capital.

At 11:10PM, the Director of Homeland Security, the President's Secret Service, Capitol Hill Police, the FBI and RCMP waited in a secure office in the Pentagon wondering if Opal Thane had guessed wrong.

If she had - with the passing of each second they expected to hear dreadful news from some other part of the country or the world.

Eric Wheeler was just as worried about his secret weapon. Where were young Elijah Clearwater and the neutralized nuclear drones?

"Yeah, Wheeler here."

"Inspector – nothing happened at any of our identified targets in New York, not even drunks in fender benders."

"Nothing happened in DC either, Opal."

Eric still wasn't sure how he was going to explain Philadelphia and the miracle that deactivated several dozen deadly weapons without incident.

"We've heard nothing from MI6, Interpol, Russia's-Kirov, Australia's-AFP no one."

"I'm concerned we should remain in place until midnight." Opal urged. "I fear we made a huge error. What if the terrorists expected us to respond and they've pushed their plan back an hour or more waiting after we pull out?"

Eric checked his watch. "You might as well stay a little longer. It'll be midnight in thirty-five minutes. We're in a command trailer in the Visitor Center parking lot. Homeland hasn't removed any people in DC yet."

After ending the cell call – Wheeler realized he had a perfect excuse to call the FBI office in Philadelphia.

"Agent Meyers."

"Good evening Agent Meyers. Inspector Eric Wheeler, RCMP with Joint Terrorist Task Team, calling from DC."

"I read the classified memo, Inspector. What can I do for you, it's late and I hope I'm done in twenty minutes."

"We've had an unexpected run of good luck in New York and DC however it may very well only be quiet-before-the-storm."

"So I understand. And you're calling about Philadelphia, I presume?" Rachel Meyers smiled to herself.

"Since there's no panic in your voice – my guess is all's well in Pennsylvania." Eric felt like he was back in high school, awkwardly asking for a date.

"Yes. Not a thing out of place. We had a slight power surge for about eight seconds around eleven, but Metropolitan Edison hasn't reported any other problems and all our lights are still on."

Eric was relieved. "Sounds good, I'll report that to everyone here. Some of us were concerned we may have guessed at the wrong cities."

To himself he thought, 'The terrorists *had* struck Philadelphia or tried to - and - they had been blocked.'

With the call ended, Eric's attention returned to Elijah. 'Where was he?'

Anxious he called the landline phone number for the hangar in Reading where the British MI6 plane was stored out of sight.

"We were wonderin if you'd ever come fer yur nephew?" The British pilot teased. "Should we let'im sleep on the sofa by er'Majesty's plane?"

Inspector Wheeler felt grateful for the pilot's humor. "Sorry he's still there. I intended to have Elijah picked up by now. Listen, I'll call the airport hotel. If you could take him there, I'll pick him up myself in the morning."

"Sure thing."

"If he's close by I need to talk to him."

"Hi *Uncle* Eric."

Wheeler smiled at his end of the call remembering how they met five months before. "Guess we both had a busy night, huh?"

Elijah had a violent coughing spell. "Yeah, kinda."

Eric didn't like how congested Elijah sounded. "I'll get you back home just as fast as I can, Elijah. Sounds like you need time with your vest."

"Don't tell Grandpa, he'll be a cranky bear."

"I'll book you a room at the airport hotel for tonight. Get something to eat, drink lots of water and get lots of sleep."

CHAPTER...41

By 5AM in every time zone all over the world *Wikileaks* had translated and posted Mario's terrifying press-release from Arabic to English, and five other languages.

> Our might can strike you down anywhere, anytime and You shall be defenseless to stop Us. Our selected targets will begin to remove all of Your history and all of Your capitals and all of Your sources of wealth, food and shelter. Soon every false establishment You have put in place since the unprovoked assault of the Crusades will be destroyed and Your punishment shall be a life of servitude.
> Qaida Kawn Jadid

None of the lead investigators of the joint task team had been to bed – and – none of the investigators had the stamina to field national and international mainstream media calls or questions.

The date on the press release was the day after the attack in Boston and Montreal. Secretly Eric was curious how the writers of this message felt now, after their target of Philadelphia had failed.

"This *Qaida Kawn Jadid* – is new?" The CIA Director looked around. "Has anyone, anywhere heard of this group before?"

Inspector Wheeler shrugged offering a theory. "I'm no linguist but qaida means base or foundation in Arabic. Al Qaeda has always promoted itself as following the foundation of the Koran.

This is only a guess, but Al Qaeda and Qaida Kawn Jadid may be one in the same."

"Kawn means new, and jadid is universe." Came the added input from Agent Adam Zaman, Opal Thane's second in command.

In a space on the meeting room's white board the CIA Director wrote–*New Universe Foundation*. "Well whoever they are, they're here and obviously able to move freely across the Canada, U.S. border."

"Whoever you have," the CIA Director looked directly at Wheeler and Thane, "working on recent immigrants, double that number. We should have research teams hunting twenty-four hours until the people who shouldn't have been let in, are identified."

From a second cell phone Wheeler contacted Grandpa Clearwater to report on his grandson's astonishing contribution. It was 3:32AM in Alberta.

"I haven't had a chance to talk to Elijah in any detail yet Rock, but *Crow Child* saved thousands of lives just over six hours ago."

"I don't know how he managed it, but he accomplished a major undertaking totally out of sight. At this moment, only the terrorists know something messed up their fourth planned attack."

"He's okay though? Before we met with you he'd only been home from the hospital five full days you know."

Eric heard the edge in Rock Clearwater's tone and felt uncomfortable. He decided not to mention his concern with Elijah's cough and avoided answering the question.

"I'll have Elijah call you from the airport hotel in Reading after he's rested completely."

Immediately after he ended the call, Eric arranged for a military helicopter to fly him to the airport hotel in Reading, so he could check on Elijah personally.

At the hotel he rushed across the lobby to the bank of elevators. When he got off the elevator, Eric could hear the youth coughing from the twenty foot distance down the hall even behind the closed door of Elijah's third floor room.

Eric knocked then let himself in with his keycard. "Have you had any sleep?"

Elijah lay propped up with several pillows behind his back on the second bed by the window. Three unopened water bottles were set on the night stand. "Darn cough. I think I got a few hours."

He began to cough again. "And don't worry." More coughing. "I drank a whole bottle before," More coughing, "I went to Philadelphia." Elijah caught his breath, "and then another one at the hangar."

Wheeler didn't like Elijah's color. "We don't have your chest vest so how does your grandfather loosen the gunk in your lungs?"

"He starts at the center of my back," he waited to catch a breath, "using the lower palm of his hand then thumps a little further up and then down, then back to the center again."

"When I was small he'd thump my chest after he finished with my back. But now I can pound my chest while my back is thumped. The stuff I cough up is pretty gross. Do ya have a weak stomach?"

"Nope. I've been to shootings and car accidents."

Forty minutes later, Elijah, could breathe deeply again. He drank more water then fell asleep almost immediately.

Eric contacted Opal Thane. "I'm making arrangements for my nephew for the day. Are we still meeting again at the Pentagon at 1PM?"

"Yes, and by all means get some sleep. I sure need to. See you later."

Wheeler was wide awake and didn't think he could relax enough to sleep.

He turned on the television to an early morning news edition of BBC America with the sound turned down low. The third news segment highlighted an investigation Metropolitan Edison planned to conduct into an eight second power surge in Philadelphia the night before.

Executives for the utility company sighted a concern their computers may have been hacked. He smiled as he fell into a deep sleep. It was still dark outside, twenty minutes before sunrise.

****

Posing as a reporter for USA Today, Lena called the Pentagon, Communications Liaison Office – eager that a new hire might answer the phone. And one did, a recent marine graduate had started his first posting only seven days before.

"Office of Communications Liaison, Marine Private First Class Malcolm Lunn speaking. How may I direct your call?"

With a French accent Lena targeted her prey. "Good morning, Marine Lunn. I am with USA Today, of Montreal office. I am new. This - my first job, only two weeks."

"I am nervous - to be a mistake." She waited hoping she sounded like someone the young man at the other end might want to rescue.

"No need to be nervous ma'am. My job is to be helpful if I am able, if not I'll find someone who can."

The marine's voice pitch and tempo had not softened. Since he remained in full military mode, Lena tried again.

"I am - look for correct person to speak. There were fires with explodings many times five days now."

"I must be accurate, without rumors. Is there someone who may help me with this?"

"Ma'am if you have a pen and paper my orders are to provide all media with the phone number for the Boston office of the FBI and the name of the contact person for all available information. The U.S. FBI is taking the team lead on both of those investigations jointly with Canadian RCMP."

Excited by what she had just learned, she politely asked for the phone number and contact name, but didn't write down either.

Their fourth temporary apartment in Wisconsin had been a perfect find. The owner hadn't needed renters she needed someone to house-sit until the end of April. By then their boat stored in the marina would be ready.

Their landlady left for Arizona soon after showing the young immigrant couple Ashur and his wife Yaida the finished third floor attic. She had checked out the couple, who claimed to be French students. Their new fake passports and driving licenses also had new names.

At the vast dining room table of the mansion on Front Street in Ashland, Wisconsin, Yaida ended her call.

"Our inside source was telling the truth. There is a joint investigating 'team' in place with FBI and RCMP working together."

"No doubt they will search immigration records for anyone who might not be who they said they were. Then they will bring those people in for questioning." She smiled at the two men formerly known as Nicos and Mario.

"Good thing for us then that Lena and Nicos Nicolas did not show up to look after this very impressive house."

All three laughed.

"If authorities manage to trace us from our apartment at the first bombing to our second apartment at the second bombing then to our third apartment - Lena, Nicos and Mario will vanish from there."

The terrorist Sargon formerly known as Mario stopped smiling. "Now, we discuss last night."

"We must determine what happened to forty-six highly tuned and perfectly designed drones."

"They did not malfunction nor did the satellite malfunction. Something happened to all of our *birds*. When I checked several of our target locations there was no trace. They disappeared – completely!"

"We know from morning television news that hundreds of authorities from several policing agencies were anticipating an 'event' in New York City or the capital of DC or both."

"The only mention of Philadelphia on any news channel was of a short electrical power surge that a utility company is investigating."

"I have contacted our FBI insider who assured me that the mention of Philadelphia was avoided at all strategy meetings."

"Where does that leave us?" Ashur frowned. "Do we move forward with our next mission as planned in two nights?"

"No, if the western nations have developed some type of counter means then it might be time to move up the date of our main mission." But Sargon decided he would only communicate with the second FBI insider, who was unknown to their first contact.

****

"Hi Grandpa. I just saw the national weather report. You got a spring snow storm last night. How much snow?" Elijah ate scrambled eggs while talking on Eric Wheeler's second phone.

They had selected a booth as far from other diners as possible in the hotel dining room. Though it was 10:30AM both Eric and Elijah had ordered a breakfast platter.

"Don't talk weather to me! How are you feeling?"

Grandpa Clearwater stood guard by his coffee maker while it dripped water into the glass pot. He hadn't slept well and woke up uncharacteristically late.

"I'm good Grandpa honest. I've had lots of water. Inspector Wheeler nags as much as you about that and he thumps my chest even harder than you do. He's going to get me a vest..."

"Wait a minute! I thought you'd be coming home after you took care of last night's threat?"

The valuable abilities *Crow Child* needed to share were one thing, but the risk to his grandson was something else.

"There's more Grandpa – a lot more. It's real bad."

Elijah handed the phone to Inspector Wheeler. "You need to explain this."

CHAPTER...42

Inspector Wheeler had no choice except to put Elijah on a Canadian military jet and return him to Alberta and his grandfather.

Rock Clearwater's argument was logical. All of the well trained, dedicated and resourceful policing and investigating agencies sharing information around the world – were still baffled.

The attack patterns the RCMP and FBI thought they had identified weren't reliable. Anticipating their next target or targets was pure speculation.

Who they were dealing with was also a guess. If Elijah had been his grandson, Eric would have made the same decision.

It had only been a couple of days, but to Elijah it suddenly seemed as if he hadn't seen his grandfather for months. He thanked the pilot then ran to the precious old man standing by their vintage farm truck. "It's so good to see you."

They hugged then Grandpa held Elijah at arm's length. "Thought you'd be annoyed with me for insisting you return."

"I should stay, but there's far more the authorities don't know than what they do know. So what will happen next and when could be tomorrow or another week or a month from now."

Grandpa looked around. "Let's get home."

The drive from the airport located on the east side of Calgary toward the west through the mid afternoon streets was far more traffic than Rock was accustomed to. When they reached the bedroom community of Bowness Grandpa relaxed.

While his grandfather maneuvered through heavy traffic Elijah had remained silent, thinking. When an unobstructed view of the Alberta Rockies filled the windshield he knew he could have Grandpa's complete attention.

"It's a lot of responsibility, I think."

"Yes it is. And you were pretty busy last fall in St. Louis. Too busy to really give what was happening a great deal of thought until weeks after."

"You had time to reflect since, but really haven't as much as you should. This situation is forcing you to."

"It was different this time Grandpa and I discovered I can do even more stuff. I just wish I wasn't fifteen – I wish I was older. I felt kinda lost."

"The stakes are even higher with *Crow Child*'s third test. And what you're able to do can leave you feeling overwhelmed. Anyone with unusual abilities often feels alone."

Grandpa turned off the highway to the county road that led to their farm. "There could be more attacks or not, but we'll deal with that if it happens."

"However, Elijah Clearwater in harm's way also risks *Crow Child* – and I'm responsible for both."

Arrow and Dart each whinnied then raced around their corral as the truck sped up the driveway. Patches of fresh wet snow contrasted against the bright green of newly budding shrubs and trees.

"Arrow needs a good run, but you're not ready yet until the doctor gives the all clear sign." Grandpa parked the truck by their back deck.

The chicks had almost doubled in size, already starting to shed their hatchling fluff. They chirped nonstop pecking at dirt.

"On the menu tonight," Grandpa handed Elijah his canvas travel bag then lifted out a bag of groceries, "is my world famous mushroom and celery soup."

He winked at his grandson. "There'll be a Caesar salad too as soon as you make one."

****

"With over fifty hours of help from Immigration Canada thirty-two names were flagged."

"Some recent arrivals from Cyprus, Greece, Italy, Turkey, Spain and Portugal fit the profile of people with likely terrorist histories that should have spotted." Blain Sol, FBI's document expert clicked a remote button to change the screen.

"There's that word *profile* again." The U.S. President frowned. "We had an election here in 2016."

"With all due respect sir," RCMP document expert Gor Vladislav rose from his seat, "and to civil rights groups, the media and general public – this is a pet peeve of mine."

"If several banks were robbed by men described to police as having red hair, freckles, green eyes, of medium height, between the ages of twenty-five and thirty-five - who else should police watch for? Who should they stop and question?"

Gor sat down again. No one in the room spoke, until Gor nodded to Blain and he resumed their joint presentation."

Blain smiled nodding in the direction of his RCMP counterpart, "Gor and I studied computer scans of all thirty-two passports. We found twenty-six forgeries and six valid passports. However the six valid documents were issued to people who had assumed the names of people long since deceased."

"In the last forty-eight hours we've been able to account for the location of everyone flagged except these three." The passport photos with passport names were highlighted on the second screen.

"These three may have altered their appearance for the passport photos, or they may have altered their appearance since. But ladies and gentlemen – Gor and I both believe these three are our lead trouble makers."

"The man claiming to be Greek, Nicos Nicolas we believe is Ashur Ahmadi, and the woman posing as his *wife* Lena, we are sure is Yaida Nasser, both are Syrian born."

"They arrived in Montreal two days prior to a third member of the trio. This fellow presented an Italian passport in the name of Mario Vito. He is known to Italian intelligence and they identified him as Egyptian born Sargon Homsi."

"The three rented a basement apartment in the home of a retired widow under their Greek and Italian names in Brockville."

"And for a touch of authenticity the husband and wife were treated for minor wounds at the local hospital the day of the attack on Brockville and Morristown."

"They also rented a basement apartment from another widow, using their assumed names in Verdun, Quebec. No record of them treated in the after math of the attacks on the elementary schools in Montreal or Boston. And no record or crowd sightings from news photos after the third attack."

"Lastly, our phony Greek and Italian immigrants were traced to a third basement apartment also rented from another widow, but this time in Hazelton, Pennsylvania."

"This location stumped us, because unless they have plans for any number of high value targets in Philadelphia we couldn't figure out why they led us to Pennsylvania."

Inspector Wheeler felt his face redden at the mention of the historic Pennsylvania city and hoped no one else in the room noticed.

"All three houses have been under surveillance since the day before yesterday morning with an undercover agent placed inside posing as a relative. However, there has been zip for any activity and we don't expect any."

"Gor and I believe the terrorist trio moved from the first apartment to the second and third apartment quickly after each incident deliberately using those names like dropping bread crumbs for us to follow."

"But their location has gone dark, so we're sure they're using different identities now."

"And just as troubling we don't know why their MO changed. We're grateful they didn't arm their drones with nuclear devices for the third attack, but it makes us concerned they're 'saving-up' for even more locations or one big one."

The Canadian Prime Minister, the CIA Director and the US President were seated side by side at the end of the long wide conference table.

The Prime Minister looked at Inspector Wheeler and Gor Vladislav then Blain Sol who was still standing at the front of the room. "What's next then?"

Blain continued. "Assuming they're using replaced passports and other new identification, we have complied composite photos of each of the three suspects," he clicked to a third screen, "with possible alterations to their appearance."

On the overhead screen each suspect had three altered photos besides their enlarged passport photo. The men were shown with glasses, facial hair, clean shaven, short hair and collar length. The woman was shown as a blond, a redhead, with glasses, short hair and long.

"These will be shown nationally and internationally on morning, afternoon and evening television news casts with every network, in all major newspapers and every post office in Canada, the U.S. and Europe for the next several weeks."

****

"Surprise! Happy Birthday Elijah!"

Startled Grandpa almost dropped the bag of groceries then he frowned at his sister Lucille.

"I know what you're going to say," Lucille rushed to her brother. "I shouldn't have done this, but Elijah turned fifteen in the hospital for heaven's sake. Besides any day is a good day for cake and a party."

Elijah ducked behind his grandfather quickly dropping his backpack into the shoe bin by the back door. No one else in the family except his best friend and cousin Jayson, knew Elijah had been away.

Fortunately Great Aunt Lucille thought he was trying to avoid her hug and kisses. She was pushy, nosey and overbearing sometimes, but he never doubted her love or loyalty and Elijah was devoted to her too.

"Rock, your wonderful soup will go very nicely with our deli style dinner plan. We have all the fixins spread out on your kitchen table so everyone can put what they want into their own unique sandwich."

She swept aside like the ringmaster of a circus, waving her left arm toward the large pinewood table. As usual Aunt Lucille was well dressed. She sewed nearly everything she wore. Her long graying hair was pinned up in a twisted braid at the back of her head.

Elijah's Uncle River took the bag of groceries from his still stunned father-in-law.

"Happy belated Birthday son," He gave Elijah a hug with his free arm.

Grandpa moved further into his kitchen to hug his other six grandchildren. Even the two younger ones were beginning to dwarf their mother, Rock's daughter, Dawn Blackelk.

James her eldest had just turned seventeen and had been driving for almost a full year. Joseph would be sixteen soon, restless to start driving too. Jayson was only a few months younger than Elijah and would turn fifteen just before summer started. Sarah was already fourteen, Spring was twelve and Jorge would be eleven at summer's end.

Rock loved to listen to the animated chatter of his energetic family when all of them got together for a meal and any celebration.

Since the western sun was still high it was warm enough eat outside on the front deck at the picnic table. Slowly everyone drifted in that direction.

Elijah's Aunt Dawn sat on the bench in the space beside him. "How are you feeling, sweetie?" She kissed his cheek. Since her brother's death she had treated her nephew as if he was her number seven.

"I feel great, truly I do." Elijah caught Jayson's wink from across the table.

"Grandpa if I promise not to gallop or even trot can Jayson and I go for a ride after we eat?"

"Oh no Arrow's been cooped up too long. He might not give you a choice. He needs a good run."

Elijah grinned. "I'll just tell him not to run." Then he laughed. I felt good to laugh.

"I have an idea Grandpa," Jayson took a bite then waved the rest of his dill pickle in the air. "We can walk Storm, Dart and Arrow to the meadow by the creek and then let *them* run."

"Sarah and I could supervise." Spring giggled with salad dressing dripping from one corner of her mouth.

"Oh no," Aunt Lucille objected. "Your mother and I want a Scrabble rematch."

Following a fox and deer trail to the creek, the boys rode bareback and the horses whined with anticipation. Scores of fresh emerging spring smells filled their flared nostrils.

"So James is driving huh. How's that going?"

"He's such a blob of dried chewing gum." Jayson dismounted, slapped Storm's rump and the horse took off head down at full gallop. Dart and Arrow followed.

"You'd think he was ten years older than Joseph and me instead of only one and two."

"James and Joseph started saving for a car. Everyone knows that partnership won't work – they're too competitive..."

Both boys started to laugh so hard they needed to stop for a few seconds.

After they resumed their walk, Elijah shared *Crow Child*'s mission. They caught up to their horses at the creek then sat in the budding grass a few feet from the shore.

"Wow." Jayson shook his head. How do you know, what you know and that its okay and it's gonna work? I'd be so scared to make a mistake."

"I *was* so scared last fall about exactly that. Grandpa said to stop for a few seconds, clear my mind and wait for *Crow Child* to tell me."

"I can do even more stuff now. I was at the airport in Reading and wondered how I was going to get to Philadelphia to a place I wouldn't be seen. I closed my eyes to pray and when I opened them I was in a park in the center of the city."

"And the huge intense blanket of light – I'd never done that before either."

Then he looked at Arrow and decided to experiment. He sent Arrow a thought in the form of a question. 'Arrow, do you like clover better or grass?'

Arrow tore at a small clump of new shoots. 'CLOVER.' He went on chewing.

The color drained from Elijah's cheeks.

"Are you okay?" Jayson was alarmed.

Elijah shook his head. His color began to return. "Do you remember the day I suggested we ride to the meadow, and I thought I heard you say a definite *No*?"

"Yeah, you were acting kinda odd even for you."

"Well, who *said* No is even odder. It was Arrow."

Jayson's mouth fell open. "No way! That's too much. *Crow Child* can talk to animals? Holy bananas!"

CHAPTER...43

We were too merciful with our third and fourth strike. Now it is time to avenge the willful death's of our ancestors by Christian invaders who butchered women, children, and burned villages. You have seven days from sunset this day to prepare to watch the rest of Your history destroyed, Your churches desecrated and Your families taken from you. The hour will be 11PM East Coast then set with every time zone across Europe and nothing shall stop us. Your only chance for survival is to swear allegiance to the teachings of our Koran – so begins Your life of servitude.

Qaida Kawn Jadid

When *Wikileaks* published the second press release it didn't seem to matter that the posted photos had resulted in a confirmed identification of the three terrorists. No one on the joint investigative team knew how to locate Ashur Anmadi, his wife Yaida Nasser or Sargon Homsi, or even where to start.

On the third level below the main floor of the Pentagon, leaders and directors of international police agencies assembled in the briefing amphitheater.

RCMP Inspector Eric Wheeler and FBI Agent Opal Thane presented all complete and confirmed data the team had gathered to that hour.

"We have Chinese intelligence officers to thank who worked quickly to confirm North Korea sold radioactive waste in the form of bricks to Al Qaeda two years ago." Inspector Wheeler began.

"Since then, two officials in the government of Pakistan secretly smuggled other elements and some expertise to create small nuclear explosive devices."

"So the first two attacks were a radioactive *sample* of the capability of Al Qaeda or this new group Qaida Kawn Jadid?"

The Director of Homeland Security spoke. "Is the design of the drones too small to be picked up by our radar or are they launched close to the targets?"

"Both Director." Inspector Wheeler answered. "From witness accounts the 'birds' as we've come to call them are between five and seven centimeters long, which is twelve and eighteen inches with what appears to be a wing style that angles back instead of straight out."

"We've had teams on both sides of the border searching houses, barns, businesses, garden sheds, chicken coups – anything within a radius of two miles of each target. Anything beyond that conventional radar might not pick up because they fly low, but the terrorists then risk having that many airborne objects spotted."

The Director of the NSA gave a slight wave in Inspector Wheeler's direction.

"Yes sir, you have a question?"

The Director nodded. "We've had three documented attacks, but the terrorist press release mentioned four."

"There's nothing in our notes of a fourth target. Has there been a fourth, perhaps a remote target that was hit with an actual small nuclear explosive device, but you're keeping it quiet?"

And, there it was the target that Wheeler had dreaded might be exposed.

"Well sir, no not to the team's knowledge. However there was an odd incident in Philadelphia that might be relevant."

Eric's heart raced so fast he could hardly get enough air to breathe.

"Agent Thane felt New York and or DC might be high value targets. But when nothing happened, I quickly started to call around to FBI offices in a number of major eastern cities to check their status. One of the first cities I contacted was Philadelphia."

"The agent I spoke with reported that the night had been quiet with nothing of note except for a short power surge that couldn't be explained."

"This is only a guess, and it's certainly after the fact, but perhaps the power surge, interfered the GPS signals and the terrorist's plans for Philadelphia." Eric shrugged.

"Nothing unusual that was airborne was ever spotted, nor was anything with explosive capabilities recovered in or around Philadelphia. Everyone on the joint-team has been perplexed by Qaida Kawn Jadid's mention of a fourth target." His knees felt weak.

The Canadian Prime Minister was sullen. "Three suspects have been identified, how many more do you guess there is, not yet known to us?"

Inspector Wheeler nodded to Agent Thane. "Initially we only searched Canadian immigration records back eighteen months to identify the thirty-two that yielded our suspected three people."

"Immediately after that, programmers created software to search both U.S. and Canadian Immigration records back three years. However that will not provide us with names of sympathizers who arrived before then or who were born in Canada or the U.S."

"Our best guess, to answer your question Mr. Prime Minister - is that terrorists can be like termites when you see one expect they have several dozen cousins."

"To execute an operation such as this one we believe there are at minimum of as many as thirty for each target location attacked so far."

Agent Thane did the math for the grim statistics. "That's at least twenty-seven additional terrorists we haven't yet identified just for Brockville and Morristown alone."

"If we're close then there's another twenty-seven for Montreal and Boston. The attack on the third targets may have included several or all of the members of the first two along with others. Our math may be 'iffy' but we feel comfortable placing the number of additional terrorists besides the three we have identified at over a hundred."

"The British Minister of Defense stood. "If I'm looking at this latest press release correctly," he checked the name again, "Qaida Kawn Jadid will escalate their aggression significantly, in a global context, so it won't be just North America. Is that how everyone else here reads it?"

Defense leaders and their military advisers from fifty-eight other counties nodded.

"A roundup of all suspected terrorist sympathizers in the UK, in secret from dusk to dawn, could be done if we used the military too. However that would still take a full ten to fifteen hours and need to be coordinated with all of the other countries represented here, today for the element of surprise to be effective."

"Then we still wouldn't know how many terrorists we missed, and we'd be guessing which targets to protect. We'd also need to have a pretty impressive press release of our own for the global media, so they don't panic the general public in a *race* for television ratings or a front page scoop."

Twenty-four hours later, thousands of terrorists suspects from Canada, America, Mexico and Europe had been taken into custody then detained in military camps.

Twenty-four hours after that security patrols had been intensified around historic buildings, monuments and in densely populated cities in numerous countries.

****

Grandpa Clearwater caught the morning newspaper headlines then read between the lines of the article below the bold print.

Rock took a deep breath thankful that Elijah was outside feeding the chickens and pigs. He wouldn't be able to keep this from his grandson for long, but he hoped to have a little time to think.

These rapidly developing, treacherous world affairs would set *Crow Child* front and center…

****

With only two days until the terrorist's deadline, Inspector Wheeler didn't want to tap into *Crow Child*'s abilities. In fact, he doubted that the gifted entity could terminate hundred's of potential targets spread over the continent of North America, the United Kingdom and Europe all in a few coordinated moments.

However, *Crow Child* seemed to have developed some 'seeing' abilities. If the entity could concentrate that gift then that in itself could assist them to identify several targets and what deadly material might be delivered by hundreds of small bird shaped drones.

Just as protective of Elijah's identity as his grandfather, Eric Wheeler decided to wait a little longer and not give in to his impulse to return to Alberta.

What fifty-eight countries faced in forty-eight hours was of vast consequence and the prospect of fifty-eight attacks needed his complete attention and experience.

But two hours later Wikileaks posted another internet press release from Qaida Kawn Jadid.

> It matters not that our faces have been identified. Our names will not help You to prevent Your inevitable fate. Pledge allegiance immediately and live in servitude or die a death as harrowing as Your ancestors visited upon Ours.
>
> Qaida Kawn Jadid

Eric read the latest posting twice then realized everyone in attendance at the multi-country Pentagon briefing had been sworn to secrecy about the confirmed names of the three main suspects.

And no new information had been provided to the press. As far as mainstream media was concerned the true names to go with faces were still a mystery. But whoever wrote the Qaida Kawn Jadid press release, knew they had been identified. How?

Then out of nowhere a disturbing idea came to him and when he was finished mulling over the consequences of moving forward he sent an email from a safe internal RCMP server.

Inspector Wheeler contacted the general who lead a special investigative unit of the Canadian military. Eric requested that the backgrounds of every senior member who coordinated tactical plans and reviewed evidence on the joint investigation team, be examined in detail as quickly as possible. He requested that as information was confirmed it be sent to him immediately.

CHAPTER...44

Elijah's cousin Jayson showed up in time for breakfast the next morning.

Both boys dived into two helpings of Grandpa's French toast made with cranberry bread and sliced almonds stirred into the egg batter.

After they ate they walked down to the horse barn to clean out the stalls.

"I could hardly sleep last night! What you can, I mean what *Crow Child* can do is so awesome."

Jayson led his horse Storm into the exercise corral then reclosed the gate. "Does Grandpa know?"

"Yeah." Elijah unhooked two pitchforks handing one to Jayson. "Dart's stall is now across from Arrow's."

"I was, like kinda shook the day I heard that 'NO'. It was distinctive and seemed to come from close by. I asked Grandpa after you left if hearing voices was a sign of future insanity."

The boys made several trips to a flatbed wheelbarrow, making a pile of the trampled, straw bedding.

"Grandpa only laughed saying a little insanity was healthy."

"But when I told him what happened he nodded. He had expected something like that to begin happening about now."

Jayson stopped with a fork full of stale straw and lumps of dried horse droppings. "Wait a minute does our grandfather have some powers too?"

Elijah shook his head. "Grandpa and members of the Sarsi First Nations council know more details of the ancient legend. The Council and Grandpa are only there to guide *Crow Child* through the time of testing."

After two more trips with a fork full of straw Jayson leaned on the long handle. "Do you only hear Arrow or can you communicate with any animal?"

Elijah pushed a stiff bristle broom to sweep out the smaller straw pieces onto a shovel. "You mean Storm?"

"Yeah Storm. I was talking out loud around him this morning when I put on his hackamore. I was kinda worked up."

Elijah stopped sweeping, closed his eyes and visualized the livestock barn on his aunt and uncle's dairy farm.

Storm walked between the two other horses then by his owner and close to *Crow Child*.

'JAMES JERK!'

Elijah opened his eyes and smiled. "James is a jerk!"

Jayson felt his legs turn to numb and he leaned on the stall gate for support. "That is w-a-y cool."

****

With new passports and appearance alterations to match, Ashur, Yaida and Sargon, boarded their motorized sail boat. Two hours later Ashur and Yaida collected their VIA Rail touring tickets bound for Vancouver, BC.

Sargon continued east sailing down the mighty St. Lawrence River. The major seaway that flanked three provinces and nine states was a water highway for commercial cargo boats, barges of international goods and personal pleasure craft.

The name on the boat's registration matched his faux Canadian Passport. And though there was more border police patrolling than usual, his boat didn't seem to attract any attention though he was pushing the speed limits, but he used the numerous freighters as cover.

The river from headwater to mouth was a formidable 744 miles. But from where he'd dropped Ashur and Yaida off to catch their train west, he only had to travel 366 miles. Still pushing his speed past 30 would take him 12 hours to reach his cargo ship, if he wasn't stopped by authorities.

Sargon was sure not even his mother would recognize him. He looked Scandinavian. Hair removal cream made his face completely smooth with no hint of black stubble. His contacts changed his eye color to hazel. With his eyebrows and hair bleached as well as his chest hair and arms he looked like someone with a deep tan after spending hours on a sail boat.

****

Six hours ticked by while Inspector Wheeler waited none too patiently for the first bit of information that trickled to his email address.

His high level contact at the military investigation unit had surprised him. There were two unexpected names that included government insiders from three of the countries represented at the secret Pentagon meeting.

The British Minister of Defense was on a watch list. The report did not go into detail so Eric assumed it was for an issue not related to the continuing terrorist threat.

The second name was for a French undercover agent working in Russia he was also expected to ignore. All other world defense leaders and their military advisors came back clear of flags.

The next list of names was for the international joint-team between RCMP and FBI – coordinated and led by Opal Thane and himself.

However, the more detailed background search found two women named Opal Louise Thane. Both women were born on the same day, at the same time in the same small town of Tifton, Georgia.

One Opal Thane was presently a resident of a local Tifton care home for adults with severe autism. The other Opal Thane was an FBI agent with the highest federal security clearance an agent could hold. No one else on the list had caused the military background researchers concern.

Eric's hands shook as he immediately typed a rush request for the next level of specialist with the joint-team to be examined. If there was one infiltrator - like termites - there was likely more somewhere working close by with access to trusted information.

No one on their team of experts in airborne weapons, or Middle East culture, forensics, forgery, bombs, navigation, commuter programming or profiling had known the photos yielded other names, except Blain and Gor.

But not even Blain Sol or Gor Vladislav – had attended the last need to know Pentagon meeting when the three terrorist identifications with other names were confirmed - only Agent Thane.

****

It was raining pellets straight down when Grandpa Clearwater and Elijah returned from grocery shopping in Canmore.

With their canvas grocery bags packed around Elijah in the passenger seat, they were so focused on moving everything into the house and not getting soaked that at first they didn't notice Inspector Wheeler. He stood in the corner under the roof eve where the new bathroom addition and the original kitchen wall joined.

There was no gutter there and water from the roof poured down the roof valley, hit the deck below then splashed back. Eric's head and jacket were dry, but his boots and jeans were soaked from the knees down.

Grandpa spotted the younger man from the corner of his eye then acknowledged him with a smile. "Good thing I really like you son, cause I know this return trip means big trouble."

Eric took two bags from Rock and one from Elijah. "I heard you made great soup."

They shuffled through the back door into the kitchen. The vintage wood burning stove warmed the room with a deep pine scent.

Eric stood close to the black and chrome cast iron antique, to shake off his chill.

"Give me those boots real quick." Grandpa tapped Eric on the shoulder. "You can smear some saddle soap on those and save the leather from drying out."

"You might peel off those jeans too. I got some grey sweat pants you can put on. They'll be a little short in the leg, but most of your modesty will be covered." Rock grinned.

Grandpa got out the cast iron skillet and cooked hamburger for tacos as Elijah cut up onions, tomatoes and lettuce.

Eric pitched in and set the table then grated cheddar cheese while he brought his reluctant hosts, current on the messages in each of the internet press releases.

At first no one said anything when Eric was done.

Grandpa set the hot frying pan on the table protected by clay tiles and two of Aunt Alice's quilted pot holders. Several tacos disappeared before the people at the table stopped crunching long enough to talk.

Elijah sipped a rare drink of soda. "Fifty-eight countries huh?"

Eric blotted salsa from the side of his mouth. "Yes. Fifty-five European countries including the UK and three in North America, Canada, Mexico and the U.S."

"When?" Elijah felt overwhelmed.

"Tomorrow night at 11PM East Coast Time and coordinated to coincide with each country's time zone."

"Gosh in the dark it's more difficult. Do you know if there are any satellites involved?"

"There doesn't seem to be. The one that sent the signal for the attack you blocked in Philadelphia was I suspect sent off-orbit. At any rate it's no longer shadowing the French communications satellite and all the others have been accounted for."

"My Commissioner believes, and I agree that if they were using satellite signals again for this global operation they'd need several and we'd spot them."

"None of this has been in the news – not even a hint."

Rock toyed with the idea of eating taco number eight. He might as well if he was going to die tomorrow night at 11PM Eastern Time.

"You know what mainstream media is like. If they got a hold of even half the information we've kept classified there'd be wide spread panic, not to mention violent crimes, and widespread looting."

"Elijah, I'd like to take you back with me." Eric gathered up his plate to rinse at the sink.

"Take me back where?" Elijah felt bewildered as he looked toward his grandfather. Then he turned in his chair toward Eric Wheeler standing at the kitchen sink.

"I'm still learning what *Crow Child* can do. This threat isn't anything like I've faced before. This menace is huge, spread out over what, half the planet? There are thousands of miles and hundreds of locations and different time zones..."

CHAPTER...45

Inspector Wheeler's military helicopter was noticed by only two local farmers, but mostly just wildlife when it lifted off in the meadow by the creek.

As he waved to the inspector, Elijah assured the officer that if he developed a defense strategy, he could be at any location the inspector chose in minutes.

"*Crow Child*, moved from the Reading Airport to Philadelphia and back with no difficulty." Elijah shrugged. "So from Alberta to DC shouldn't be a problem either."

The rain had tapered off with only a light mist still lingering in the cool afternoon. As Elijah walked back to the house he stopped several times to lift his nose to the air. The scent of new grass, budding trees and blossoming wild flowers was dense and sweet.

Elijah went straight up to his loft bedroom to think.

If there was a solution to stopping multiple small nuclear attacks on multiple countries in multiple time zones then *Crow Child* would know – he hoped. If not then perhaps there wasn't one.

It was *Crow Child* who had created the vast intense blanket of fire-light that blocked the drones from reaching their targets in Philadelphia.

But try as he might Elijah couldn't clear his mind enough to relax and let the wisdom of the six thousand year-old *Crow Child* fuse with the overwhelmed fifteen year-old Elijah Clearwater.

After thirty minutes, he gave up and decided to take Arrow out for more exercise since he had been cleared to ride again by his doctor.

To the west the clouds were breaking up over the Rocky Mountains with random patches of blue showing through. Elijah wanted to include Dart out too, so he attached one end of a lead to her halter and the other to Arrow's halter.

Elijah rode bareback. They trotted out through the gate following the driveway beyond the back deck and then between the chicken coop and pig barn.

Rock watched his grandson ride in the direction of the meadow. His heart ached for the youth whose fate was to juggle the burden of persistent, troublesome health with an ancient destiny.

In another year Elijah Clearwater and *Crow Child* would no longer be distinct – they would be one-energy. People would still see the person named Elijah, but the mystical transition would be complete.

As the eastbound figures grew smaller the protective, guiding grandfather turned away from the kitchen window confident that *Crow Child* would somehow prevail.

Elijah's destination was the meadow by the creek. He always seemed to think better in the meadow. But this time he chose to go the long way taking a deer path south through the trees first.

Part of the path was a long gradual climb up hill. Seeing a break in the trees Elijah stopped Arrow and Dart dismounting at a ridge that overlooked the peaceful valley below.

When he let out a deep sigh both horses moved to stand on either side of him. He wrapped his arms around Dart's neck then Arrow. He felt comforted by their presence.

Again Elijah tried to clear his mind. 'How?' He asked silently. 'How does *Black Crow* protect so many people in so many places all at the same time?'

A breeze flowed between the branches of budding trees, kissing fresh spring leaves. *Crow Child* felt the breeze on his face.

The forest remained silent until two crows landed on a branch of a sixty foot spruce. When they bickered over where to perch on the branch, the restful silence was broken.

Elijah looked up toward the noise however the branches were too thick to see them clearly. He looked around for a stick to throw, to make them fly away and argue somewhere else, but Arrow bumped his arm with his nose.

'NO...'

'THEY BRING MESSAGE'

Elijah took a deep breath and spoke aloud. "Interesting that my destiny is not tied to a grand bird of prey like the hawk, or the falcon, or the eagle – it's the crow."

'THEY ARE YOUR ARMY'

'THEY LIVE EVERYWHERE'

'HARNESS THEIR INTELLIGENCE'

'USE THEIR VAST NUMBERS'

Then Elijah understood.

And when *Crow Child* acknowledged their presence both birds left the spruce branch flying in the direction of the meadow...

By the time Elijah and the horses arrived in the meadow the ground on either side of the creek was black with ten thousand crows awaiting *The Crow Child*'s instructions.

Crows by nature cooperated in an organized network both remote and populated that covered entire cities, rural farmland, forests, desert and semi tropical locations.

Crow Child remained on Arrow scanning over the vast carpet of black energy. He communicated with thought.

'Decide among yourselves who shall leave this valley to recruit cousins for Mexico, west and east coast America, or patrol the coasts of Canada – while others network in the islands of the United Kingdom – and still others travel to France, or Holland, Portugal, Italy, Poland and the other fifty European countries that need our help.'

'The threat is imminent and targeted at all life. The threat is a machine made to look like and fly like a bird. The head of the mechanical bird carries a toxin that shall poison as well as destroy with fire.'

Crow Child hung his head for several seconds. When he lifted it to address the massive flock of crows his heart was heavy.

'The makers of this threat lied. Their warning deadline was for 11PM – but they intend to strike at 11AM East Coast Time. That allows us only seventeen hours for our network to be in place…'

A low tone twitter travelled from bird to bird. In a minute, random groups of crows began to rise and take flight heading in several directions.

Another minute later an enormous black mass of beating feathers lifted off as one, their wings grabbing air.

Rising high above his head the legion of crows scattered in the sky for the far reaches of North America, the United Kingdom and Europe.

****

The FBI agent who called herself Opal Thane, had managed to vanish.

To Inspector Wheeler that meant someone in the Canadian Military investigation unit had warned her.

Since the General's special research investigators numbered only eighteen, finding a specific leak would be easy. And it was. That morning the General counted only seventeen who showed up for work.

At the DC apartment one block from Dupont Circle, of the woman who called herself Opal Thane - Homeland Security investigators found what Wheeler expected them to find - nothing useable.

Any documentation she hadn't had time to burn in her fireplace, Opal had literally washed. FBI and Homeland Security Agents discovered soaked and completely unreadable papers in her dishwasher and washing machine. Hundreds of wet pages were stuck together in several large clumps.

After Eric left the Clearwater farm, his Commissioner had informed him that he would remain joint-team coordinator. Since he'd been in on the investigation from the beginning of the terrorist attacks he was now the only one who knew everything.

Under other circumstances that kind of faith in his abilities might have been a compliment. However two dozen American investigative policing agencies as well as two dozen collective agencies across Europe looked to him for direction. And as weary as Eric was, there was no time to enjoy flattery or to rest.

Inspector Wheeler was the last person to leave Opal Thane's apartment. Cameras had been set in key locations to record anyone who might return, with remote monitors set up across the street, for swift apprehension.

Wheeler descended the stairs of Thane's second floor apartment to the street below. So much had changed in only a few weeks.

Essentially the upper half of Planet Earth was on lockdown. In every targeted country every available active military or reserve military personnel were pressed into service to supplement the entire list of other civilian policing agencies.

To keep crime and panic to a minimum the media was given only half the information that in turn was reported to the average citizen who only knew half of what was pending.

As the hours slipped by streets and avenues became almost deserted. People had been asked to remain inside with their doors and windows locked and blocked, to stay alert, be armed if they already owned a weapon, but otherwise let the authorities do their job.

It was 5:10PM when Eric got a text from Elijah, using his grandfather's new cell phone.

Sitting behind the wheel of his borrowed DC Secret Service car Wheeler was relieved after reading the text:

> GOT AN IDEA MIGHT WORK – WHERE ARE YOU EXACTLY? STILL GREEN
> W/THIS TRAVEL THING…

Eric sent a text response:

> IN A BORROWED BLACK CAR PARKED ON CHURCH STREET –TARGET
> TOO SMALL? TRY DUPONT CIRCLE IT HAS A PARK…

A homeless man sat down on a bench under a spreading magnolia tree to enjoy the second half of his cheese sandwich. He had settled in relieved and happy that no one else was anywhere near him.

However after he had retrieved a water bottle from his backpack he was no longer alone. At the other end of the bench a nice looking young teen sat smiling at him...

CHAPTER...46

"Sorry to disturb you, sir." Elijah stood. "I was waiting for my uncle."

He gave the surprised man a half wave as he walked to the center of the circular park to search for Eric's car.

Two lanes of traffic moved in, around then out again channeled from five major arteries exiting on the opposite side. But at rush hour with the directive to head home and stay indoors, most vehicles were barely creeping.

Elijah didn't have his grandfather's cell phone, but he did have *Crow Child*'s navigation skill. He began walking due east taking P Street then north on 18th Avenue. He found Inspector Wheeler stuck at the lights on the corner of Church Street and 18th.

When Elijah tapped on the passenger door window, the season investigator jumped.

"I nearly had a heart attack. How'd you find me?"

"I didn't find you *Crow Child* did."

"Of course. I don't suppose *Crow Child* can get us out of this?" He made a broad wave across the glass from the inside of the car's windshield.

"Wish I could. Cause I'm gonna need a large open field that's remote." Elijah pursed his lips, searching for the right words, but there wasn't any way to ease what he needed to say.

"I don't know how you do these things, but all of the target countries need to be prepared with everyone off the streets much sooner. We don't have until 11PM tomorrow night the terrorists will attack at 11AM tomorrow morning."

Wheeler felt his entire body lose all feeling, relieved he was stuck in traffic. "What!"

Eric began to shake. "For sure?"

Elijah nodded.

With deep breaths Eric steadied his hands. "Let me know if I can move another foot or two." Then he bent his head over his phone and the inspector sent a group text marked urgent:

NEW INTEL INDICATES ATTTACKS SET FOR 11AM TOMORROW-*NOT*-REPEAT-*NOT* 11PM SEND GLOBAL ALERT...

"You got any other surprises for me?"

Elijah looked up at the sun visor above his head then back to his friend and nodded again.

They had been through so much together and now they both carried the weight a large portion of the world on their shoulders.

"Okay, what?"

"A few surprises."

The traffic began to move and Eric made the decision to turn right and drive in the opposite direction of the commuters from the suburbs trying to leave the city.

He had no idea where he was going, but that didn't matter. Wheeler had no specific place to be at that moment.

"Are your surprises more distressing as discovering the terrorists lied with the intention of attacking a full twelve hours sooner?"

Following 18th Street north, the pace of the traffic was slow, but steady. As he drove, the inspector noticed what to him seemed like a gathering of a greater number of crows in trees and on roof tops than he'd ever seen before.

"One for sure."

Then Eric thought he knew. "About five this afternoon, I spotted eight or nine crows sitting on the roof of the building across from Opal Thane's apartment. Then while I waited for you to–arrive – several more joined the first group. And then even more began to accumulate in parks and on other roof tops. Is that you?"

Elijah nodded. "Crows are everywhere, in every country. They're smart, courageous, resilient and protective. They're *Crow Child*'s army."

The inspector shook his head. "That's amazing, but how do they stop several incoming drones with nuclear capability?"

Elijah was quiet.

They drove by restaurants, condos and government buildings leaving DC behind. Crossing into the state of Maryland there were more and more colonial style two story homes with gardens that became a more common view - replacing freeways with patios of potted plants.

Eric spotted an off ramp for highway 29 to Baltimore. "Ever been to Baltimore?"

"No sir."

"Me either, but according to the sign it's only another thirty-nine miles. We should stop for gas and pick up plenty of bottled water for you then get some dinner. Who knows when we'll eat again?"

He handed his cell phone to Elijah. "Text or call your grandfather. Let him know you're fine. And tell him too that you have a peculiar plan we hope will work."

Thirteen miles out from Baltimore they stopped at a gas bar and truck stop. The café was busy and it looked to Eric like it was a favorite of long-haul drivers.

At a corner booth a waitress with bright orange hair dyed from a box kit brought two glasses of ice water. "Have you had time to look at the menu gentlemen?"

Elijah smiled looking up and wondered how she got her hair to match her fingernails and lipstick. "I'll have a grilled cheese on rye and a bowl of tomato soup please."

"Well aren't you adventuresome." She winked at Elijah. "And you sir?"

"That sounds good to me, I'll have the same." Eric folded one of the plastic covered menus and put it back in the rack on their table with the condiments.

"You two need a little more zip in your life!" The waitress laughed. "I'll get those out ta ya real quick now. Anything else ta drink besides water?"

"Coffee with cream for me."

"I'll have orange juice, no ice, please."

"Okay, gentlemen." She walked away shaking her head.

Eric leaned forward. "You can coordinate millions of crows in several countries? You do have a plan, right?"

"I think so. The crows are on the lookout for the launch locations."

"The terrorist's drones had to come from somewhere. And since there were several at a time they had to have been assembled then launched from a location large enough to hold them, but still not attract attention."

The waitress brought their beverages.

"When grandpa and I looked at a map of all four attack targets, the first three followed the Saint Lawrence river, which is also a major seaway for large commercial cargo ships. The fourth was also easily reached from water, along the Atlantic Coast."

"Stupid!" Eric made a fist and thumped his forehead.

"We searched a two mile then three mile radius from each target site, for places where the drones could have been launched. Never ever thought the drones might have come from a boat. Aw!"

"Back to my plan." Elijah was interrupted by the arrival of their soup and grilled cheese.

"Just so you guys know this, if you feel even more daring after you're finished with your main course, we have every flavor of pie ever invented. More coffee, sir?"

"Yes, thank you."

Elijah downed eight of his digestive enzymes, so his body could deal with the cheese. Then both of them ate and talked quickly, without tasting much of their food.

"I believe that the interior of Canada and America is safe, but the west and east coasts, including Mexico are vulnerable – as are – all European countries that border oceans, seas and deep water bays."

"I keep seeing fishing boats, sailboats, tugboats and a ship with a Greek mariner's license number. Authorities rarely stop tugboats they're the workhorses of shipping lanes and harbors. And a commercial cargo ship flying a Customs-Clearance flag wouldn't be stopped by police patrol either."

Eric frowned. "So the crows are gathering along all coastlines?"

Elijah nodded. "That's just the first line of defense. What ever gets by the thousands of very irate crows will be tackled by the next line. The idea is to send every drone into water, especially salt water, which should disable the mechanism."

"If you're wrong?"

"If I'm wrong then we'll have a third bunch of crows on look out all over every major city and historic site to alert other crows of any incoming intruder. All the crows need to do is clip even the edge of the drone's slightly for it to lose forward momentum."

"Crashing to the ground may still trigger its ignition response, but I'm betting that the GPS and the detonation are linked. If the drone doesn't reach its programmed destination then it malfunctions."

"At least I hoped so, because the tops of the drones are not radioactive. That was only done with the first attacks to give everyone the wrong impression, but what they do have is just as extreme."

"There's some sort of live spore encased in each drone. So not only will property be damaged but tens of thousands of people in fifty-eight countries will be made extremely sick and severely weakened. Some may probably die."

...fifteen hours to targets...

CHAPTER...47

In the café parking lot Eric sent out several urgent texts that went to key contacts. It was an alert to all authorities of *his* new theory – which thankfully to everyone else in all fifty-eight countries, seemed to make sense.

Then he pointed the car back toward the U.S. capitol. "Baltimore will need to wait."

Elijah drank water until he was sure his kidneys would explode. Inspector Wheeler was worse than grandpa and his doctor put together. He was so full of fluid they had to stop three times so Elijah could empty his blander.

When they reached DC it was 9PM, but Eric kept driving. He knew of several miles of rural land in central Virginia that would be fairly isolated enough for *Crow Child* to transform unseen.

Pulling off the highway down a two lane paved rural road in Stafford County Eric checked them into a local family owned motel, Carnation Cottages. "We'll need some sleep – if that's at all possible."

When they opened the door what greeted them made their day absolutely perfect. The room was a visual feast.

Eric shook his head. "On a hunch I actually booked this amazing time capsule for two days."

Each cottage was the same size twenty feet by twenty feet. They had been redecorated in 1973 with red shag carpet, set off by black velvet and silver foil wallpaper. There were two four poster queen size beds painted a high gloss black, with black and white checked comforters. Red ceramic lamps with red shades stood on either end of low four foot long night stand set between the beds.

Elijah rushed to check out the bathroom which had last decorated in 1957. It had black tile around a pink cast iron tub-shower, with matching pink toilet and two pink sinks set in a long narrow vanity with a Formica top of black and pink stars on a white background. Two large pink glass lights hung over each sink.

"Well Inspector," Elijah's head was just visible around the doorway. "If you liked the bedroom, you're really gonna like the bathroom, but we may need to keep the lights off."

As much as their cottage was a well needed amusing relief they both remained edgy, battling exhaustion.

Ever since Elijah tuned into the threat of an attack set for an earlier timeline Wheeler became anxious. If the terrorists would move the attack up a full twelve hours would they, move it up a full, twenty-four hours?

After they finished checking in Eric sent an urgent text to every member of his team to alert all their European contacts in each target country. They needed to expect anything suspicious much earlier, perhaps even that evening. He cautioned they remain prepared to coordinate their local time with either 11PM North American East Coast Time or 11AM.

Along the east coast of North America 11PM came and went and then midnight came and went and no multi-layered attack occurred.

Elijah was puzzled. With millions of crows in place what was *Crow Child's* role? He'd never before considered that *Crow*

Child might not need to transform and he drifted into a shallow, troubled sleep.

Inspector Wheeler stretched out on top of the quilt on his bed fully dressed. He sat up with three pillows stacked behind his back, still communicating with key members of his U.S. Canadian joint team.

The only light that remained on was a soft pink glow from the partially open bathroom door.

Several times Wheeler dozed then jerked awake – startled by his strange surroundings. Eventually he too drifted into a shallow, troubled sleep.

…ten hours to targets…

****

The cargo liner 'Bright Light' was anchored in the Atlantic Ocean in international water just beyond the U.S. twelve, nautical mile limit.

Marine registration of the 965 foot container ship had been certified as being exclusively Greek with no change of hands in its twenty-nine years at sea. The inspected cargo was stress-graded Polish lumber.

In a false storage hold below the lumber was a supply of assembled drones. This attack would not rely on a single satellite – this group had their own implanted homing device.

Over the course of the last two weeks their mass of loyal followers had deposited tiny electronic receivers in hundreds of key locations. And now they were ready.

Sargon Homsi made a predawn inspection of the several rows of grey seagull shaped drones. There was room on the deck of the ship to set them out to lift off simultaneously.

His heart raced with anticipated excitement. He would supervise the launch of all 216 drones, from the Atlantic side - personally.

Yaida was in one of four boats. Three fishing boats and one tug were spaced several hundred miles apart in the Pacific Ocean along the west coast of Canada, the U.S. and Mexico. From those locations 160 drones were set to cruise to their targets

Ashur was positioned in international waters to the south off the Gulf Coast. From his placement he could send eighty-seven programmed drones to the east coast of Mexico, to all of Florida and each Gulf Coast state.

…five hours to targets…

****

Elijah woke up first - coughing.

Like Inspector Wheeler he had fallen asleep in his clothes on top of the checkered comforter.

Sitting up, he was able to breathe easier. He retrieved his puffer from his inside jacket pocket. After a minute his breathing wasn't as labored.

From their hastily purchased drugstore supplies, Elijah brushed his teeth then rinsed his mouth. Splashing his face with cool water helped – a lot.

Back in the bedroom, Inspector Wheeler sat on the side of his bed. "We need to give your back a sound thumping, right? Can't have *Black Crow* passing out."

"I'm pretty sure I'll be okay, honest. Can I give Grandpa a call?"

"Sure." He looked at his watch, feeling far too calm for a man facing impending doom. He handed Elijah his personal cell phone as he went into the bathroom.

"I'm good Grandpa truly I am. I drank more water than a whale yesterday. I took enough enzymes before I ate and hardly had a cough this morning, so all I needed to use was my puffer."

He listened to his grandfather then responded. "Yeah I know. It's gonna be a big day."

"I expect the crows will be able to stop drones coming from the smaller boats offshore. I woke up realizing that only *Black Crow* can stop the main ship – the one that sends out all the commands."

"I'll be careful." Elijah the youth closed his eyes. "I love you too Grandpa."

When Inspector Wheeler came out of the bathroom Elijah was gone. It was still fairly dark outside, less than an hour before sunrise.

Eric sent another urgent text for everyone to be alert to an attack that could come much sooner than 11AM. He and Elijah suspected that soon after the shock of loosing much of their leadership – the next in command of Qaida Kawn Jadid could step up and accelerate the mission.

...four hours to targets...

Due east of Washington DC, on latitude 38N *Crow Child* felt the presence of a major vessel anchored fifteen miles away.

Crow Child stood on the deserted shore between the Maryland towns of Salisbury and Crisfield. There was no reason to wait and so many reasons to strike immediately. And the cover of predawn darkness was perfect.

Stepping into the water *Crow Child* merged with the ocean. At the bow of the cargo ship 'Bright Light' - *Black Crow* rose above the surface.

In a rush of energy the ocean began to churn.

Crow Child's entire being expanded.

The ship began to sway.

A flash of intense white light surrounded Crow Child transforming his physical form to that of an enormous black crow with a wingspan that surpassed the length of the ship.

Black Crow's vast form filled the open space.

With one sweeping flurry Black Crow stepped into the air, rising higher and higher over the cargo ship below him with fire and light…

Terrified deck hands ran for cover below. On the ship's bridge Sargon was petrified at the sight of the apparition before him.

Spreading out Black Crow's fire-light surrounded then dissolved the entire ship and its' cargo. All persons on board were plunged into the open ocean.

The intense white light altered to violet sending a second massive wave of wind that sucked the air from the lungs of the hundreds of screaming men.

When air to their lungs returned all of their voices were mute.

Twenty miles north the captain of Coast Guard Cutter *Georgia* noted an odd bright light in the distance.

She immediately reported the latitude and longitude of the light to her Commander at the Pentagon. "Should we investigate sir? We were advised to be alert to a possible attack by the terrorists much sooner than 11AM."

After checking directly with RCMP Inspector Wheeler, her naval commander was assured the powerful light was part of a planned offensive against the terrorists–designed to catch Qaida Kawn Jadid by surprise.

...threat to targets immediate...

CHAPTER...48

In a heartbeat all communication with Qaida Kawn Jadid's dominion ship, ceased.

Ashur thought his fishing boat's radio was down, but he couldn't reach Sargon by cell phone or anyone else on the cargo ship, 'Bright Light'.

Following the alternate leadership directive – Ashur did not hesitate to ensure Al Qaeda's mission.

Every vessel anchored off the shore of all target counties was ordered to pull anchor, move in and launch their armed drones.

Within minutes of Ashur's commands 116 fishing boats, sailboats and tugboats travelled from international waters to inside the seven mile mark on the coastlines of each marked country.

From those locations, the sound-of-rain echoed across waves of water that ran along miles of deserted coastlines.

Hundreds of preprogrammed drones lifted off from the decks of each boat in set groups heading for their inland targets.

For the waiting defense force of crows the distinctive sound-of-rain was their signal.

Across Europe, across the United Kingdom, across North America, millions of crows left tree branches, roof tops, fences, park grounds, and beaches.

The skies littered with thousands of programmed mechanical drones were outnumbered by millions of calculating, and determined live crows.

Exactly one mile from the shores of Wales, Ireland Scotland and England, soldiers patrolling at noon were startled by the sight of clear blue skies suddenly filled with tens of thousands of crows flying feverishly out to sea.

From nowhere a mighty force heaved the terrorist's smaller boats off the UK coast, in a massive swirl of water. The deckhands were blinded by a fiery bright light before being tossed mute into the ocean.

In Holland, France, Italy and Spain, police and military personnel took cover under trucks and armored vehicles.

The sky over their heads was filled with millions of crows passing above them leaving from the coastlines like black darts.

Trapped by a fiery white light that made clear vision by their crews impossible, Qaida Kawn Jadid's assembled fishing boats, sailboats and tugboats were tossed by a force of wind that capsized them all.

Just before sunrise, along the Gulf Coast massive numbers of crows defending their home territory flew out to attack hundreds of disguised drones.

Ashur dropped his binoculars in shock at the sight of countless black birds he believed to be Western drones.

Rushing for cover he was temporarily blinded by an intense white light then tossed overboard by a sudden, fierce storm.

An hour before sunrise on the west coast of North America, Yaida did not see the enormous black blurr of crows that responded to the distinctive sound-of-rain coming from the drones.

She only heard a commotion.

With no idea what caused the clamor a few miles from her boat she was stricken by a fiery white light that surrounded her tug.

Hers and the other three boats had released their drones to a failed fate.

CHAPTER...49

Eric couldn't answer either of his cell phones fast enough.

Calls came in by the dozens from agents and military personnel.

Reports from the military positioned along every coastline from all fifty-eight countries confirmed sightings of massive numbers of gathering crows that flew out over open, ocean.

No drones had been sighted anywhere that attacked any location in any of the threatened countries.

As word spread it seemed clear to police and military personnel that the odd behavior of so many crows may have blocked the terrorist's planned attacks.

One police officer commented, "We heard an odd sound, like, the-sound-of-rain which seemed to provoke the crows."

Members of Wheeler's joint-team, agency directors and military leaders wanted to know if the odd behavior of so many flocks of crows could have been a factor. If so what had the birds done? If not then where had the drones gone?

Inspector Wheeler couldn't answer any of these questions, yet. He was too apprehensive about Elijah.

Black Crow and the vast crow defense had neutralized almost two thousand armed drones, sunk 121 small boats, and one cargo ship in twenty-seven minutes.

The fifty-eight country threat had been deactivated three hours and twenty-three minutes before the original …threat to targets… of 11AM East Coast Time.

Attempting to avoid more probing questions into the curious flight of so many crows, and several unexplained white light incidents - Eric suggested that the director of Homeland security locate an expert on crow behavior, for some insight.

Hiding out in their motel cottage Eric paced the room only half paying attention to the bomb expert talking at the other end of his second cell phone. All the while his mind asked, 'Where was Elijah?'

He opened the door and checked outside then heard coughing behind him. When he turned around Elijah lay on the floor at the foot of his bed. Eric abruptly ended that conversation, rushing to help Elijah sit up.

"I was hoping to be *on* the bed." Elijah coughed. "Guess I'm lucky I landed in the right room, huh?" He coughed again and smiled.

Inspector Wheeler pulled a footstool away from the chair by Elijah's bed. "How about we give your back a good thumping."

****

There was virtually no trace of the cargo ship 'Bright Light' nor any of the other smaller vessels the terrorists seized to launch their armed drones.

Weather experts studied wind, water currents and temperature patterns to explain the number of fluke storms along several coastline locations.

But none of the boats were recovered. Not even parts of the boats were recovered. There simply was no trace of any maritime material.

Bomb experts theorized the lack of any recoverable fragments may have had something to do with the reported fiery white light. Perhaps the terrorist's own explosive material destroyed their boats?

Naval ships from NATO on search patrol with military ships from seven of the fifty-eight threatened countries found and rescued several surviving terrorists at sea, floundering to stay afloat.

The terrorists they brought into custody would not talk because they could no longer speak.

There were plenty of downed drones to recover. Naval bomb experts from the UN, NATO and numerous member countries were naturally interested in their construction and inner workings.

However biologists, zoologists and ornithologists were at a loss to explain the concentrations of crows that had gathered along the coastline of only the threatened countries.

It was agreed by every expert interviewed that crows were protective of their territory and of each other, but that still didn't explain how so many had gathered at exactly the right times at exactly the right places…

EPILOGUE...

April, 2019

Great Aunt Lucille gave her nephew Elijah a hug. "Well you're having a much better birthday this year - you're not in the hospital."

"Sixteen is pretty special, and so is getting your driver's license. Now all you need is a car, or a truck, or something with a motor."

Crow Child grinned accepting a plate with a slice of lemon flavored cake. "I have Arrow."

Eric Wheeler and Grandpa sat across from *Crow Child*. Eric scooped ice cream and Grandpa passed around mugs of steaming tea.

"Or," Eric winked at *Crow Child*. "You can always *think* of a destination…"

Aunt Lucille frowned. "What are you talking about?"

Crow Child took a few bites then walked with his plate of cake out the front room door onto the west deck.

The sun was an hour from setting. Streaks of pink and orange colored the edges of stratus clouds that stretched just above the horizon.

He listened with a slight smile to the background banter of his Great Aunt Lucile. She complained to Eric and Grandpa about the risks of planes and trains. "Your own car is the only way to travel…"

The sound of her voice faded as *Crow Child* closed his eyes absorbing the energy of that day's vanishing sun.

This was a '3' year.

This was a year of disruption and of change.

For those who were selfish change would bring fear, for those who were selfless change would bring relief…

Elijah

Always know

That no matter where

You are

Or

What you're doing

The moon

You see at night

Is

The same moon I see too

So know that when you look up

I'm thinking of you…stb

Many people are under the mistaken impression that crows were viewed as the harbingers of death in Native American [and many] cultures, but in fact that is not true. We do not know of any Native American tribe in which crows were seen as omens of death. Indeed, just the opposite. Seeing a crow was and still is considered good luck by many tribes. In Native American folklore [and scientific studies] the intelligence of crows is portrayed as their most important feature. Crows are often linked with the raven, a larger cousin of the crow that share many of the same traits, but they are distinct.

[Bog Archives of *BlueFeatherSpirit*: Native American Crow Gods and Spirits

Cystic Fibrosis [CF] is an inherited medical condition that affects the secretory glands, including the sweat glands and mucus glands such as the lungs, pancreas, liver, intestines and sinuses. [data site: *MedicineNet.com*]

The distal obstruction syndrome [DIOS] previously known as meconium ileus equivalent [MIE] is a condition unique to cystic fibrosis. The syndrome occurs in about 10-22% of patients [Dray et al 2004]. It may present at any time after the neonatal period, but the incidence increases with age becoming more common in adolescent and adult patients. The recurrence rate is about 50%.

Effective preventative measures may include prophylactic laxative therapy and a diet high in water and water content foods [fresh fruits & vegetables] to void dehydration. Medical intervention measures require the immediate introduction of pancreatin and the continuous administration of a GI lavage solution [Gilljam at al 2003]. [data site: *cfmedicine.com*]

Maps and other graphics that appear in this fictionalized literary collection were reprinted from graphics sited by public sources available online.

Made in the USA
Middletown, DE
30 January 2020